Alice Darwin lives in a little Victorian house in Surrey, with her husband and their black Labrador puppy. She used to work in a residential care home for the elderly. When she's not making up stories in her shed at the end of the garden, or walking the dog, she is a writer and journalist and has written over twenty original features for the BBC.

Rokitansky is her first novel.

www.alicedarwin.com

Alice Darwin

CHAPTER 13 BOOKS

CHAPTER 13 BOOKS

First published by Chapter 13 Books 2014

Cover by John Chandler at Chandler Book Design

Alice Darwin asserts the moral right to be identified as the author of
this work

A catalogue record for this book is available from the British Library

ISBN: 978-0-9928782-0-7

This novel is a work of fiction. Any resemblance to actual persons, living
or dead, events or localities is coincidental.

For my Daniel

A beginning

ONE

Moira stared at the fifteen year old girl in her bedroom mirror. She neither liked nor knew what she saw. She could hear them talking about her down below. Muffled, displeased voices. She washed and dressed then cautiously crept downstairs, lingering on the bottom step, uneasy and unnoticed. The front door slammed and Mother muttered and blasphemed. She stood still where she was and listened to Father crunch his way across the snow-covered gravel driveway. A driveway much like the one leading to the house next door. A house which looked much the same as all the other houses on the street. A street lined with the same houses, filled with the same people doing the same things at the same time, over and over until the beginning skipped past the middle to an end.

Moira shuffled her way towards the kitchen door and stood, unconsciously chewing on her lower lip. She watched Mother, hunched over the kitchen sink, her hair scraped back into a small knotted bun. The odd grey wisp escaping in a static dance about her elf-like ears.

"Morning," Moira whispered. The word lingered in her

throat, as though not quite ready to be born into the world. A hushed statement of the time of day rather than a satisfying greeting of any kind. She forced the word out of her mouth and watched as it flew away on wary wings in the direction of Mother's good ear. The word landed safely at the designated destination and Mother stopped her furious scrubbing. Without turning to face her daughter, her body stiffened, then sighed and released some words of its own.

"You don't have to do this you know," said Mother. And now that the words were out there, floating in the space between them, she turned to face Moira. Their eyes could not and would not meet. "It's not too late to change your mind," Mother added. It was as though the words themselves drained and exhausted her. There was nothing more or less to be said. Moira stared at Mother, who in turn stared at the floor. The floor had nothing to say. It was time to leave, so Moira left the wordless vacuum and returned to her room to fetch her things.

They sat in the taxi. There were things to be said now that the journey had begun, but Moira knew that Mother would never say them in front of the man driving the car. She was grateful then for the ten minutes of peace the snow and a cancelled train had bought them. Her leather seat had retained the heat from the previous passenger, it was strangely comforting to feel the warmth of another human being, albeit indirectly. The driver puckered his dry, chapped lips and performed a lacklustre whistle for the duration of what was always going to be an uncomfortable journey. His eyes met with Moira's in the rear view mirror to confirm that all was far from well. Their final destination echoed the sentiment as the driver pulled up outside the hospital. Mother disliked hospitals. Mother disliked whistling. She grumbled at the fare, there would be no tip.

Moira climbed out of the car and was hit by a wave of apprehension. Mother bum-shuffled across the back seat and followed her daughter into the outside. She mumbled an empty thank you and slammed the car door a little harder than was necessary. They stood still then for what seemed like a long time, while life moved on around them.

"Well come on then, unless you've changed your mind," barked Mother. Willing and able to make a scene, now that the audience had driven away. Moira had not changed her mind. Mother didn't require an answer to know that. "Selfish through and through, just like your father. There's nothing wrong with you, you're just an attention-seeking little bitch." The words stung. She looked at Mother then. Reluctantly, their eyes met. Moira could see her mother's fear, see her anguish, see her guilt. Mother could see that Moira had no intention of turning back, she had come too far now. Neither could cry, though both felt that they should. Mother's face relaxed and softened ever so slightly. The army of angry lines around her mouth temporarily ironed themselves out for the sake of appearances. "Let's go in then, get this over with," she said, before abruptly turning on her heel and leading the way towards what the day had in store. She was not a thoroughly unkind woman. She was capable of love once, but life had changed her, as life sometimes does.

The air felt cold inside the hospital. They registered at

the desk and sat down next to each other but far apart. Mother sighed and glared and fidgeted. They both wanted to speak but were too scared to try. Words can be spoken and unspoken. Important, though sometimes unnecessary.

"I'm going to call Father," announced Mother and left Moira alone with the bare waiting room walls. Moira wanted to ask her to stay, to confess that she was afraid, but the words got stuck.

"Moira Sweeney?" read a nurse from a clipboard. She was younger than Mother but shared the same serious expression and heavily lined brow.

"Yes," said Moira. This felt like school.

"Follow me," said the nurse. Moira looked around for Mother. The nurse, who had already begun walking stopped and turned back to check on her progress. She frowned back at Moira, the lines in her forehead accelerating into folds of deep creases. Her expression said many things, it said, "I'm tired and irritated and hurry up." So Moira did. She followed in the footsteps of the nurse's white squeaky shoes, along sterile corridors and into an unmarked room. She stepped inside and held her breath without meaning to as the door was closed behind her.

The windowless room smelt of talcum powder and was eerily lit by a flickering fluorescent tube. Moira was aware of a lock being turned. A silver-haired man in a white coat sat at a desk squinting at paperwork. He removed his glasses and rubbed them with a grubby-looking red spotty hanky. After a swift but thorough examination, he placed them back on the end of his large bauble of a nose. He squinted at Moira momentarily before returning his attention to the crumpled piece of A4 in his fingertips.

"Come in, come in," he said with a veil of forced cheer. His other long pale hand conducted her closer. "I'm Doctor Goodman. Just reading this letter here from your GP. Step behind the curtain and take your clothes off, there's a good girl. I'll be with you in just a moment," he said. He forced the words out of his mouth as though the effort to expel them exhausted him. With each syllable he grew less able to disguise his weary tone. Moira followed his nicotine-stained finger to a curtained area and did as she was told. She wondered three things; why a doctor would be stupid enough to smoke, whether by taking her clothes off, he had meant everything, or to leave on her socks and pants, and whether Doctor Goodman was indeed a good man or a paedophile in disguise.

Moira removed and carefully folded her clothes into a neat pile. She stood and waited and stared down at her own nakedness. She jumped as the squeaky shoed nurse whisked back the patterned curtain. Her hands instinctively flew to her breasts, uncomfortable with her own nudity and not used to it being observed by others.

"And your knickers," said the nurse, scowling impatiently at the triangle of navy material. Her voice was sharp and snappy and reminiscent of a cloth against glass when cleaning windows. Moira unhappily removed the last item of clothing and stood ill at ease on the cold tiled floor. An army of goose bumps gathered on her skin and her small nipples hardened and pointed at the doctor, willing him to get on with whatever he was going to do. He stood then, rather robotically as though he had things on his mind. His chair scraped angrily across the floor in protest. He pulled back what remained of the curtain blockade and a ripple of displeasure formed on his brow like a critic faced with a substandard work of art. They both stood and stared at her then, frowning in unison. The doctor spoke and the nurse scribbled down his words into permanence, whilst nodding and shaking her square-shaped face at the clipboard.

"How old are you now, Moira?" Doctor Goodman asked her breasts.

"Fifteen," Moira replied to the floor, "I'll be sixteen tomorrow."

"Normal height for age..." said the doctor to the clipboard. "No excessive facial hair." *What a relief*, thought Moira, though she could have diagnosed that part herself, she had eyes and a mirror.

"Hands by your sides, please," he said, his tone impatient, but kind. "Small breasts have formed. There is a mass of pubic hair, indicating that puberty has started or at least tried to. Hop up on to the bed for me and spread your legs, good girl." Moira obeyed his command without question and turned to stare at the wall. There was a poster of a skeleton and a map of Italy. She wondered if this was where the doctor liked to go on holiday. There was a sound of stretching plastic.

"Female genitalia of normal appearance from the exterior," he said before tapping her on the knee with a gloved hand. "Now I'm just going to do a quick internal examination. You have nothing to be afraid of."

Moira was afraid.

6

"It shouldn't hurt."

It did.

"You might feel a little uncomfortable, just try and relax," he said.

She couldn't. Pain had entered the room and he was screaming inside her head. Instinctively Moira snapped her legs shut. The doctor gently opened them again and continued to examine and hurt her. The nurse stood and stared as though this was completely normal, like she was watching something mildly interesting on the television but was considering changing the channel during the next commercial break. Moira stared up at the ceiling and focussed her attention on a small broken spider's web, dancing in the heat from the radiator below. Finally he stopped. Moira tried not to cry as she listened to the sound of stretched plastic, a man's footsteps, the screech of a pedal bin opening its metal jaws and the light thud of the doctor's gloves swallowed inside, used and discarded. The bin snapped closed, its contents redundant and forgotten.

"I'm going to need to do an ultrasound," sighed Doctor Goodman, as though this were the most inconvenient thing to happen to him that day. The nurse momentarily put down her clipboard and wheeled an old-fashioned computer with a small TV screen towards them both. Then she took a tube from the shelf and squirted some cold transparent gel onto Moira's tummy. The doctor took what looked like a small car window scraper and pushed it down onto her abdomen, spreading the cold gel all over her skin. The doctor and the nurse both stared at the small screen, screwing up their faces in displeasure, but Moira couldn't see what they were looking at. The doctor pushed down harder in frustration at whatever he didn't see, rolling the instrument of pain backwards and forwards as though he was ironing and doing his best to straighten her out.

"I can't really tell what I'm looking at," he said crossly. "A rudimentary uterus perhaps?" he asked nobody in particular. The nurse had returned to scribbling and shrugged her shoulders. Moira saw her hand make the shape of a large question mark with her pen. "That's all for now, Moira. Get dressed and sit in the waiting room. Send your mother in, there's a good girl," said Doctor Goodman, before taking the clipboard from the nurse to read what she had written he had said. Was she a good girl? Did the doctor calling her good make it true? Was he a good man? She didn't know the answer to either question. She knew she wanted to go home. Not the home where she lived, but the home in her head. A home she imagined from books and films and longing.

Moira returned to the room for waiting and sat with her fingers in a white knuckle knot on her lap. She sat rigid and still while the hands of the hospital clock stuttered forwards. Time passed, the pain didn't. Just when she thought maybe Mother and Doctor Goodman had forgotten about her, the sound of squeaky shoes echoed down the corridor.

"Follow me please," said the nurse once more. Her gut said to run to the exit, but Moira was an obedient breed of girl, it wasn't in her nature to do the opposite of what someone had asked. She stood and followed the nurse as instructed, back to the room she had recently left. Everything was the same as before, but different. Mother was there this time, sitting opposite the doctor. Her expression was hard to read, twisted and wrong.

"Everything is fine," said Mother.

It wasn't.

"Doctor thinks you just need a little operation, to see what's what." Moira nodded. She didn't need an operation to know that she wasn't like everybody else.

She reluctantly removed her clothes for the second time that day and put on a hospital gown that gaped open at the back. She thought perhaps it was broken but the nurse insisted it was all the rage in the gynaecology ward. Moira wasn't entirely sure what a gynaecologist was. She guessed it meant a fanny doctor and wondered why on earth anyone would ever want to become one of those.

Moira lay on a cold metal bed in her open-backed gown. A porter, in a uniform the colour of dry mud, wheeled her from one part of the hospital to another. She was perfectly capable of walking, despite what the doctor had done, but was grateful for the ride nonetheless. As they travelled down a labyrinth of identical looking corridors, the rolling view of discoloured, magnolia ceilings made her feel dizzy and nauseous, but she didn't complain. In a small room with grey walls, a softly spoken man with tired eyes injected something cold into her arm. The edges of the room went from grey to black. Moira's circle of vision got smaller and smaller until there was only nothing.

Pain awoke and enveloped her. Moira opened her eyes and surveyed her surroundings. This was a new room. A bedroom, but not hers. The pain cradled her firmly in the metal bed, assisted by well washed, white hospital sheets. Her eyes blinked and adjusted to the light before finding Mother and Father, huddled in the corner with sad faces.

"She's awake," said Mother. She disappointed them then, by surrendering to sleep and allowing the throbbing discomfort to close her heavy eyelids once more.

When she opened them again, it was clear that more time had passed, but how much or how little was uncertain. Mother and Father had been joined by Doctor Goodman, who sat on the bed and held her hand. She tried to sit up a little, to get a better view of the final act. The pain sliced between her legs and tore into her tummy, spreading over her body like a glass of spilt milk. She wanted to tell them, but she couldn't speak, couldn't move. She daren't look under the sheets to see what had happened down there.

"How are you feeling?" asked the doctor. Without waiting for her words he continued to spew his own. "I'm afraid I have some very sad news Moira. You have a very rare condition called Rokitansky syndrome. I feel I must confess I've never seen anything like it, but I've spoken to a colleague in the city and he has confirmed what is wrong with you. We will refer you there for some treatment in due course; they'll be able to tell you more about the condition. From what I understand and from what I've seen, in your case it means that your womb did not grow as large as it should. That's why you haven't had any periods. It is probably best if you think of it as not being there at all. The good news is, we didn't find anything unexpected down there, you are otherwise a normal, healthy young woman. The bad news is that you won't ever be able to have a family of your own." Moira processed his words. She couldn't move, she couldn't speak, she could only hurt. The doctor paused then, and stared hard at Moira to try and ascertain if she had heard and understood him. He decided that she had. "I'm very sorry," he added, patting her hand. He was wearing a comforting smile that didn't quite fit his face. After delivering his news and apology he made an awkward departure, leaving his words and a faint smell of talc behind.

Mother and Father came closer to the bed. Not too close. They looked at her with red, swollen eyes, searching for who they thought she had been.

"We'll get through this, together," said Father from a distance. Moira couldn't help thinking that they had never been further apart.

"Everything is going to be okay, you'll see," said Mother. "We are here for you," she added. And then they were gone. They left with the tears they had shed for themselves and the girl they had known.

Moira was left alone with her pain and their sorrow. She reached for her bag at the side of the bed without knowing what she was looking for, careful to keep her body still while her hand explored. She rummaged inside the bag until her fingers found a small, circular, compact mirror. She opened it and cleaned the glass with a corner of the white hospital sheet. She stared for a long time at the reflection and what it showed her. A tear burst its banks and rolled down her cheek as Moira recognised the girl in the mirror. She saw herself. She closed her eyes and silently cried. She had known deep down for as long as she could remember that something was wrong. What she didn't know, was what happened next.

TWO

Tori was rudely awoken by the sound of the alarm. She opened her eyes to squint for the source of the offending noise and silenced it. A solitary tear, independent of motive, formed and slid down her cheek. She brushed it away as though it had never been, as though it wasn't one of many. Her head ached with a subtle throb and she could still taste last night's Malbec on her breath. Harry's arm slipped under hers and pulled her to his chest. She felt safe, she felt loved. To the untrained eye Tori's life was a public exhibition of contentment. She lived in a small but perfectly formed home, she had a good job and a loving husband. Everything was just as it should be. Almost.

"We should get up," she whispered.

"Five more minutes, it's Saturday," he mumbled into her ear. She turned to face him and slowly traced the outline of his jaw with her index finger, enjoying the feel of the stubble. It was almost exactly ten years since they had met as students and he hardly looked a day older. Her hand, in contrast, looked like that of an old woman, her skinny, wrinkled fingers wrapped in tight, dry, paper skin. She withdrew it from the foreground and banished it under the sheets for spoiling her view. They had both wanted to be writers back then in their twenties, filled with hope and optimism at that age when you really do believe you can be anyone you want to be. Harry had succeeded in making his dreams a reality. His first book did reasonably well, well enough for him to quit his job as a teacher. The second book was a bit of a flop, but his third, the one he was writing at the moment, was just brilliant. She had read the first draft and she felt sure their money worries would be over once it was published. Her dreams had not come true, not yet. There were other things she wanted more, and one of them needed to earn a regular income. Tori had started writing a novel of her own, but she couldn't finish it; she didn't know the ending. For now, she was a travel writer who rarely left her desk in an office full of strangers in the city.

"There is so much to do," she said, her mind nagging her eyes to stay open.

"Relax, today is going to be fine, everything will be okay, just five more minutes, I'm so tired, okay?" he said, his eyes still closed. She studied him then, watched the way he breathed, felt the warmth of his body wrapped around hers. He was a good man. She could never quite comprehend what she had done to deserve him or why he was here. She was all he ever wanted and less, so much less. She heard her mother's voice interrupt the thoughts in her head, "We are born alone, we die alone, everything in between is just an illusion." The recollection of the words triggered an involuntary shiver. This was not an illusion, this was real. She wasn't alone, she was loved. She permitted her drowsiness to smudge the memory.

"Okay, five more minutes," she said, feeling her body and mind relax once more. She was tired too, so very tired of sleepwalking through life, trying to remember how to breathe without it hurting. Trying to remember how to be. Struggling to silence the thoughts and fears that consumed her. Waiting for answers to questions that could never be asked. Her eyelids, swollen and heavy from the tears she had shed the night before, surrendered themselves shut and she slept again.

Fear crept into the room and into their bed and woke Tori once more. He whispered in her ear and then shook her awake. She sat bolt upright in panic. It felt like she had only rested her eyes for the briefest of moments, but when she snatched her mobile from the bedside table she realised just how late it was. Panic immobilised her limbs as consciousness reminded her why it had been so important to get up early this weekend.

"Fuck!" yelled Tori, throwing off the covers, leaping out of the bed and knocking over the empty wine bottle and glasses from the night before. The glass smashed and she felt a stab of pain in the little toe of her left foot.

"Fuck!" she screamed again, like a Tourette's sufferer with a very limited vocabulary. She sat back down on the bed and examined her foot which was now bleeding big red blobs onto white cotton blotting sheets.

"What? What time is it? What's happened?" asked a confused and disorientated Harry. He reached for his glasses and sat up in the bed.

"It's ten o'clock, he'll he here in a couple of hours and I've cut my bloody toe," Tori churned out, her words tripping over themselves in their hurry to enter the room and be heard.

After a brief frown and a bewildered silence, Harry shrugged away the confusion.

"Fuck!" he yelled and leapt out of his side of the bed. The Tourette's that morning was contagious. "Don't panic," he said panicking. "Everything is going to be fine." He grabbed his robe off the back of the bedroom door and crouched down to examine Tori's foot. "It's just a scratch," he said unconvincingly, "I'll clear this up, why don't you go and have a quick shower, and don't worry, we have plenty of time," he lied. "You know we'll have to stop swearing all the fucking time when we have a baby in the house," he said with a grin. Tori's face cracked into a smile she reserved only for him.

"If we have a baby," she added, the smile vanishing as quickly as it had appeared.

"When," Harry whispered, staring deep into his wife's eyes. He kissed her on her forehead, then made his way downstairs to find the dustpan and brush. Fear was waiting for him in the hallway and gave him a good hard slap around the face. His expression changed as he told himself to be strong for Tori's sake, and tried to bury his own thoughts and feelings sufficiently deep to not resurface. Harry ignored the pain those thoughts caused him and hurried on to start tidying away their lives.

Tori stood under the shower and let the warm water attempt to wash her worries away. She scrubbed hard at her skin, until it was red and sore, but it made no difference and she had known that it wouldn't. Steam filled the room but it didn't cloud her judgement. She knew the risk she was taking. She turned off the shower and stepped out onto the bath mat. After roughly drying herself with a too small, frayed white towel, she wrapped it around her body before snatching her toothbrush from the cup on the windowsill. She brushed her teeth so hard that her gums bled. She spat the blood out into the sink and watched as the clear water whirled it around the white porcelain, before sucking it down and away as though it had never been. She wiped the steam-covered mirror on the bathroom cabinet with her hand and was startled by the face of the woman who stared back at her. She looked older than she remembered. Old and tired. The neat line of her eyebrows forming a uniformed frown. Did she look good enough? She didn't know the answer and was too afraid to guess.

Time ate away greedily at the hours that were left until it was full and fat. Tori dressed twice before deciding on what looked best, what would look good enough for the visitor. She pulled her long dark hair back into a ponytail and disguised her face with makeup. She was careful to create the right look, a good image. Mindful not to do anything that might somehow ruin her chances. Ruin their chances, she corrected herself. This was for both of them. She opened the bedroom door and stepped out onto the landing, briefly pausing to look at the mess in the spare bedroom. It was Harry's office really. There was a sofa bed for when guests stayed the night, but the main focal point of the room was his large writing desk, covered in precariously balanced piles of books and scraps of scribbled on notepaper. All of this would have to go one day, they would need the room and he would have to write somewhere else; the shed maybe. She hurried down the stairs and grabbed the hoover from Harry. Without words he placed the nozzle in her hand, like a well-practiced relay runner and hurried upstairs to wash and change himself. Being himself today felt like an unworthy option. Tori vacuumed furiously, sucking up any specks of dirt and unsuitability. She washed up, tidied away, lit the fire and dusted the packed shelves. Their home was crammed full of books and longing. Just as she began to think everything might be okay, the doorbell rang. The visitor had arrived. He was early.

Harry flew down the stairs and saw the terror in Tori's eyes. He held her face in his hands, his lips brushing her forehead, kissing the fear away. Love rushed down the chimney and into the room, it soared and encircled them, forcing them closer. Fear fled into the cupboard under the stairs. Tori and Harry stood perfectly still and held each other. Contrary to popular myth, time rarely does stand still. The doorbell rang once again. Harry held Tori's hands in his to stop them from shaking. He kissed her once more and whispered, "I love you." Then he walked towards the door, removed the chain and twisted the lock. He opened the door and offered a welcoming smile as though this were just another day.

The visitor stood on the doorstep, glanced at Harry, then at the file in his hand. He was a good couple of decades older than both of them, a large man, who looked like he had a fondness of beer and a healthy relationship with pies.

"Hello there, David, is it?" said the visitor. A light breeze carried doubt into the hallway to join the conversation. Harry frowned, his shoulders tensed and shifted ever so slightly towards his ears.

"Erm no, it's Harry, can I help you?" The visitor returned his frown and then let his eyes fall back to the file. The corners of the visitor's mouth turned upwards, a slight flush crossed his round cheeks.

"Sorry, you're right, David was the last chap, Harry you are," he said with an odd chuckle. Harry, slightly flummoxed but relieved to have got his own name correct, hoped the rest of the visit would go more smoothly. "I hope I'm not too early, I had a cancellation and came straight here from my last appointment," said the visitor. He was early, but they had been waiting a long time for today and they were ready. Tori and Harry jointly stole an unconscious breath. The visitor stepped into their home and into their lives.

The three assessed each other quickly and quietly. The visitor followed Tori through to the front room and took the seat that he was offered. He lifted a battered black leather briefcase up onto his ample lap and snapped it open, removing a fat wedge of paperwork from inside. The room felt cold and foreign despite being filled with familiar things. They sat surrounded by photos of friends and family, overseeing the situation as it was about to unfold. The faces in the photos smiled on encouragingly.

"How was your journey here?" asked Tori, trying to distract them all from the silence that had filled the room. The visitor gave her his answer but her heart was beating too loudly to hear anything he had to say. "Will you be seeing any other couples today?" she added when the silence threatened to swallow her once more. She didn't hear his response to either question but studied the way his mouth moved as it answered and noted how his top lip curled downwards when he spoke and upwards when he listened. His words sat redundant and cold on the wooden floor. Tori sat on her hands whenever she noticed they were trembling and reminded herself not to chew her lower lip. Harry reached out and put his hand on hers and she felt an instant calm wash over her. She knew she could do this with him by her side. Together they would get through it.

"So..." said the visitor, ceremoniously relocating the angry pile of paperwork from his ample lap to the coffee table. It formed a sturdy pine and paper border between them and him. His lips made a smacking sound as he searched for the words he hoped to deliver and they waited to hear. "So," he repeated once again before deciding how to conclude the sentence, "...you are hoping to become parents."

"We are," answered Harry for them both.

"And you're interested in surrogacy?" asked the visitor. Hearing the S word out loud shocked Tori. It bounced around her head colliding with all her own words which popped on impact like over-filled balloons. It was a dirty, rude little word. Something from a foreign dialect that she couldn't quite pronounce. An illegitimate word from a language she wouldn't speak and could barely comprehend. This was all her fault. She was broken beyond repair and now this dirty secret of a word was their only hope. It chugged through her mind like an out of control steam train. Surrogacy. Surrogacy. Surrogacy.

"We've explored all the possibilities and after a great deal of thought we think surrogacy is the best option for us to have a family of our own," said Harry. It sounded so less awful when he said it, his voice purifying the meaning of the letters arranged in order to form the words she couldn't speak. They were words he had rehearsed. They sounded good out in the open. Harry pressed Tori's hand in his and squeezed a little consciousness back into her.

"Yes," she managed to whisper in agreement. Harry's love turned a key inside her. Tori's true self awoke from a coma of doubt. The words that had been unsure, uncertain and uncomfortable only seconds before, flew out of her mouth forming paper-chain sentences which danced above their heads. Her other self sulked and sat back in the shadows of the heavy, suffocating childlessness. That self was plagued by longing for something, for someone she feared she would never know. Questions were asked, answers were given. Smiles were exchanged and hope popped round for a long awaited visit.

"So...I've read through your application letter and I understand this is your only option to have a child of your own. I'm pleased to say we'd be happy for you to join the agency, subject to medical and criminal checks, and hopefully we'll be able to help you find a surrogate mother and get you that baby."

Tori felt a weight on her chest lift a little and the crack in her heart begin to heal. Harry squeezed her hand and held her together.

"Is there anything else we need to do?" asked Harry.

"Just the payment...if you don't mind," came the swift reply.

"Of course," said Harry, reaching for his cheque book. He wrote down some numbers representing cash that he didn't have but that his overdraft would cover. Then he signed the thin slip of paper before handing it over and hoping that the money might buy them some happiness.

"Lovely to meet you both," said the visitor before making his way out of their home and their lives and down the garden path. He took their hopes, their dreams and their money with him.

They held their breath and stood still as stone, until they heard the sound of an engine starting and the visitor's car driving him away from their vulnerability.

"Did we do okay?" asked Tori, closing the door now that it was safe to do so.

"We did great, you were brilliant," said Harry, wrapping his arms around her.

"*You* were brilliant," she said, reaching up to kiss him.

"I love you," he said. He still looked at her the way he had when they first met. She hoped he would always look at her that way. She reminded herself how lucky she was for all the things she *did* have.

"I love you more," she whispered and buried her face in his chest, catching a glimpse of their reflection in the dining room mirror. She stared at the glass a second longer than was necessary to process the image of the happy couple that gazed back at her. She looked just long enough to see the smile disappear from Harry's face when he thought she could no longer see. She did love him, more than she thought was sensible sometimes. She hoped their love was strong enough to survive this. She wished she knew that it would be.

THREE

Mrs Brown opened her eyes. It was an effort, as was almost everything nowadays. She wondered where she was. Then wondered why she had wondered. She was in the same place she always was when she woke up, her bed. Her eyes struggled and strained to adjust to the bright light slicing through the crack in the curtain. The house was silent. Pain had been to visit in the night and woken her early. She felt him all over her like an unwanted lover but he mostly settled for holding her hands in his. She looked down at them, two tight angry fists, slowly opening flowers of crooked bony fingers, white knuckle thorns and paper-like petals of skin over blue vein stems. She reached for her glasses on the bedside table and slipped them up onto the end of her nose. Her head felt too heavy as she tried to sit up, as though it might just roll off her neck and down onto the floor. Her fingertips found the reading lamp which shed some light on the matter.

Her pupils adjusted themselves to wakefulness and light, allowing her eyes to find the face of her husband, or at least a photo of his face on the dresser. He looked happy and brimming with youth. She remembered taking the photo as though it was yesterday, but of course it was a long time ago now, back when it was just the two of them, when they were happy. She glanced over her shoulder at the right hand side of the bed. The sheet was smooth and flat and neatly tucked in place. She missed him. Still, there was no point moping about the place. She knew it wouldn't be long before they could spend some time together. Life went on, at least for some at Godalming Lodge, and this building and its elderly inhabitants were her life. Until she could find a full time replacement manager to run the place she was stuck here day and often night, trying to do all of the things that needed to be done. She heard the things the staff said about her when they thought she couldn't hear. They all thought she was too old for the job, mainly because she was. She missed her own bed, her own family, and her own life, but as she kept reminding herself and her husband, this was only temporary. He thought she was mad, working so hard at her age, but he understood her reasons. In so many ways, her work gave her a reason to live.

Mrs Brown sat up. It felt like a major achievement. With effort she swung her legs around to the side of the bed and eased her feet into her fur-lined slippers. The cold mornings and Mrs Brown's arthritis did not get along. Sitting up had been relatively easy, now came the tricky part. She gently started the rocking motion, slowly at first, backwards and forwards, forwards and backwards on the edge of the bed, gaining momentum until, with the help of her clawed hands she launched herself into an upright standing position. She waited the few seconds required to determine whether the launch had been successful. She didn't fall back down onto the bed and smiled to herself at getting up on the first attempt on such a cold Monday morning. Or was it Tuesday? Her memory sometimes played tricks on her, but she liked to think she still had a full set of marbles. Running a residential care home for the elderly certainly required them all.

Now that Mrs Brown was officially up, she could get on with her day. Like most days, today was bound to be busy, her time was no longer her own. Until a new manager could be found, it had become easier to live on site with the residents from time to time rather than commute backwards and forwards every day. There were never enough staff and this way she was always close by if there was a problem. She surveyed her surroundings. She hated this room. It was like a floral-covered prison cell. Though she was free to come and go as she pleased, she felt trapped in here, suffocated. How many people had died in this room, in this bed? She shuffled towards the oversized bay window on painful toes and drew back the curtains, permitting the bright sunshine to render her briefly blind. Her tired eyes blinked revealing snapshots of a cloudless blue sky, the outside world looked entirely agreeable. With tremendous effort she opened the window and the sound of birds' chatter broke the still silence. The floor above creaked, joining in the chorus with an out of tune melody, momentarily snatching her attention from the glorious outdoors. Nobody was walking overhead, the house was simply stretching and yawning away the night that had been and gone. Ancient floorboards, groaning like old bones, bored and bending with the prospect of another day much like the last. Mrs Brown willed the window to open further and greedily gulped the cool air that surged into the room. The house had a certain staleness to it. It was more than a smell, it was an aftertaste of talcum powder, piss and a lonely despair that no potpourri could disguise. Even when she left the house she could still smell it on her clothes and in her hair. They were all just waiting for the end together, some knew it was coming, nobody knew when.

The garden was looking quite splendid, protectively encircling the proud old building. The grounds of the lodge were as impressive as the house itself. Unlike the crumbling bricks and bodies within, it didn't show its age. These walls had stood on this hill overlooking the town below for over a century. These rooms had held and warmed a wealthy family of shipping merchants and their decedents before the property was emptied and sold. The impressive country estate had itself retired to a quieter, simpler existence and was reborn into a place where people came to die. The walls were solid and trustworthy and had seen a great many things. They protected those inside from all of the elements, including reality. The walls kept the residents' darkest secrets, heard their final thoughts and prayers and hid the tears shed for hopes and dreams never realised.

Mrs Brown shuffled her way past the unmade bed towards the en-suite. She pulled the cord to illuminate the small bathroom, there was no window. The extractor fan hummed and whirred into action. She found the sound comforting. It reminded her of home and was part of a daily routine which held her together. She gripped the sink to steady herself. The reflection of an elderly woman stared back at her from the mirrored door of the bathroom cabinet. They gazed quietly at one another, sussing each other out. Mrs Brown never failed to be shocked by the sight of the old lady in her bathroom each and every morning. She looked as tired as she felt. Time had carved deep lines into her once youthful face and her thinning grey hair was in a delicate, wispy plait that fell over her shoulder. She squinted through her thick spectacles to get a better look at the woman she knew to be herself but failed to recognise. It was the eyes that gave her away. Somewhere behind them she could just make out a shadow of the girl she had been, the woman she grew into. The pale skin around her eyes was translucent and timeworn. She did not like what she saw, so opened the bathroom cabinet, banishing the elderly stranger and revealing a small pharmacy of pills. She didn't take any, she couldn't remember what they were for. She made sure the little bottles of tablets were in a straight row, arranged according to height. It was something she did every morning and something which Rosie the nurse called OCD. Mrs Brown didn't know what OCD meant. She called it neat and tidy. She washed her face and popped in her teeth.

Mrs Brown shuffled back into the bedroom, pulled open the dresser drawer and examined the neat rows of socks and knickers. She wondered how many other people had stored their underwear in these drawers and thought better of thinking about it. They sometimes did her laundry for her when she stayed, which was kind. She made sure her clothes were washed separately from the residents' belongings. She didn't want her nice things to be washed in with theirs, floating around with their vomit stains, dribble, piss and shit. She found a vest and a healthy portion of guilt in the bottom drawer; it wasn't their fault they were so disgusting, they hadn't always been. She was grateful for the nurses who worked so hard to deal with the messier side of old age. She mainly had to deal with all the staffing issues, paperwork and visitors, so had more than enough of her own shit to deal with.

She closed all the drawers, determined to seal her guilt back inside for the day. She had selected a pair of lilac cotton knickers, amused and ashamed by their tent-like size, she pulled them on, one leg slowly after the other. In the wardrobe she found a nice summery cotton dress to match the optimistic weather outside. Everything she now owned was washable at forty degrees; there was no time anymore for fancy frills or fuss. Pulling the dress on was an effort. Pain rose up with the hot air through the floorboards and stabbed at her body. She fought with the dress to pull it up and over her head, her fingers shaking disobediently like frightened little twigs as she struggled with the buttons. She wrapped her trusty cream cardigan around her shoulders and was ready for what the day had to offer. She closed the window and picked up the pile of paperwork that she had meant to finish the night before from the desk. She would take it to the conservatory, it was lighter in there and she could keep a closer eye on everyone.

Mrs Brown stepped out of the laughable sanctuary of

her room and peered down the barren hallway. The stale air of the corridor flooded her lungs. There was nothing she could do to stop herself from breathing it, from breathing them. Like smoke from a bonfire, the stench of decay clung to her and followed her around from dawn until dusk. A constant reminder for all who entered Godalming Lodge, they weren't so very different from the residents who lived within. A warning to all that their time would one day come and was inevitably closer than they might think. Life wasn't too short, it was too fast. If you didn't keep up, you would get left behind, and spend your life alone looking back over your shoulder at all that could have been. Mrs Brown carefully and cautiously put one foot in front of the other towards the new day, looking forward, not back, for fear of what she might see.

FOUR

Moira slowly opened her eyes and stared at the artex ceiling. She focused on the swirls and patterns and found comfort in the silent shapes. Since she came home from the hospital, these brief moments between sleep and wakefulness were the most precious, safest time of the day. Unknowledgeable seconds to be enjoyed, before memory reminded her who she was and what she would never be. She breathed a silent sigh and wished that she had not yet found out what she already knew. Her sixteenth birthday had been and gone, spent in a lonely hospital bed with little cause for celebration. It didn't matter. It was best forgotten about.

Moira carefully manoeuvred her left arm out from under the duvet without moving any other part of her body. Her fingers spidered over the surface of the bedside table, before locating the old fashioned alarm clock and lifting it in front of her face. She squinted her eyes until they obeyed her brain. They translated the hands of the clock to contribute to her decision-making on the matter of getting up. It was seven-thirty. If she was going to school today, it was time to get out of bed. She sat up too quickly and the pain ripped through her. It had been five days since the operation and it still hurt when she moved. She was tired of sitting around the place, and bored with the self-pity her parents encouraged and imposed upon her.

Moira washed herself and poured her limbs into her uniform. She checked her reflection front and back twice, to be sure that nobody could see the giant pad between her legs beneath her school skirt. The bleeding had almost completely stopped, but mother would be angry if she got any more blood on her virgin underwear or the white bed sheets.

She made her way downstairs, where the house was unusually quiet for the time of day; no kitchen sounds, no radio, no voices to greet her ears. Mother and Father were sitting in silence, together but apart at the kitchen table. They stared at her as though an unwelcome stranger had entered the room, fearful but protected in a bubble of twinned solitude.

"Let me handle it," muttered Mother under her breath. The words were meant for Father's ears only, but an unexpected breeze drifted through the open kitchen window, it caught the words and hurled them in Moira's direction. They were mere whispers by the time they reached Moira, who still stood statue-like in the doorway. She blinked with understanding, well aware that she was the 'it' and curious to discover how she was about to be handled. Father's eyes accepted Mother's words, they avoided his daughter and turned down to frown at the table.

"Good morning, how are you feeling?" asked Mother, a bizarre forced cheerfulness in her tone. She tried to smile at her daughter. It had been so long since she had done so, that her face twisted with confusion.

"Okay," said Moira, wanting desperately to leave this place and go to school. "Thank you for asking," she added, afraid to say the wrong thing, careful to use words that would be deemed to be polite, anxious to avoid confrontation. Mother had been kind to her since the operation, Moira didn't want the ceasefire to end.

"Come and sit down, darling, I see you have dressed for school, but are you still in pain?"

"I'm okay," lied Moira and sat down opposite them both.

"Good, that's good," said Mother. "We just wanted to sit down and have a chat with you before you go back to school. Would you like some breakfast?"

"No."

"No thank you," corrected Mother, a flash of danger in her eyes.

"No thank you," repeated Moira.

"Your father and I having been thinking about how best to handle your situation." There was a pause then, an empty vacuum for Moira to fill, but she didn't have the right words to fit the space, so it remained barren. It was like a square desperately trying to fit with a circle, another invisible gap widening between them and her. In the absence of a response, Mother took a deep breath and continued. The words which came out of her mouth had been carefully considered and rehearsed.

"We think it is best, for now at least, that your...condition, remains a family matter. Father and I don't think there is any need for your friends or teachers to know about the hospital appointment or what the doctors have said. We have decided that they would only judge you if they knew the truth. You are too young to decide how best to handle the situation and Father and I agree that not to talk about it, with anyone, is the best way forward for all concerned." It was the most that Father and Mother had agreed on in years, thought Moira.

"Why?" was the only word to form and pop out of her mouth and into the room in response to Mother's suggestion of secrecy. It bounced off the wall and landed in the centre of the table amongst the breakfast things, which would not be touched.

"Why?" Moira said again, a little louder this time. She had not meant to repeat herself, but the first why had seemed so lonely and afraid. The twin why landed inside Mother's coffee cup, then echoed around the room, desperate to be heard by ears that would listen.

"Well, because Father and I want to protect you. The world is a cruel place, Moira, and children can be particularly unkind. There is no need for anyone to know that you are different. And if they don't know, they can't be mean to you."

"Why would they be mean to me?" asked Moira, confused.

"Because you are different and if you let them know your weaknesses, they will hurt you. Father and I don't want to see you get hurt. Do you understand?" Moira nodded but didn't understand at all. She felt their shame and it became her own.

"Everything happens for a reason," said Mother. This was one of her favourite things to say. She only ever said it when things were really bad. And she never elaborated further on what the reason for everything happening actually was. Moira was tempted to question the favoured statement, but decided three whys were enough for one day. "Your condition is nothing to be ashamed of," said Mother. The truth was a lie and forced a further unexpected silence. Mother had inexplicably run out of words. Sensing there was more to be said, Father chose to add some without permission.

"It is best if we just keep this a family secret. Do you understand?" said Father. *No*, thought Moira.

"Yes," she said. She understood that they were ashamed. She understood why.

Father drove Moira to school. Normally she would have walked but Father had insisted, making her return to reality even less natural. Mother had made her a packed lunch, something she hadn't done for years. In trying to make her feel normal, they had made everything strange and different. They wanted to protect her from any more hurt, but pain was now her shadow and had spread to her heart and mind. They had only noticed her fragility when she was already broken.

At school, Moira's body continued its routine; it stood when the bell rang and walked to wherever it needed to go. Her mind however, was far, far away. Her friends and teachers all seemed to believe her story about being off school with a tummy bug and Moira quickly learned that living a lie was remarkably easy. They collectively put her quietness down to still feeling a little under the weather. At lunchtime, she quietly ate the sandwiches Mother had made without any awareness of what was inside them. She chewed absentmindedly, whilst listening to her friends' happy chatter. The food kept lodging in her throat, causing her to cough and making it hard to swallow. She drank a can of what could have been cola or lemonade to wash the food down, she didn't know and didn't care which.

Moira felt a heavy sense of shame in the changing room that afternoon. She reluctantly peeled off each layer of her uniform, embarrassed by the imperfect body hidden beneath. The other girls giggled and gossiped and behaved as though removing their clothes was just routine. Moira fretted about the pad between her legs and pulled up her gym knickers under her school skirt, hoping that nobody would notice. She turned to face the wall and hid her body from the others, hurriedly pulling the grey-white t-shirt over the training bra Mother had bought her last summer. Moira had never been comfortable in her own skin. She had always hated her body and now she had good reason to. It had failed her. It hadn't done what it was supposed to do, what the other girls' bodies had successfully managed. She sat on the bench while her classmates chatted and changed at their leisure, filling the air with gossip and cheap spray. Her eyes found the floor, but jealousy and curiosity encouraged them to pay more attention to their surroundings. Many of the other girls were standing about in their underwear. Moira found herself gazing at their bodies, their breasts in particular, almost all of which seemed larger than her own. She stared down at her feet, her flat chest doing little to hide the view and wondered if they knew, if secretly they all knew that she was different.

An angry looking Ms Searle appeared in the doorway. The born-to–be-single gym teacher entered the changing room looking less than satisfied. She had the body of a young man, the face of a sunburnt turkey and the personality of someone who was distinctly displeased with the mediocre hand life had dealt them.

"I don't know which part of 'be ready to go in five minutes' you silly girls had difficulty understanding, but for those of you with smaller brains than my pet goldfish, let me make myself clear. Anyone not changed, stretched, outside and ready for cross country in sixty seconds will be running the course in their underwear. Do you understand?" she barked, her eyes piercing through each and every adolescent. A murmured response groaned through the sweaty, sock-covered floor. It was not enough to satisfy Ms Searle.

"Shall we try that again?" she snarled, the edges of her words a little sharper now, slicing through the air. "Thirty seconds left now, do you understand?"

"Yes, Ms Searle," chanted the choir of hastily changing pubescents. Gratified, for now at least, Ms Searle went outside to wait in the cold, determined to humiliate and belittle anyone who dared disobey her. She was not a happy woman. Her world was a sad and lonely one.

The gaggle of girls, all thankful to be dressed in more than just their underwear, began the long and arduous route that their unhappy teacher had mapped out for them moments before. It was to be a particularly long and gruelling run, mostly uphill through muddy woods. Unknown to the girls, Ms Searle had recently broken up with a lover, was struggling to pay her mortgage and was terribly worried about her mother who had suffered a stroke the previous month. She translated her own pain into a cross country run around a murky, deserted lake and a dark, muddy forest. No doubt at least one of the students would get lost along the way. Ms Searle felt her whole life had been one giant wrong turn, but fear told her she was too old and it was too late to start again or ask for directions.

Moira began to run. She ran away from the school, away from her friends, and away from herself. At the start of their journey, the group of girls ran as one. Twenty-eight sets of legs, a steady rhythm of trainers and plimsolled feet pounding the muddy school field that led out to the neighbouring park and forest. As the minutes and the miles stretched out before them, the pack began to break down, a few pushing out ahead, a steady group in the middle, and a handful of girls, including Moira, who started to fall behind. Under normal circumstances, cross country was something Moira would have excelled at. But, only a few days after the operation, she was still gripped by pain and with every step, the agony intensified. The doctor had said not to exercise for at least ten days, but Mother didn't think anyone at the school should be informed and a note would only draw more attention to the unmentionable truth. Mother told Moira not to make a fuss and the memory of her words played on a repetitive loud loop in her mind. Her feet knew what to do and continued onwards around the lake and upwards beyond the hill and into the shadowy woods.

Time seemed to stretch. Moira's feet grew sluggish and weary, tripping over themselves and struggling to remember the part they were to play. Her mind allowed itself to run on ahead, while her body slowed down, held back by heavy, cumbersome limbs that had long since forgotten the way. Before she thought to remember where and when she was, Moira found herself completely alone. She came to a complete standstill beside a lightning-struck weeping willow and stared in horror at a small trickle of blood as it ran down the inside of her thigh. Rain had surreptitiously started to fall. It mixed with the tears that now fell freely from her eyes and streaked her face. Time became an unknown, she ran and ran and cried until there was nothing left. Alone in the woods in the darkness, she fell to her knees and allowed herself to feel how she felt. Her chest hurt, her lungs temporarily reluctant to expel the air within, her body it seemed had forgotten how to breathe. It did not matter where or when she was anymore. She curled into a ball on the forest floor and held herself like someone else should, like nobody had. She held the self she had finally let herself be and at some point, after the wind and the rain and the tears and the mud had had their way with her, she let herself sleep. She switched herself off.

FIVE

Tori circled the compact car park like an eagle-eyed robin. The surgery was busier than the local supermarket and the clientele even more aggressive. Not wishing to be late for her appointment she negotiated into a tight spot, turned off the engine, removed the key and reminded herself that breathing was a necessary pastime. Tori wasn't afraid of doctors, she just didn't like them. Nor did she trust them. Any of them. But this should be a simple case of in and out. All she needed was a signature and a referral, how difficult could that possibly be? She checked her reflection in the small visor mirror, slowly moving her head to inspect each part of her face as it was impossible to see it all at the same time. Her long dark hair sat down and relaxed upon her shoulders, her make up discreet, her eyes wide but tired, her camouflage complete. She bared her teeth, checking for lipstick she had forgotten to wear. She looked good. Good enough. She grabbed her bag from the empty passenger seat. Harry had offered to come with her but there was no point in them both sitting around aging in a germ-filled waiting room. There would be plenty of time for that later on, she presumed, she hoped.

The building was rectangular and sterile. Its internal

40

walls were plastered with posters and leaflets, an information overload of various illnesses, diseases and medical conditions one would hope never to catch. The first obstacle was the reception area. There were two desks, two receptionists and two queues. There was no time for a considered choice as the sick were still piling in behind her. She opted for the queue to the desk on the left, and soon wished that she hadn't. The ailing line snaked slowly forwards with a hiss of coughs and sneezes. Unanswered phones rang loudly in the background, like an unstoppable alarm warning those in the queue not to get too close. Tori's new shoes crushed her toes and hurt the balls of her feet. She stood in line, shifting her weight from one foot to the other, trying to alleviate the pain. She wished she had chosen to wear something else. She wished she had made a different choice. After an uncomfortable amount of time, Tori reached the desk.

"Yes?" said the receptionist without looking up. Her mouth was twisted downwards, her lank blonde hair was greasy at the roots and her eyebrows had been over plucked into angry thin lines. She looked as though she had never been loved or loved in return. Doubt washed over Tori, making her increasingly apprehensive. She found her voice and encouraged it to find some words to stammer at the unfriendly woman behind the glass.

"Hello, I have an appointment to register this morning," she said.

"Name?"

"Tori."

"You're late."

"I've been in the queue." Their eyes met and agreed not to like each other's owners.

"Take a seat outside the nurse's room, Room Five, down the corridor," barked the receptionist.

"The nurse? I need a see a doctor, I have some forms that need to be signed. I spoke to someone on the phone..."

"Have you been here before?" interrupted the receptionist.

"No." Tori wouldn't be here now unless she really needed to be.

"Then you need to register. Registration is done by the nurse."

"Can I make an appointment to see a doctor afterwards then please?"

"No. Not until you have registered. You can try and make an appointment then but I expect we will be full. It is very busy today. It is always very busy. What do you want to see a doctor about?" Tori froze. It was as though the whole clinic was suddenly silent, everyone's eyes were on her, their ears eagerly listening for her answer.

"I'd rather talk about it with the doctor," whispered Tori, leaning over the desk ever so slightly, trying to convey the personal nature of her visit. The receptionist recoiled, leaning back as though physically repulsed.

"If it isn't an emergency then I'm afraid you will have to come back tomorrow. Next!" she shrilled, concluding their exchange. Tori reluctantly followed the signs to Room Five and sat in the empty seat outside the door, not knowing what else she could or should do. Fear allowed her to feel defeat and she had not yet reached the first hurdle. She wondered whether they could really do this, whether they, whether she, was strong enough. The receptionist didn't know how hard it had been for Tori to come there that day, to take the first step. She didn't know how much more difficult she had just made a situation that was already impossibly hard.

Time passed and was lost in a jumble of fear and thoughts. Her name was called and her legs stood, allowing her feet to walk towards the door. Tori found herself entering a small, square room. The plump nurse who had called her name spoke with a kind Irish accent. She smelt of pharmacy perfume and mints. She weighed Tori, took her blood pressure, scribbled ticks and crosses on a questionnaire and asked her a series of non-invasive questions, until,

"Any medical conditions or operations in the past that we should know about?"

"No," said Tori. It was a well-practiced and convincing lie, she almost believed it herself. There was simply no point in wasting both their time, the nurse wouldn't understand and definitely couldn't help. Tori needed to talk to the doctor, not the kind nurse or the unkind receptionist.

"I have some forms that I need the GP to sign, that's why I came today..."

"I see. Do you have an appointment?"

"No, and the receptionist didn't seem to think I could get one. It's just that I have to work tomorrow..."

"I understand, let me see what I can do," she said with an empathetic smile and left the room. She reappeared moments later. "All sorted, you'll have to wait a wee while I'm afraid, but Doctor Patel has an appointment free in forty minutes or so."

"Is Doctor Patel a woman?" asked Tori, not really sure why it mattered.

"She is indeed, last time I checked."

"Thank you very much."

"Not at all, you're welcome. Good luck," said the nurse, sensing that Tori could use some, regardless of what it was for.

Tori sat and waited. It wasn't the first time. It wouldn't be the last. She cursed herself for not bringing a good novel to read. Her eyes searched the room for a source of entertainment and evaluated the occupants of the chairs around her. There were children with their intolerant or indifferent parents and some elderly patients. Not a great deal in between. Time passed slowly and after an hour or so Tori's name was finally called for a second time. She entered what was a larger square room than before and closed the door, sealing herself and her fate inside its walls. She noticed the large window, a good source of natural daylight or perhaps an emergency exit of sorts, she pondered. She took the seat that was offered and introduced herself. Without any previous notes, the GP could do little more than listen, which she did, impatiently, intensely and without expression until Tori ran out of words.

"I've never heard of your condition," said Doctor Patel. She was neither friendly nor unfriendly, a slender and serious looking woman with a hint of grey around her temple. She wore a dark supermarket-bought suit and a frown. Tori wished Harry was there.

"It's quite rare," said Tori.

"And I've never come across a patient who wanted to try surrogacy either," said the doctor. The S word. She said it as though it was dirty and had left a sour taste on her tongue. There was a silence then. It stretched from the door to the window and filled the room. As though perhaps the appointment was over and that was that.

"Have you not considered adoption?" asked Doctor Patel.

"Yes of course...we've given quite a lot of consideration to all the options, but if it is possible, and I know the odds are against us, but if we can, then I would like to try for a baby of our own."

"I see," came the reply. Tori felt the cloud of doubt that hung over the room lift a little. "But surrogacy, especially with a stranger...it's all very...strange. I mean have you and your husband properly looked into all this? The agency you mentioned, are you sure it's all above board? I don't know a huge amount about the subject but for starters I thought it was illegal to pay for someone to carry a baby." Doubt was replaced by a hint of anger and Tori did her very best to make it lie low. She looked over at the window, imagining herself climbing through it, away from this place and this ignorant woman.

"It is illegal, sort of. The payment we would make is for the surrogate's expenses...travel etc."

"Fifteen thousand pounds worth of travel? I don't wish to sound unhelpful, but this all sounds very risky and very

45

strange. If you want to pursue surrogacy, do you not have a sister or family member or friend even who might be able to help, rather than a complete stranger? How do you know they won't keep the baby and what if they do? I've read about that happening in the papers. Surely legally they would be entitled to do so? They would be the mother after all..."

"I would be the biological mother," Tori interrupted. The woman had used the word strange once too often and her insensitivity was enraging. "Harry, my husband, would be the biological father."

"And legally?"

"Legally...she, the surrogate would be the child's mother when it was born, but only until a parental order was granted, which only takes a few weeks and it is practically unheard of for surrogates to try and keep the baby with host surrogacy."

"Host surrogacy?"

"Yes, using my eggs and my husband's sperm," said Tori. She wanted to stand up and leave, but she couldn't, she needed this awful woman to help her.

"You've lived in the area for a couple of years, but haven't registered until now, why is that?" asked Doctor Patel, intent on continuing her interrogation.

"I haven't needed to, I haven't been sick," replied Tori simply.

"Do you know you're overweight?"

Do you know you're a bitch? thought Tori, but did not let the words enter the room.

"No..." she said, slightly taken aback and mentally

searching for a defence, "I'm only a size twelve, I thought that was fairly normal."

"Dress size is irrelevant, your BMI based on your height and weight is over what it should be. Do you drink?"

"Yes, but just at weekends, we know the chances of success are better if we drink less so we've already cut back," said Tori. It was only a tiny white lie, today was a week day and she was definitely going to have a drink tonight. Her head began to ache, pain pounding her temples to compete with the discomfort that the too-tight shoes were causing.

"Okay. Well it sounds like you have done your homework, I'll need to do some of my own. There are two options for local hospitals for IVF, but you need to understand these things take time. I will have to write to them and explain your case and see if I can get you an appointment, but there are no guarantees that I will be able to do so and even if I can, they might not be able to help you with your particular situation. And then there's the PCT who will have to decide about funding, I really don't think you'll get any. IVF has been around for a while, but it is still very much in its infant stages. Success rates aren't great and with the added complication of surrogacy...I just don't know what is possible. I've been a GP for twenty five years and I've never come across this before."

"I understand. I had some forms from the agency that I need signing."

"Without your notes and without the consent of your husband, I'm afraid I can't sign anything today."

"Why not?"

"I don't know anything about you or your husband, you could have something wrong with you or be mentally unstable for all I know." Tori wasn't mentally unstable but was starting to feel that way.

"The form is just to say that you are my GP so that they can contact you if they need to. It isn't about medical conditions or suitability. I've waited a really long time to do this, to come here."

"Then I'm sure you can wait another two weeks. It will give me time to read through your notes and talk to some colleagues. If I am going to help you with this you will need to learn to be patient. This won't happen overnight, if it happens at all that is. Make another appointment for two weeks' time at reception on your way out."

Tori nodded, stood and thanked Doctor Patel for her time. She went to reception, queued and made another appointment as instructed. She left the building, walked to the car, opened the door, and sat down in the driver's seat. She reached into her bag, her fingers found her phone. She called Harry, but he didn't answer. She started the engine, then immediately turned it off. Tiny little spits of rain exploded on the windscreen. She observed them quietly, her eyes joining the dots to form shapes that meant nothing at all. The miniscule dots grew large and fat until their own weight dragged them downwards in a row of watery stripes. The shower was rapidly followed by a full on downpour, producing a river of angry liquid streaming down the windows. The rainwater prison held her hostage, obscuring the view of the outside world, which carried on all around her. A solitary tear escaped her right eye and trickled down to her chin, leaving a glistening, moist trail on her cheek. It was the first of many, as though there was an invisible tap that could not be turned off. Tori couldn't run or drive away, she couldn't see through her tear-filled eyes or the rain-covered windscreen. There was nowhere to hide, so she sat and she cried until there were no tears left and the rain had stopped. She wished she could leave the pain of the words that had been spoken behind in Dr Patel's room, but they were in her head forever now and she would have to take them home to share the pain they had caused with Harry, to lessen the heartache and halve the hurt.

SIX

Mrs Brown shuffled her way towards the conservatory, which doubled up as her office. Every day, come rain or shine she could be found in her chair at the far end of the house, rustling through type-covered papers in the forgiving morning light. It was a good place to work. The sun shone and danced upon the walls, throwing a flickering woodland canopy over the tired furniture. Mornings were the quietest time in the old house, the only time when the residence was at rest. The stillness of the conservatory was perfect for concentrating and contemplating the day ahead. Her preferred vantage point also had the added benefit of adjoining the main lounge, so that Mrs Brown could keep a short-sighted eye on the residents at the same time as sorting through all the mail. There was no email in this house, only printed fonts or handwritten pages penned with joined up, ink stained words. Words mostly about the past, occasionally about the present, rarely about the future, for it was a future many here knew they would never know.

The journey from Mrs Brown's bedroom to the conservatory was positively epic. Her limbs had long since resisted any form of long distance activity before lunch time. Today however, was a good day. With perseverance and a pinch of stubbornness, she eventually made it to her seat. She eased herself into the chair and delighted in the blanket of silence that settled around her. Nobody else was up yet. This was her quiet time. It was a chance for solitude before the rest of the cast took their places on the set of their daily lives.

She cast a sleepy eye about the place. Everything was as it should be; quiet and tired and still. A little bit like some of the residents. There was a series of small couches, armchairs, sofas, footstools and coffee tables; mismatched, time-worn furnishings that didn't belong together. They were like lost pieces of multiple jigsaw puzzles, thrown together to be forgotten in a battered old box. Some of the residents didn't think they belonged here either. It saddened Mrs Brown to know that some of them might be right.

It had always fascinated her that the majority of the residents would choose a chair upon arrival at the home and then sit in that same seat every day until...well, until they left. Everyone had different requirements; some liked to sit with others, some liked to sit alone. Some sat on chairs so low that they were completely unable to get back up out of them afterwards. Others insisted on several cushions in order to sit just high enough to look down their noses at their companions. She studied their expressions sometimes. It was as though they were glaring at disagreeable strangers who they would meet for the first time every day for the rest of what was left of their lives. Mrs Brown's mouth felt dry, she licked her lips and wished she had a cup of tea.

Tea and coffee were served twice a day in the lounge; first at eleven, to give everybody a little something between breakfast and lunch and then again at three, on the dot. The afternoon tea was served promptly or a certain madness came over the place. Residents would begin to stare, mesmerized by the hands of the grandfather clock from as early as two in the afternoon, counting down the minutes until the trolley would arrive. If it entered the room so much as a minute late, there would be audible complaints for the rest of the day. Tardy tea would not be tolerated. Mrs Brown liked a good cup of tea, especially with a biscuit to dunk. She wouldn't touch the coffee, hated the stuff, just the smell of it made her feel sick. She smiled to herself as a memory of Mr Brown came to her. He liked nothing more than returning to bed on a Sunday morning with a cup of hot coffee and the newspapers. He would slurp the hot, black liquid loudly, methodically reading the first few pages of black print, while she casually flicked through the supplements. When his cup was empty, he would abandon the half-read newspaper and cuddle up to her, his face close to hers so they could kiss. Then he would roar with laughter as she recoiled from his coffee breath. She would laugh and scream and pretend to fight him off, whilst he held her tight covering her face in coffee-flavoured kisses. She longed for him to hold her like that again. To be together wrapped up in nothing but sheets and happiness. There had been so many things she had taken for granted back then.

Mrs Brown came back to the present. She misplaced the

smile that had formed on her face but retained a feeling of contentment as she observed the quiet room, enjoying the stillness of it once more. Of course it wasn't perfect. She had long believed perfection was a myth, something that only occurred when love blocked out the imperfections of life, allowing you to only see the best in a person, a relationship, or even a room. Everything in this room was revoltingly floral, the cushions, the carpets, the curtains and the walls. But, despite the stale air, the place was at least tidy and clean. She spotted an empty Lucozade bottle. Her eyes fixed on their target and made it feel very unwelcome indeed. Mrs Brown had never really cared much for Lucozade. She did not like the orange colour of it or what the sticky liquid represented. It was a drink she associated with ill health, a suitable partner for a bunch of grapes on the bedside table of a hospital ward. The residents weren't sick, just old, and last time she checked old age was not an illness, it was a fact of life. Lucozade tasted like warm fizzy death if you asked her, not that anyone ever did. Mrs Brown believed there was a proper place for everything, she hated mess. This was not the place for an empty bottle of fizzy drink, nor was it the place for a random pair of renegade slippers which she spotted next to the armchair in the far corner. Every resident owned at least three pairs, two of which normally remained unworn. They were the gift of choice on birthdays or Christmas. Mrs Brown wondered whether there was a resident walking about the place with bare feet. It seemed unlikely. Then she considered that perhaps the owner of the slippers no longer lived here, perhaps no longer lived at all. That might be why the offending footwear had remained unseen and unnoticed, sitting there in the corner, empty and cold, like two unclaimed suede twins making the place look untidy. Mrs Brown paused her bemused curiosity just long enough to peer down at her own slippered feet. She should have put her shoes on really before coming in here. This was after all work, not home. Her fancy little fur-lined slippers were just so cosy and warm. She still couldn't remember who had given them to her, Mr Brown perhaps. He had always bought her nice things.

A sound from upstairs interrupted her thoughts. The residents were waking and stirring. She must get on with the paperwork, there was never any time once the rest of the house was awake and constantly making demands of her. The sound of activity reminded her that her time was not her own. She picked up the first letter on the pile and held it at various distances from her face until her eyes agreed to read the words that were printed on it. They weren't happy words. They made her frown and forced her to look away for a moment. Perhaps she should come back to this one, get through some of the others first, something a little less painful to read perhaps. She put the piece of paper down, her hands trembling ever so slightly as she did so, her mind erasing the words from her memory one by one in the reverse order from which she had read them, banished to her subconscious for another day, another time. The faded wallpaper caught her eye, successfully distracting her once more by peeling away ever so slightly at the tops of the walls. The escaped floral flap danced lazily in an invisible stream of heat from the radiator below. She added the possible redecoration of the house to her ever growing list of things to do.

Her attention was drawn away from the decrepit distractions of the room into the outdoors as she turned to gaze through the window. A spider's web shimmered in the early morning light on the outside of the dimpled glass of the decaying sash. A blue butterfly, the colour of sky, fluttered into the web and was temporarily halted. It looked so exotic and colourful, as though it couldn't possibly belong here. It flapped and twisted but soon became permanently entangled and gave up its struggle. She wondered if the butterfly knew where it was and the fate that awaited it. If it was aware of its surroundings it seemed effortlessly content just waiting to die. She looked away, it was not in her disposition to meddle with nature. A cloud covered the sun and the room darkened, along with Mrs Brown's mood.

Her mind was all over the place today, she needed to steady it, gather her thoughts together and train them to be as still as the room in which she sat. She closed her heavily creased eyelids for the briefest of moments to smell the freshly picked tulips on her bureau. They smelt of summers past and made her smile. She made a mental note to thank Bert the gardener for bringing them in from the garden for her. He was a good man and a loyal employee. She opened her eyes and almost leapt from her seat with fright.

"Morning, Mrs Brown, how are you today?" asked Rosie, one of the nursing staff. Her name clear as mud in large letters on a badge on her lapel. Mrs Brown didn't care much for Rosie. She was a rotund young girl whose ample cheerfulness was frankly unnecessary. Mrs Brown could never quite fathom what the girl had to be so jolly about, given the work she had to do around the place. Rosie's job description included washing and dressing tired old bodies and wiping their wrinkly, saggy, damp bottoms. Her fat face was still fixed with a permanent smile, despite the retch-inducing smells and general unpleasantness of it all. The girl spent her working day surrounded by decay and despair and ultimately death. Rosie's job was not a pleasant vocation by any stretch of the imagination. Mrs Brown found herself on many occasions not dissimilar to this, completely bamboozled, trying to figure out exactly what the girl had to be so damned happy about. But Mr Brown had liked her. Mr Brown always liked the nice ones. Mrs Brown had always found the nice ones deeply irritating.

"You alright, Mrs Brown?" persisted Rosie in that loud West Country drawl of hers. That was another thing that Mrs Brown detested about the girl, her inability to speak anything vaguely resembling the Queen's English and her insistence on communicating with all the residents in a very loud, slow, deliberate manner. It was as though Rosie thought everyone in the house was either deaf, stupid or both. The girl didn't reserve this speech pattern for the residents, she used it when addressing anyone over the age of sixty, including Mrs Brown who felt old enough as it was and certainly didn't like being spoken to like a fossil. She was, after all, the girl's boss, and was of the belief that a little respect could go a long way. Mrs Brown had often fantasised about dismissing Rosie, that would surely wipe the smile from her happy, round face, but alas, she could never quite bring herself to do so. Her conscience would never forgive her and besides, however irritating, she couldn't fault the girl's work.

"Yes, I'm fine, dear," replied Mrs Brown at last, while opening up the morning paper. She deliberately avoided eye contact and hoped the cheerful cow would sod off and dress someone.

"You're up nice and early today, would you like a cup of tea?" said Rosie, her cheeks living up to her name. Tea...now then, that was a good idea, Mrs Brown had meant to make some...

"Yes, dear, with two sugars..."

"And a dash of cream, yes I know. Be back in a jiffy," finished Rosie. Mrs Brown watched as the girl retreated to the kitchen, supposing that she wasn't all bad and at least had some uses around the place.

SEVEN

"What were you thinking? Haven't you put your father and me through enough already?" screamed Mother. She paced up and down the tired, creaking floorboards of their front room. Her angry heels pounded mercilessly at the already threadbare carpet. Father was also present and at the same time absent for this telling off. He sat and stared at the groaning floor. His sad eyes cried out to be somewhere, anywhere else. Moira's eyes said something similar but were too tired to convey the sentiment with such clarity. She felt bad for making them sad and angry again. It hadn't been her intention.

Moira felt dreamlike. Her life no longer seemed real, not since Doctor Goodman had held her hand and told her the truth. She was glad in a way for the delusional state of mind she had involuntarily adopted. The reality of the situation caused her more pain than she thought she could bear. She had been woken a little earlier in the evening by the flashlight of a kind policeman. He was not alone. There were other policemen and other flashlights and when they had found her in the darkness, curled up on the forest floor, still wearing her gym kit and surrounded by mud and dry dead leaves, they had been happy. Their eyes had danced with a mixture of success and relief. The happy policeman had wrapped a blanket around Moira, carried her to his car and driven her home. Mother, on the other hand, was not happy to see her at all. Mother's eyes did not dance, they stared and then they cried and then they adopted their standard wrathful gaze. They were sad, angry eyes and looked ever so disappointed. Moira had fallen asleep in the forest, she did not know why or for how long. She was still desperately tired and wanted very badly to sleep some more.

"Why did you do it?" barked Mother, now that the policeman had departed. He had been thanked for his delivery then briskly shown the door.

"I don't know," whispered Moira, afraid of the dance she knew would now follow.

"Let's try again. Why did you do it?" said Mother, a little louder this time. The pacing shoes came to an abrupt stop and Mother came to a standstill. Her face directly in front of her daughter's, emitting irrepressible fury.

"I don't..."   In one swift movement Mother's hand pulled back and swung. The sound of the slap hit Moira almost as hard as the pain of it. Mother had never hit her before. She had hurt her with words, but never smacked or slapped her. Father woke up out of his trance. Everything stopped, everyone stared. Mother cried, as though she were the one who had been hit.

"I think it is best you go to your room, Moira," said Father. Moira didn't hear him, but her feet understood and carried her tenderly up the stairs. Her unholdable hand held her face and her knees knocked a little from the cold of the forest and the cold of her home. Mother continued to cry and Father dutifully comforted her. Moira entered the limited sanctuary her bedroom had to offer, and cried alone. She closed the inadequate door firmly but quietly behind her. She wished the door had a lock. She looked at herself in the mirror. The red shape of Mother's hand was still painted on her cheek. She sank to the floor and waited for something that would not happen.

More time passed, though how much, Moira could not be sure. The clock on the bedside table was broken, as was she. Her eyes had stopped their crying. Her puffy, swollen face had ceased to sting, but the insufferable pain lived on inside her, it wore her like a jacket. She stood and walked to the window, ignoring the discomfort from the damage down below. It had been dark when she came home, it was still dark. The sound of crying downstairs had stopped. The thin glow of light from the hallway that had shone under her bedroom door was gone and only the glimmer of street light through the open window illuminated the room. Everything was the same but something had changed, something was missing; she no longer felt afraid. She found herself double checking, but the fear that had beset her for as long as she could remember was definitely gone. Before she had time to think it over and before the fear had time to return, she put on her shoes, pulled on her coat and climbed out of the bedroom window.

She stepped out on to the garage roof, carefully made her way to the edge and slowly lowered her body downwards. She couldn't quite reach and her fingers were struggling to hold her weight. She closed her eyes and let go, allowing her body to drop down until both legs stood shakily at the side of the house and she could feel the solid ground beneath her feet. She stared up at her bedroom window, at how high up and far away it looked and marvelled at how quickly she had escaped from it. She had often fantasised about doing this but never dared dream she ever could. There were so many things she wanted to run away from, so many things she never would. A cold wind blew and doubt joined her thought process, questioning the sense in her actions. Mother was angry enough as it was. The thought of her mother made her start walking, leaving the house she grew up in and doubt behind. She knew where she was going and she knew what she needed, she would not turn back now. Love did not live here. She could not find something that was not there in the first place.

The streets were deserted, the houses that lined them were quiet and dark. The world was asleep. A boy she had grown up with, grown apart from then grown to love, lived a little over half a mile away. It did not take Moira long to get to where she was going. The boy slept oblivious within the bungalow on the street where he lived. The street was lined with homes made of bricks where other people slept, all drowsily content to be unaware of the visitor outside. She knew instinctively which house was his, she had been there before, though not like this, uninvited, in the middle of the still night. She knew the boy cared for her and she needed to feel wanted. She crept up the driveway and around to the back of the house, where he lay in his room, dreaming of some other place. Her right hand made a small fist and before she could stop it or consider what to do, it performed an autonomous knock on the window pane.

She waited. Nothing happened. She thought about turning around, retracing her footsteps and going back to the house in which she lived. But her hand had other ideas. It formed another fist and knocked on the window again, harder this time, more determined to be heard, making a loud tapping sound on the glass. Silence resumed and she stood and waited.

A light came on in the room behind the pane of glass. A shadow formed on the curtain, the shape tightening and defining itself as its maker drew closer. The impenetrable wall of cotton was slowly peeled back at one corner of the window and a curious boy peered out into the darkness. His eyes found hers, but they did not smile, they looked confused. His eyes asked, "What are you doing here?" Then his lips formed the words which asked the same question, barely audible behind the glass barrier between them, but she interpreted the language he offered all the same.

She could not give a suitable reply as she did not know the answer, so instead she stared blankly back at him as though she were a garden statue, a ghost haunting his dreams. He frowned, then drew back one side of the curtain fully and opened the window.

"What are you doing here?" he whispered again. "Do you know what time it is?"

"No..." she said eventually, realising that she did not. Finding her voice was a struggle. The words inside her head did not want to come out. Either it was too late or too cold for them, but they wanted to stay right where they were.

"No, what?" asked the boy. His voice was a little louder now, though still hushed so as not to wake the neighbours or his parents. His eyes looked confused, slightly wary.

"No, I don't know what time it is...I'm sorry, I'll go," she said, her eyes filling with yet more tears. He rolled his eyes.

"Don't be stupid, come in, just be quiet, will you, you'll wake the whole house." An ever obedient Moira did as she was told and quietly climbed inside, allowing the boy to help her down onto the floor. A sharp pain somewhere new in her body informed her of a bloody gash on her right knee. She wondered how and when it had got there and stared at the dirt on the palms of her hands. The boy quietly shut the window, closed the curtain and gestured to his bed. She took a seat on the edge while her eyes adjusted to the light. He was wearing stripy blue pyjamas, they were slightly too large for his teenaged frame, his bare feet poking out underneath. Their mutual innocence and tiredness was charming. She had never seen him in anything but his jeans and t-shirts. She had never seen his feet before either. They were ugly looking, with long finger-like toes. She pulled a face while staring at them without really meaning to. The boy sat down next to her, a little too close. He instinctively edged away a fraction, a mess of hair sticking out in all directions, framing his head in an auburn halo. He had sleep in his eyes and a spot on his chin that had been picked until angry and red. He looked tired and worried. They had grown up together but he looked like someone she did not know.

"What's going on, Moira? We had the police round here earlier this evening asking when I last saw you. My dad went mental. My mum called your mother before bedtime and she said you'd been found in the woods. Now you turn up here in the middle of the night and knock on my bedroom window at..." he looked at the alarm clock next to his bed, "three o'clock in the morning. Are you okay? Do you want me to call someone? This is all a bit nuts," he said and scratched his head.

"I'm cold, can I get under the covers, please?" Moira asked. She was aware that her teeth were chattering though did not know when they had started to do so.

"Are you crazy? What if one of my parents walks in?"

"As you said, it's three o'clock in the morning," she said staring at his eyes, which looked anywhere they could to avoid meeting hers.

"Okay then, just for a little while, until you warm up," he said, and stood up so she could get into the bed. She removed her shoes and let her jacket fall to the floor. He climbed in next to her and tentatively put his arm around her beneath the duvet cover. They had never touched like this before. She felt the love she needed to feel. It felt nice. It felt warm and safe. Moira's eyes felt heavy. Sleep was coming.

"What happened?" asked the boy. His mouth was so close to her ear she felt his breath as his words hopped out.

"Just stuff, that's all," she said. It made no sense but she did not know what to say and the truth was not an option. He took his time considering her answer and she hoped it would be enough, she had nothing else to give him. She didn't have feelings for the boy. She didn't have feelings for anyone. But she appreciated how his feelings for her made her feel.

"Are you okay?" he whispered. She was close to sleep now. She could tell from the slowness of his breathing that sleep had come for them both. She was too tired once more to resist it.

"I am now," she whispered back. The boy withdrew his arm and she felt panic rise up inside her. It was unnecessary. The boy turned off the bedside table lamp and held her once more. She felt warm. She felt safe. She felt loved.

EIGHT

Tori awoke one minute before the alarm was due to sound. She silenced it before it had a chance to be heard and began her morning routine. She went to the bathroom, lowered the seat that Harry had left up and emptied her bladder. She brushed her teeth, washed her face then stepped on the scales.

"What are you doing?" asked Harry, appearing in the doorway. He was unshaven and looked as though he hadn't slept.

"What does it look like?" replied Tori, without looking up.

"You don't need to weigh yourself every bloody day, there's nothing wrong with you the way you are," replied Harry. He entered the room and lifted the toilet seat back into the upright position.

"She said I was overweight," replied Tori. Harry did not need to ask who. This was not a new conversation. This was not a new routine.

"By a couple of pounds and you're certainly not anymore."

"I need to get ready for work," she said and kissed him as she left the room. Their morning dance was over, the

66

well-practiced choreography complete.

Tori's office was a small, cramped affair. The windows offered spectacular views of the city, though there was rarely a spare moment to look out of them. One long desk filled the room and was divided into individual workspaces on either side. Her magazine was one of many that worked out of this building under the same umbrella organisation. The publication was hurriedly produced each month by eight people and she was one of them. There was an editor, a deputy editor, an accounts manager, two designers, a secretary who was absent most of the time and two staff writers, of which she was one. The job was neither what she thought it would be nor what she hoped to be doing with her life. She was a travel writer who rarely travelled anywhere other than to her office and home again. She certainly didn't have time to partake in pointless debates with her colleagues.

"I just don't see how two gay men, regardless of whether one of them is a multi-millionaire pop star, can be allowed to pay a woman to carry a baby for them. It's not just wrong, it's sick," said one of the designers sat opposite her. "Anyone want a coffee? Tori, can I get you one?"

"No thank you, tastes of socks and smells revolting," she replied absent-mindedly.

"I think surrogacy in general is wrong," said the voice to her right. It was the voice of her boss. "It's just not natural. If people can't have children the normal way then they should just adopt." he added for good measure. Tori felt light-headed and slightly sick, this couldn't be happening and yet it was. The S word was something she didn't discuss with anybody. It was private. It was safer that way. She was afraid of the word, of the sound it made, of what people knew about it, of what they thought it meant. The word had a habit of sneaking up on her when she least expected it. It would catch her off guard in a newspaper or on the radio and now in the office. Some secrets were made to be kept. Some words were best not spoken.

"Well, I don't think a rich woman should be allowed to pay a poor woman to get pregnant and carry a baby for her, just because she doesn't want to get fat or go through childbirth—which is why most of them do it," said the voice to her left. Tori looked down at her hands which were trembling ever so slightly. She examined her thin fingers on the keyboard in front of her with an intensity sure to silence the room in which she sat. The skin was lined but soft, and lightly tanned. The polish on the nail of her index finger slightly chipped. Her engagement ring slightly twisted too far to the left. She turned it straight.

"Anyone want a chocolate chip cookie?" said the girl opposite, opening up a small round tin. It had a pretty floral pattern that was not quite symmetrical, lovely despite its slight imperfection.

"Tori?"

"What?" said Tori, a little abruptly. They had reached the crescendo in a conversation in which she did not wish to participate. She needed this to end. She longed for silence and wanted to run away.

"Cookie?" asked the girl, waving the tin under her nose.

"No. No, thank you," said Tori.

"You and that diet, honestly I wish I had your

motivation," said a voice she did not hear. Tori stared at her screen and continued to type. The words in front of her made no sense and were soon clouded by watery eyes. Time was cruel and turned slowly towards the end of the elongated day.

Tori stood on the tightly packed Tube and stared at the woman and her swollen belly. The train came to a standstill and the doors reluctantly opened, spewing an army of tired passengers and allowing her to escape. She fought her way through the commuter-crammed station, searching for a platform and a carriage that would assist her exodus. She was tired of the bloated city, but that was where the work was, and they needed the money. It was a long commute at the best of times, but tonight it felt like she was quite literally going nowhere. No closer to the life she had dreamed of when she was younger. No closer to the baby she longed to love and no closer to home. She sat motionless and silent, staring at nothing out of the dark windows of the slow moving train. She waited and tried not to worry. The doctor had said worrying and stress could significantly lower their chances of success. She worried about worrying. When she wasn't worrying, she was waiting. Waiting for one doctor to write to another, waiting for test results, waiting for appointments, waiting for funding, waiting to have a baby of her own. The train stopped again without reason or apology. She sat and waited once again, helpless as always to do anything else.

The train came to a lazy standstill at Tori's destination, long after they had been due to arrive. It spat her out at the station and continued onwards, making its own way towards somewhere better, its journey delayed but protected by a self-assured predetermined final destination. No surprises, no wrong turns, no unknowns. She left the station behind and let tired feet walk her home. She wished she had worn flat shoes. Words went round in the carousel of her mind, she was too tired to silence them. Her feet came to a standstill and her fingers reached into her handbag to find the keys. There was no need to look for them. This had been her routine for long enough, she knew it well.

The warmth of the house rushed to greet her. She dropped the keys back in her bag and placed it on the sideboard in the hallway. She could hear music in the kitchen and the sound of Harry cooking. Something pleasant reached her nostrils and an unfamiliar appetite, which moments ago was all but forgotten, reintroduced itself. She slipped off her shoes, took off her coat and hung it on the back of the door, before following her senses to her husband. She stopped in the doorway and smiled at the scene before her. She was instantly reminded of all the things in her life she was grateful for. And Harry, wearing her polka dot apron, stirring something in the wok and singing along badly to Amy Winehouse was one of them. He sensed her presence and looked up, smiling when he saw her, his dimpled cheeks flushing, his glasses a little cloudy with steam.

"Hello, I didn't hear you come in. How are you?" he asked. He stopped his stirring momentarily to walk over and kiss her on the cheek.

"Tired, fed up, but happy to see you."

"What's up?"

"Oh, nothing, everything....you know. People at work were talking about surrogacy today, in a very negative way, it upset me."

"Oh darling, that's only because they don't know what they're talking about. What did they say?"

"The usual, surrogacy is wrong, unnatural, evil, we're going to hell etcetera," she said, staring at the floor.

"That's just their ignorance, they don't understand, that's all. If they knew someone going through it, if they knew you were going through it, they would understand it better and would probably feel differently. Don't be too hard on them," he said, lifting her chin with his finger until her eyes met his own. She pulled away a little. They both noted the withdrawal.

"I know, I know, it was just hard hearing the words. I've known these people for years, I think of some of them as friends. I couldn't believe what I was hearing and I couldn't wait to get out of there." Tori shifted her weight from one foot to the other.

"Well, you're home now," said Harry.

"There was a pregnant woman on the Tube home too," she added.

"It happens," said Harry, returning to his wok.

"You don't understand, you get to stay here all day, away from all the constant reminders. They're bloody everywhere, big, fat, waddling pregnant women, it's like they're breeding or something. Anyway, this particular whale had a badge saying, 'Baby on Board'. London Underground now make badges for pregnant women...and women wear them...can you believe it? She stole the seat that should have been mine. I was going to offer it to her anyway, but she just shoved her bump in my face, pushed me out of the way and took the seat. I'm not even convinced she was pregnant to be honest. Just fat. I wanted to punch her, Harry. I actually wanted to punch her. Do you think that's normal?" The words had rushed out of her, almost tripping over themselves in the process. She felt lighter, better for having shared them with someone.

"No, sweetheart, I'm not convinced that's normal, but I love you anyway. Was everything else okay today? Any exciting new commissions from your tit of an editor?"

"Yes. Rioja."

"The wine?"

"The region, fool!"

"Cool – well, there you go! You wouldn't be able to go to a wine region if you were pregnant now would you?"

"Can't go there anyway, he wants me to write it from my desk again..."

"You're kidding."

"I kid you not."

"Maybe it's time to quit, you know, if you're not happy..." Harry ventured.

"Good one," Tori muttered. "Anyway, it makes sense for me to hang on in there for the maternity pay. The magazine has stolen five years of my creative juices, five years of my life! It's the least they can do. Besides, if I quit now then how would we pay for everything?" Harry stopped stirring. Their conversations about money were the ones he tried most to avoid. They made him feel inadequate. They made him feel like he was failing her.

"We'd find a way," he ventured, pessimistically hoping his words were simple enough to end the exchange.

"We'd find a way to pay for the mortgage, the car, the fertility treatment? I love that you're a published author now but until you finish the next book, we haven't got a hope of paying all the bills without my salary."

The fragmented conversation drew breath. Harry sighed and pretended to need something from the other end of the small kitchen, pointlessly looking inside the cupboard furthest away from her. She pretended not to notice his retreat. He closed the cupboard door and turned to face her, a safe distance between them now. She stood and stared expectantly. She was still so beautiful, even if she couldn't see it herself. Watching what she was becoming, what this was doing to her, broke his heart. He reluctantly prepared to say the words which needed to be spoken, that he had waited to deliver. As though putting them off could make them less true, more unnecessary.

"Which is why I am going to go back to teaching for a while, just until we get back on our feet. I spoke to the school today," he said, and came to stand in front of her. She held on to her own words, unsure if she had heard his correctly. There was an uncomfortable silence while they both stared at each other. Harry broke the spell and looked down at the kitchen floor.

"What about your writing?" she whispered.

"I'll do it in the evenings," he said, and kissed her gently on the forehead.

She smiled, they were the words she had been waiting

to hear but had never wanted to incite them.

"Wine?" asked Harry, already opening the drawer in search of a corkscrew.

"We probably shouldn't..."

"Course we should..."

"The doctor said..."

"The doctor said to cut back, not to cut it out altogether. One glass isn't going to hurt you or our chances of having a baby," said Harry. He held her by the shoulders then and forced her to look him in the eye.

"Actually I did read a glass of wine a day is good for you, even when you're trying. It relaxes your body, contains a whole bunch of antioxidants, reduces the risk of heart disease and some say it can slow the progression of diseases like Alzheimer's," she replied.

"Well I've heard everything I need to know...shall we?" he asked.

"Okay then, I suppose it can't hurt."

"How about some Rioja?" said Harry before uncorking the bottle of red and pouring them both a glass. Tori took a sip and let it slide down her throat. She felt better already.

"Now then, I want you to take that," he said, pointing at her glass, "and go sit down in front of the fire. You are to relax and do absolutely nothing until dinner is served, which will be in approximately fifteen minutes, or until the smoke alarm goes off. That's an order, wife, off you go."

The next day began the same way as the last. The alarm

sounded, Tori was awake before it went off and had been staring at the ceiling, worrying and waiting. She switched off the alarm, and began the morning ritual. She slipped out of the front door and began the walk along the lane to the station. It was still dark. Everything was as it had been when she walked home the night before, the same as it would be when she came home later that day. She walked along the platform, stood and waited.

When the train came, Tori sat in her usual seat and observed the familiar faces of strangers around her. As they hurried closer to the city, the sun started to rise. The light hit the buildings and bleached the sky until it was a mix of pale pinks and blues. The further away the train got from home, the busier it became. The more people who crammed on board, the more lonely Tori felt. Nothing was wrong but nothing was right. She tried to feel happy, but she could not remember how.

NINE

Mrs Brown opened her eyes. Had she been dozing? She was sure she had only rested them for the briefest of moments, but the grandfather clock in the conservatory informed her it was just after eleven. This would never do, what if the residents had seen her sleeping on the job? Godalming Lodge was literally sucking the life out of her, there just weren't enough hours in the day to get everything done and she never slept properly here. She missed sleeping in her own bed, in her own house with her husband. She wished Mr Brown would return soon, things just weren't the same without him by her side. She scolded herself for snoozing and scanned the letters in front of her, trying to pick up where she left off. Just as she gathered her thoughts and was ready to proceed, a sweet young voice invaded the peace and quiet.

"Hello, Mrs Brown, how are you?" The melodic words entered the room on a carefree breeze. They wrapped themselves around Mrs Brown and hugged her with a friendly affection she had grown quite unaccustomed to. They warmed her and lifted her spirits. She smiled inside and raised her eyes to see who had delivered the floral-scented words. A vision of loveliness stood before her. She remembered this girl, she had seen her before, though she could not remember why or where. There were so many residents, here one day, dead the next. It was simply impossible to remember each and every one of their relatives, but this girl, this visitor, she would be no trouble. Mrs Brown knew deep within her heart that she was nothing but happy to see her.

"Hello there, I'm very well thank you, do come in," she said. The visitor came closer. She looked young...thirty or so, Mrs Brown guessed. "Please, take a seat," she said. She wasn't so welcoming to all visitors. There were some she deliberately never had the time to talk with. Only the select few were permitted to join her in the conservatory. "Now, what can I do for you?" said Mrs Brown politely when her visitor was seated.

"Oh, I just thought I'd pop in and say hello. I came to visit my grandmother and we had such a nice talk last time I was here, I'm Emily, do you remember?" Mrs Brown tried desperately hard to remember, but couldn't. There were so many visitors, always coming and going. Just like the residents, always coming and going...although when the residents left, they did tend to leave for good. Mrs Brown had been brought up by a strict mother. She was trained to be polite and honest at all times, but self-taught to tell the odd white lie when strictly necessary.

"Yes, of course I remember, dear," Mrs Brown lied, "How could I forget a pretty young thing like you? How was your grandmother? I do hope she's happy here?" The girl seemed nice enough but Mrs Brown wished to eliminate all possibilities of a hidden agenda before

77

entering into any further pleasantries. Experience warned her that the relatives of elderly patients so often complained....even more so than the residents themselves. Sometimes Mrs Brown just wished everyone would accept old age with the grace and dignity she intended to display herself, when the time came, and she was well aware that the time was not so very far away.

"I think she is happy enough," said Emily. "She misses her old home sometimes, but deep down I think she knows it is better to be here now and get the care she needs. Her old house was just too big for her to manage on her own. And she misses my granddad too of course."

"Is he not a resident here?" enquired Mrs Brown, never one to miss a business opportunity.

"No. He passed away last year," replied Emily, an uncomfortable expression materialising over her porcelain features.

"I'm sorry to hear that," said Mrs Brown, reaching across her bureau to pat the young woman's hand. "It can be hard, adjusting to life in residential care and relinquishing one's independence, but I'm sure your grandmother has done the right thing and this is an excellent home, even if I do say so myself."

"These flowers are beautiful, were they a gift?" asked Emily, changing the subject. Mrs Brown sensed her guilt and sympathised with it. Seeing loved ones move into a care home could be terribly hard for the rest of the family; so many were burdened with guilt at the thought of abandoning the very people who brought them into the world. It was hard to shun the care for the parents and grandparents who had loved you and cared for you when you had needed them. In this modern, time-poor society, looking after elderly relatives was practically impossible and predominantly unheard of, but guilt often lurked within these walls; guilt of the children who visited, guilt of the parents who asked them to, guilt of the children who didn't. Mrs Brown felt Emily's stare and realised she had been daydreaming. She didn't know what was the matter with her today, her mind kept flitting. She wondered if she was coming down with something and inadvertently raised her hand to her brow to feel for the temperature she suspected before answering.

"Yes, a gift from Bert the gardener, he is too kind to me and puts fresh flowers on my bureau at least once a week. I am spoilt! I must remember to thank him later. The garden is looking quite splendid at the moment, I'm sure your grandmother will have been enjoying it too – we make sure all the residents take a walk around the grounds at least once a day, weather permitting. Stretch their legs and get some fresh air..."

"Yes, she often says how much she likes the garden here," said Emily politely.

"It is good of you to come and visit her so often, some poor dears never see a soul."

Mrs Brown tried to focus on the girl, but she had so much to do, she couldn't help wondering how much more of her time she was required to give. Surely the girl would sooner spend the time with her grandmother, rather than sit here making idle chit chat. *Perhaps not, we all deal with difficult situations in our own way and none of us are really qualified to judge which way is right or wrong*, thought Mrs Brown. Her wits seemed set to wander today, her mood seemed unpredictable and she was feeling out of sorts. Her mind was on a one-way path of over thinking and heavy contemplation and it wouldn't be disturbed. The girl's lips were moving, but she couldn't hear the words they formed. She nodded politely at the appropriate junctions, but was already on her way to somewhere else.

Her mind dragged her back in time to when her own mother was nearing her final days. She would never have moved into a residential home for the elderly and Mrs Brown would never have dared suggest such a thing. It wasn't for everyone, she supposed. Her mother had been a cruel woman when she was growing up, but she had softened, at least a little, with old age. Mrs Brown had done her very best to care for her when she could no longer care for herself. Some people simply could not and would never relinquish their independence in that way. Some people wanted to die in their own homes, and she could understand that. It was so much better when the residents came willingly. It broke her heart when someone new arrived, delivered by a regrettable power of attorney, often having their homes sold for them by their nearest and dearest, with neither their knowledge nor consent. You could always spot a man or woman who was here against their will. The pain of it all hung over them, the hurt hunching their shoulders, clenching their fists and lining their faces. They were the powerless and the angry. Despair followed them from room to room, with the daily routine of eating, sitting, shitting and sleeping. They sat in the same seats each day, filled with an unspeakable sorrow and sighed impatiently while they waited to die. It wasn't fair. But then life frequently wasn't. For some, death was a long awaited relief. The girl's voice came back into reception.

"I try to pop in once a week or so...it is hard sometimes with work and everything, but I enjoy seeing her, I think it lifts her spirits and she's great with advice. I was telling her about my wedding..."

"You're getting married?" interrupted Mrs Brown.

"Yes...in a few months' time. We just booked the venue, it's all very exciting," said Emily, proudly displaying her left hand. Even without her glasses, Mrs Brown could clearly make out the rock weighing down the beautiful girl's finger.

"That's wonderful news. I'm sure you will have a magical day, I always wanted a summer wedding."

"You did have a summer wedding," interjected the girl. Mrs Brown froze, replaying her own words and then those of Emily. The girl was quite right, she had married in the middle of a warm, sunny May, a long time ago now. She hadn't forgotten, just got her words in a muddle, that's all. Wonderful memories of the day she married her husband came flooding back. The taste of champagne, the feel of the designer dress she had spent a month's wages on, and the look on her husband's face when their eyes met at the wedding ceremony. He thought she was beautiful, she never understood why. She put her confusion down to tiredness and smiled broadly in an attempt to cover the mistake and recover her composure.

"That's right, we were married in May. But how did you know, my dear?"

"Oh, you mentioned it last time I saw you. It sounded so romantic," beamed Emily.

"It was. It really was a wonderful wedding," said Mrs Brown, lost momentarily in the memory. "I'm sure yours will be an equally special day."

"I hope so," said the girl.

The bell in the hallway began to ring signalling lunch time. Mrs Brown couldn't fathom where the morning had gone, but like it or not, the hours had been forever stolen from her.

"I'm so sorry, my dear, that's the lunchtime bell, you will have to excuse me as I have work to do. You're more than welcome to stay if you like? Once all the residents have eaten I'll probably have a bite to eat myself. It's pasta day today and cook does a superb impression of a lasagne..." said Mrs Brown. Herding everyone into the dining room was a major task and required all hands on deck. She struggled to her feet. The pain shattered her right hand and shot up her arm as she pulled herself vertical. She grimaced but chose to ignore the reminder; she already knew she was getting too old for this malarkey.

"Thank you, but I have to get back to work myself. It was really nice to see you, though," said the lovely Emily girl. She hugged her then and kissed her on both cheeks. She smelt of blossom and her skin was soft as a peach. Mrs Brown felt a surge of love and a sprinkling of happiness dust over her. What an enchanting girl. Her grandmother should be very proud.

"Lovely to see you too, dear, do come and see us again soon," said Mrs Brown. It was her habitual departing phrase for visitors, but on this occasion, she truly meant it.

TEN

Moira was woken by the sunrise creeping through the cracks in the badly drawn curtains. The sun shone a beam of light on the floor. The beam yawned wide and travelled to the side of the bed, it crept up across the sheets and onto Moira's chin. The light spread up over her face to her lips, round her cheeks, along the ridge of her nose and finally to her closed eyes and opened them. Once open they examined her unfamiliar surroundings and processed where she was. The boy's room smelt strange, musty, not like her bedroom at home. She looked over at the clock on the bedside table and saw that it was six o'clock in the morning. The boy's arm was still firmly locked around her, quiet snores escaping from his open mouth. She slowly lifted his log-like limb without waking him, then slipped out from beneath his grip, getting up and out of the bed. She pulled the covers back over the boy who was her friend, carefully and quietly tucking the sheet under his chin. She lightly kissed his forehead, it was a kiss of thanks and love. Without doing very much he had helped her. He had let her in and he had held her. In the morning light she realised that was all she had needed. She slipped on her trainers and left the room. She walked down the dimly lit hallway, past the kitchen, past the lounge, past the bedroom where the boy's parents slept and past the dog basket where a furry Shih Tzu raised her head and issued a low growl. Moira ignored her, she had had her fill of angry bitches. She opened the front door, stepped out into the morning light and walked away.

The air was cool and clean and fresh. She could see her breath, little smokeless clouds which vanished almost as soon as she made them. The redundant chimneys along the street looked down on her disapprovingly, they had given up smoking for the summer, many had given up for good. Moira pulled the zip of her coat up as high as it would go, lowering her chin just under the upturned collar and burying her cold hands deep into her pockets. The dewy scent of damp lawns and vanilla scented aubrieta replaced the smell of the boy in her nostrils and on her skin. She retraced her footsteps with unconscious precision, her feet carrying her back to where she didn't want to go but where she nevertheless belonged.

Getting back into the house without being caught by her parents was something Moira had failed to think about the night before. She hadn't done much thinking at all, she had just let her feet and her heart carry her away. She decided to go in through the front door and listen to whatever music there was to be faced. She slotted the key into the lock and turned it with the precision and expertise of a veteran cat burglar. She slowly pushed the door open, just enough for her to be able to slip inside. She closed the door behind her, carefully stepping over the doormat, not wishing to disturb the unopened mail. Some of her breath escaped her and she realised she had been holding it. The house was calm and silent. She wondered whether she was in the right building, given that all the houses on the street looked the same, but then reminded herself that the key had fit the lock. There was no movement upstairs or in the kitchen. By now her father would normally be getting ready for work and Mother would be clanging and clanking dishes. Not wishing to miss the opportunity to get away with her inconsequential disobedience, Moira crept quickly and quietly up the stairs, missing the third and seventh, which she knew tended to creak. Once inside her room, she slipped out of her coat and shoes and climbed under the covers of her bed. The sheets were cold, but smelt familiar, they smelt of home. She lay there for a while like that, still and cold and silent. She worried then that something had happened to her parents and even considered checking on them until she remembered that it was Saturday. At the weekend nobody in this house, or in any of the houses she had passed on the way home, was awake yet. This was a time for sleeping and so she slept.

"Moira, are you getting up any time today?" The words forming Mother's voice interrupted Moira's slumber. She awoke abruptly from her dream, unsure of where she was or what had happened. Mother stood on the other side of the closed bedroom door. Waiting.

"Yes, I'll be down in a moment," Moira managed to say. She heard Mother's footsteps back away from the bedroom door and retreat down the stairs. Moira sat up, more tired than before. She gathered her senses and made her way downstairs to find out what the day had in store for her.

She walked cautiously into the kitchen over stone tiles that were painfully cold beneath her bare feet. Father sat at the table, reading the newspaper and occasionally spooning what looked like porridge into his mouth. Mother was in her usual position, by the sink. Everybody waited for somebody to speak.

"How are you feeling today?" asked Father kindly.

"Okay," said Moira, sitting down opposite him at the table. For a moment things felt normal.

"Did you sleep well?" asked Mother. Her Marigold gloves worn like she was preparing for surgery. Moira took a deep breath.

"Yes, thank you," said Moira, then stared down at the table. The words danced around the room, she hoped they were the right ones. It seemed the events of yesterday were not to be spoken about.

"Good," said Mother, the gloves were coming off now and she was walking towards the table. "We managed to get you an appointment today. It wasn't easy at such short notice I can tell you and at the weekend too, but the doctor was very helpful."

Moira was afraid to ask who the appointment was with or what it was for.

"After yesterday, we thought maybe you should just rest, but the doctor thought it might be good for you to talk to someone," said Mother. She looked down at her daughter and stroked her hair away from her face. Moira felt sad at her touch. The mark on her face from where Mother had hit her was gone, but it would never be forgotten. Moira realised they did not really know each other. She missed the mother she wished she had and felt guilty for not being the daughter Mother wanted her to be. Moira couldn't look Mother in the eye, she stared at her hands in her lap and waited for more words.

"It might be good to talk," encouraged Father. Mother and Father looked at each other then, an unspoken conversation going on between them.

"Why don't you go and get dressed and then I'll drop you off," said Mother, before gently kissing Moira on the forehead. For a moment it felt like she might love her again. They wanted her to talk. Just not to them.

Moira sat in the small square room. The emulsioned walls were emotionless white. There was a small curtained window, a table, a lamp, a box of tissues, a clock on the wall, two chairs and a closed door. Moira sat in her chair. It was not comfortable. She looked at the man she was supposed to talk to, sitting opposite her. Mother had said it would only be for an hour, but it already felt like an eternity. He was old and faded with a plump tyre of fat around his middle. Everything about him was a shade of grey, from the hair on his head to his laced shoes. She really did not want to talk to him about anything at all.

"How are you feeling today, Moira? said Grey Shoes Man.

"Fine, thank you. How are you?" she replied. It seemed a polite response. He sighed at her answer so she supposed, unlike her, he was not fine. He looked weary and every time she spoke he looked more so. He said she should try not to answer his questions with questions of her own. She stared at the clock. This was hard work. It felt like she had been here for hours already, but the clock on the wall insisted it had only been five minutes.

"Are you angry, Moira?" he asked. This was a peculiar question indeed. She was starting to feel angry that she was here. This wasn't her idea of a fun weekend.

"No. Are you?" she asked. He raised an eyebrow over his spectacles. He did look rather peeved. He did not answer, just sighed and scribbled some more illegible writing on his pad of paper.

"How did you feel when the doctor told you that you would never have children?" he asked. She did not answer. He stopped his scribbling and looked up. His eyes staring into hers. She looked away, but not before seeing a flicker of contentment wash over his grey face. They both sensed he had finally asked a good question. They both waited to see how she would answer it. She avoided his gaze and stared at his grey trousers with their strange little pleat up the middle of each leg. They were too short for him and exposed a stripe of white hairy leg between the fabric and his socks. He sat like a woman. A silly, fat old woman.

"I'm not sure," were the words she chose to provide him with. They both knew they were inadequate. Grey Shoes Man put his pad down on the table and leant closer to her. The gesture was supposedly friendly but she wanted to lean away, her body already pressing into the back of the chair. He had large bags under his eyes, as though he hadn't slept for months. She wondered what was keeping him awake at night and thought perhaps he should try talking to someone about it.

"Come now, you must have felt something," he urged.

She sat in silent thought and tried to remember what she felt, then tried to figure out what he wanted to hear.

"I felt sad," said Moira.

"You don't look sad," said Grey Shoes Man.

"Do you want me to look sad?" asked Moira, wondering if she might be allowed to leave if she cried. She presumed that was what the unused box of tissues was for.

"I want you to talk about your feelings. I'm trying to help you," he said. For a moment he seemed so sincere she almost believed him. She knew he believed the words he was saying, but that didn't mean she had to. "Do you want to talk about it?"

"No."

"Why?"

"Because I don't," she said. She meant it, she didn't.

He looked momentarily defeated. He didn't look like he had a lot of money. His grey shoes were worn down on the heel and his glasses were a decade out of date. She doubted they or he had ever been in fashion. His breath stank of stale coffee and she was not surprised by the lack of a wedding ring on his left hand. Perhaps he didn't earn a lot of money. Perhaps they didn't pay him much because he wasn't very good at the job. A whole lifetime of Mother instructing her never to talk to strangers and now she'd sent her to be locked in a room with one.

"Sometimes talking can help," he ventured.

"I don't know you," she replied.

"Which means you can say anything you want to me. Everything we talk about inside these walls is confidential. Do you understand? Nobody else will know."

"Will Mother know?"

"No," he said. Silence filled the space between them, allowing him time to think up his next words.

"How did your parents take the news?"

"They cried."

"Have you cried, Moira?"

"Yes."

"With them?"

"No."

"Why?"

"I don't know."

"Are you ashamed of your condition?"

"Should I be?" She sat up straight and stared hard at him then, this grey-shoed stranger. How dare he ask her questions about something he knew absolutely nothing about? He didn't have a clue about anything, this was a complete waste of both their time. Anger sent blood rushing around her damaged body, her hands clenched themselves into fists and her head started to pound at the temples with frustration. The man was nothing but a silly, fat fool. She stared at the clock. The hands hadn't moved. Perhaps it was broken. A bird in flight caught her eye. It came to rest on the window ledge, eyes darting, tiny feet hopping in unison, coming closer to get a better look, blue-flecked feathers warmed by the sun. Its beak tapped silently on the glass, as though it wanted to come in almost as much as she wanted to get out.

"Moira, you are doing it again. Please try not to answer questions with questions. Is there anything that is upsetting you, anything you are worried or wondering about?

Anything you want to ask me about our session together?"

"Yes."

"Go on."

"When can I leave?"

ELEVEN

Tori awoke to the sound of birdsong. Her eyes followed the movement of the gently billowing curtains. They had been blown into a ghostly dance by the window that had been opened to cool them in the night. She turned her body to face the silent performance, transfixed until a thick curl of her hair tumbled down over her face, obscuring her view with a barcode of dark strands. She took a moment, as though not sure what came next. Today was going to be a good day. She told herself that most mornings, in the hope that one day it would be true. She rolled onto her back and allowed her eyes a few moments to study the ceiling before moving from the warm and comfortable bed. She sat up and rubbed the sleep from her eyes, enjoying the sensation of it grazing her cheek. Harry's side of the bed was empty. She could hear him pottering around downstairs. She stood lazily and went to close the open window and draw the curtains to a static frame upon the stage of outside. She stared at the wind-blown trees, their skinny branches waving back at her, she ignored them and turned back to survey the room. She started to make the bed then decided it could wait. They were only going to climb back in and unmake it again in a few hours' time. She abandoned the sheets, dumped the pillows and headed for the bathroom; there was so much to do today, she just wanted to get on and do it.

Tori stepped into the shower, distracted by overthinking the day ahead, trying to anticipate the unpredictable. She shivered a little with fear, which seemed to make the hot water feel cold. She shaved her legs, cutting herself just below her right knee. A tiny droplet of blood formed, swelling until fat enough to burst its own banks and trickle down her leg. It made the journey only to melt away in the shower water, before repeating the process all over again; an angry traffic light, urging her to stop. Pain peered behind the shower curtain. She pretended not to see and let him watch. She washed her hair and studied the soapsuds as they gravitated towards the plug hole. She hoped she might be able to wash her pain away with the dirt if she just scrubbed hard enough.

Dressed in a stylish loose fitting outfit and ready to face the music, she made her way downstairs. The smell of burnt bacon alerted her senses to Harry's breakfast making. She turned into the kitchen just as the smoke alarm started to screech. Harry stood red-faced, holding a frying pan in one hand and a tin of baked beans in the other. His glasses rested low on his nose as he held the tin close to his face to read the instructions. Despite looking hot and bothered he was unfailingly handsome. She kissed him on the cheek then grabbed a tea towel and began furiously fanning the alarm to silence it. She could see Harry's lips moving, but couldn't hear a thing over the insanely loud beeping. If the neighbours weren't already awake they would be now.

Harry opened the oven door and smoke billowed out, Tori smiled and opened the kitchen window, allowing it to disperse. As it cleared the culprits were revealed, four lumps of charcoal that she suspected had once been sausages. The smoke alarm relented and Tori surveyed the damage.

"I couldn't hear you, what did you say?" she asked.

"I said I love you," said Harry. Tori smiled.

"I love you too, darling, but why are you trying to destroy our kitchen?" she asked, taking the frying pan out of his hand and giving him a hug.

"I wanted to make you breakfast."

"Well never mind, I'm not really very hungry anyway, I think I'm too nervous to eat," said Tori, allowing her thoughts to wander towards their visit to the hospital.

"There's nothing to be worried about," said Harry, kissing her forehead and hugging her closer. "It's just an appointment with the specialist, to find out what's what."

"An appointment we've waited six months for."

"Exactly, the wait is over...this is a good day. How about I admit defeat with the fry up and make us some cereal and toast?"

"Are you sure you're up to it?" asked Tori with a grin. "How about I help?"

"Okay, I'll let you help, but only to demonstrate my firm belief that together we can achieve anything, okay? Even Coco Pops!"

The journey to meet the specialist felt long. Their local hospital didn't help couples who required surrogacy, so after a number of disappointing meetings with doctors who couldn't help, they had had to look a little further away for a hospital and a doctor who would. Finding a hospital that would help them had been hard. Getting an appointment had been harder still. Harry parked the car and they made their way inside, they were ridiculously early. They followed the signs to the Assisted Conception Unit and walked up to the reception desk, hoping someone inside would indeed help them to conceive.

"Name?" barked a hungry looking receptionist, without looking up from her computer screen. Her face had been in the sun too long and her earrings were two heavy, garish hoops of metal weighing down her stretched pink lobes.

"Victoria," stammered Tori. Harry squeezed her hand. She wondered why all of this was so very terrifying. Her stomach rumbled loudly and she wished she'd managed to eat a bit more breakfast after all.

"Take a seat," muttered the woman behind the desk, the sound of her witch-like nails tapping angrily at the keyboard.

Tori and Harry found two seats in the corner of the crowded waiting room. It was impossible not to notice the other couples sitting patiently all around them. Most of the women sat with large, swollen tummies and the men displayed proud, self-confident smiles. The women turned the pages of well-thumbed magazines, while the men stared transfixed at their mobiles and Blackberries. The walls were covered with posters of pregnant women and charts about pregnancy. Tori didn't know what she had expected, but she hadn't anticipated being confronted by so many mothers to be. This was an assisted conception unit she reminded herself, finding it hard to know where to look. She supposed all of these couples had been assisted by doctors, hidden behind closed doors, in corridors not too far away. She hoped that they would be assisted too. Tori looked at Harry, who stared back at her as though she were the most perfect creature in the room. Even if, by the looks of things, she was the only woman here with such complicated imperfections.

Time moved slowly. The longer they sat waiting and worrying, the stronger their fear became; it filled the room until it was too sizeable to dismiss. Tori stared at the floor, desperate for a point of view where pregnant women were out of frame. Harry, like the other men, stared at his phone. Fear filled both their heads, and when they were called to room four, it came between them. They paused in front of the door and looked at one another. There was no need for words. *I'm scared, I need you,* said Tori's eyes. *I'm here, I love you,* said Harry's. He took an unconscious deep breath and knocked lightly on the heavy wooden door.

"Come in," called Doctor Sydney. She smiled warmly at them both as they entered the room. Her kindness melted their fear just a little. "Please, take a seat," said the doctor, looking up from her screen. She met their anxious gaze and gestured to the two solid looking chairs in front of her large, messy desk. Doctor Sydney looked young for a doctor, but older than Tori and Harry. The woman had shiny black hair, tied neatly into a short ponytail, and wore trendy looking reading glasses. She took them off and slipped them on top of her head, as though they were sunglasses, revealing large, kind, brown eyes, the kind of

97

eyes that could see and know everything.

"Nice to meet you both," said the doctor genuinely, offering another broad smile. "Now then, I've read through your notes. The purpose of today is to assess you physically, to be sure you are fit and well and medically able to proceed down the path you have chosen. I understand you've decided to explore surrogacy as an option to have a child of your own. That is something we may be able to help with at this hospital, we should at least be able to get you started along what will be a very long road. But before then we'll need to carry out a few tests...on you both. Victoria..."

"Tori, please," interrupted Tori.

"Tori, I'd like to do a scan to see what's what. Harry, we'll need to do a semen analysis and you'll both need to do a series of blood tests I'm afraid."

"That's fine, we were expecting it," said Tori, in a voice that sounded unlike her own.

"Good. Well I'd like to do an ultrasound on you this afternoon, Tori, you'll need to come back later with a full bladder. This leaflet is for you about what to expect. I'm hoping to see everything I need to see with the ultrasound, but I might need to do a quick internal scan, just to warn you. Harry, this jar is for you, if you could possibly return your sample when you come back to the hospital this afternoon, that would speed things up. These forms are for your blood tests."

"What are the blood tests for?" asked Harry. He had never been particularly fond of needles.

"I just need to check Tori's hormone levels, she'll need to

come back a few times over the next few weeks and repeat the tests to establish when she ovulates. And you both need a few tests just to check that you're both healthy and don't have anything nasty that might hurt the surrogate or your baby. Does that all sound okay?" asked Doctor Sydney, slipping her glasses back onto her nose and typing something on her computer. "Have you found a surrogate yet?"

"No, but we've been approved by the agency. We've paid the fees and we're on the waiting list," said Tori.

"Jolly good," said the Doctor.

"And do I....erm, fill this here at the hospital somewhere?" asked Harry, referring to his jar.

"No no, most people go home," replied Doctor Sydney with a barely noticeable wrinkle of her perfectly straight nose. "Just remember, we need the sample to be as fresh as possible, so best to return your pot no later than sixty minutes after ejaculation. Who is driving?"

Harry wasn't entirely sure why this was relevant...

"I am..." he replied.

"Fine, well if you could hold Harry's jar between your thighs on the way back, Tori, that would be a good way to replicate body temperature and we'll get a more accurate result from the analysis."

"Okay, I can do that. So we'll see you later?" said Tori.

"Yes, two o'clock. Just remember, full bladder for you and semen sample from you," said the doctor without looking up from her screen.

"Will do. Thank you," said Harry. They left the office with their leaflets, forms and instructions. Harry carried his sample pot, a little embarrassed at the prospect of having to fill it.

"That woman is like Mary Poppins on drugs," said Harry once they were out of the ACU.

"Shhh! Someone might hear you," snapped Tori.

"What's the matter with you?" said Harry.

"Nothing. It all just seems so...clinical. What if the scan isn't okay later, and what if my hormone levels aren't right and what if..."

"What if, what if. We can what if for the rest of the day if you like, but that isn't going to make us feel any better and it won't make a blind bit of difference to the results. What if my sperm are swimming in the wrong bloody direction? At least this doctor sounds like she knows what she is talking about. Look, we've come this far, we just need to be patient a little bit longer, have all the tests they want us to have and then take it from there...okay?" said Harry. He held her shoulders and stared down at her, until her eyes met his. Tori looked up at him, she knew he was right, but she did not feel quite able to shake off the burden of anxiety. She no longer remembered how it felt not to worry.

"Okay," she said. "Are you okay?"

"With this?" said Harry, gesturing to his pot.

"With all of it. With going back to work on Monday?"

"I said it's fine. We need the money. It's teaching English to a bunch of middle class kids, how hard can it be? And it's only for a few months. Please stop worrying about everything."

"Okay," she said, only too aware that while his words

said one thing, the look in his eyes said another.

"Good. Right. Well, let's get you home so you can drink until you're fit to burst and I can...do something in this silly little jar. Come on, race you to the car...no? Okay, we'll just walk then," he said, taking her hand in his and leading her towards the exit.

"Love you, don't I," she said, letting him lead the way.

"Love you more," he replied, trying to be strong for her. Trying to be strong for them both. She held his hand tightly, hoping he would never let her go.

TWELVE

Mrs Brown was tired. Her weariness wrapped itself like an insistent vine around every inch of her body, creeping all the way up to her neck, so that even breathing seemed to require a level of effort. Her limbs ached and her feet felt heavy and clumsy. She needed so badly to sleep, but she just didn't have the time. The residents were mostly fed, apart from Judith at table two and Edward in room six. Judith had been refusing to eat for twenty four hours now. She stared vacantly at the walls and drooled a little, globules of spit gathering at the sides of her downturned mouth, before dripping down to form a disgusting sticky mess on her chin; it was revolting. Edward was bedridden after suffering a minor stroke last week and would need to be hand fed in his own room, once everyone else had been dealt with. Mrs Brown contemplated being too tired to eat, but thought better of the notion and sat down in the far corner of the dining room, away from the others. Watching them while she ate troubled her and tended to put her off her food.

"Hello, Mrs Brown, can I get you a portion of shepherd's pie with gravy?" said Glenda, sticking her long face around the swing doors to the kitchen. Glenda the cook was a broomstick with arms, and Godalming Lodge's very own non-domestic goddess. Mrs Brown could never fathom how someone who spent all day surrounded by food could remain so stick thin. Although, on reflection, Glenda's offerings did tend to be rather unappetizing; she supposed the woman could quite easily resist her own cooking, most of the residents did.

"I thought it was lasagne on Wednesdays," queried Mrs Brown. It was the only half decent meal the woman was capable of making.

"It is lasagne on Wednesdays, but this being Thursday and all, it's shepherd's pie for lunch. Do you want some or not?" said the broom, in a rather hoity toity manner. Mrs Brown felt her mind made up for her in that moment to sack Glenda. The only area of indecision on the matter, was whether to sack the woman for her below bog standard cooking capabilities, her inability to know what day of the week it was, or her ridiculously long face.

"Glenda, it is most definitely Wednesday, but if shepherd's pie is what you have made then yes, I shall have some," said Mrs Brown, before silently complimenting herself on not being more derisory to the woman.

Glenda retreated back into the kitchen and returned moments later with a steaming plate of minced meat, potato and gravy. It was a clear cut case of service without a smile.

"Thank you," said Mrs Brown. She said the words deliberately loudly and a couple of the residents turned to stare. She ignored them and looked down to examine her food, a dog's dinner if ever she saw one. The steam rose from her plate, casting a welcome haze across her vision, for which she was mildly grateful; she hoped the food might taste better than it looked. It didn't. It reminded her of school dinners. It tasted of a memory long forgotten, for just a moment the years fell away and she felt like a child again. She longed to be free of all the burdens that time and age had gifted her with. She wanted to be able to run and leap and jump in the air without fear of breaking a limb. She yearned to redeem the ability to look forward, not back and a chance to be rid of all the admin and red tape. The thought of the correspondence and paperwork piling up that needed seeing to, brought her back to the present and her uneaten shepherd's pie, rapidly cooling on the chipped, white plate in front of her. She ate a few bites and put down her knife and fork. She hated to waste food, but she couldn't eat any more of it, even if she wanted to, no wonder Judith was refusing to eat. She washed away the taste with a glass of water and made a mental note to advertise for a new cook at the earliest given opportunity.

When the residents had all been safely returned to their afternoon sitting positions, Mrs Brown took her seat in the conservatory. She popped her reading glasses up onto the end of her nose and took out the paperwork, determined to sort through the lot that afternoon. Just as she had started drafting the advert for a new cook, Rosie's foghorn call burst through the room, shattering her concentration.

"Afternoon, Mrs Brown," she said gingerly.

"Hello, Rosie," replied Mrs Brown in a monotone, without looking up and barely concealing a heavy sigh.

"I wondered if you might have time for a little walk in the garden?" stammered the girl. Mrs Brown stared at her long and hard from above her spectacles. She wondered what it might be like to have just a moment's peace. She wondered what it was that Rosie wanted to talk about that couldn't just be said in here. She put down the papers and reluctantly pulled herself up and out of the chair.

Out in the garden Mrs Brown took the path towards the pond while Rosie shuffled along beside her. The breeze brushed Mrs Brown's soft grey curls off her face and refreshed her after the disappointing lunch. She breathed deeply then, drinking in the freshness of the outdoors and enjoying the warm sunshine on her skin. Stiff pinecones that had strayed onto the path surrendered themselves, apologetically sinking ever so slightly into the rain-softened dirt underfoot. She took a childlike pleasure in the sensation, deliberately recreating the encounter whenever their location matched her stride. It was good to get out, although it would have been an altogether more pleasant experience had she been alone. Rosie's hay fever caused her to sneeze every few moments, scaring away the birds and making Mrs Brown jump with each outburst.

"So, Rosie, is everything okay?" prompted Mrs Brown, during an interval of Rosie's spluttering.

"Oh, yes thank you, Mrs Brown," said the girl.

"You're not finding the work too hard, the hours too long?"

"No, I love my job. Don't get me wrong; it's hard work, very hard work at times, but it is so rewarding. I worked as a barmaid before this, and although it worked out better paid, with the tips and everything, I'm definitely happier doing this sort of work," said Rosie cheerfully. The penny finally dropped with Mrs Brown as to what their little garden chat was really about. They made their way through the rose bushes and the older, wiser woman's impatience got the better of her.

"So, you think you should be paid more, is that it?" she asked, desperately trying to speak in a pleasant tone and hide her exasperation.

"No! Well yes, it would be nice, I mean it is a bit of a struggle sometimes and I do think I work very hard, harder than some of the other staff, but I know these are tough times and I'd never dream of asking," blathered Rosie like a whimpering sausage dog. Mrs Brown could feel her blood pressure rising and could hear her doctor's voice echoing in her mind about not getting stressed, taking it easy. This place, these people would be the end of her and she knew it. She wasn't a begrudging woman, far from it. She would love to pay all the staff more, of course she would. She'd double, triple their salaries, (excluding Glenda), if it were a viable option, but the home was already struggling to break even this year. What with the recession, she had been forced to keep the care home charges at the same level two years running, despite a dramatic rise in the cost of keeping the place going. There were several residents with outstanding bills at time of departure, whose families either couldn't or wouldn't pay and the building, as well as its inhabitants, was in a constant state of disrepair. The roof had recently started leaking and the staff were frequently complaining about the smell of damp on the top floor. She had been too scared to get a quote for it to be fixed, because unless it was free, she simply couldn't afford it.

They rounded the corner past the last rose bush in an uncomfortable silence. Mrs Brown found herself in deep thought, so much so she almost walked straight into Bert the gardener. After the initial shock, she felt a flush of pink cover her cheeks and a rare smile stretch across her heavily lined face. Bert in return smiled down at her, his teeth white and above all, real. His tanned hand reached up to remove his sun hat while his eyes dazzled and bewitched her. She felt a surge of guilt about Mr Brown, but reminded herself that he wasn't here. She wasn't doing anything wrong after all, just exchanging pleasantries with a young man who happened to be very handsome indeed.

"Hello there, Mrs Brown, you're looking lovely as ever if you don't mind me saying so, how are you today?" She felt her blush intensify.

"Good afternoon, Bert, I'm very well and I wanted to thank you for the beautiful flowers in the conservatory, they made my day, they really did," said Mrs Brown.

"Good, well I'm glad you liked them."

"I did, very much so, and the rest of the garden is looking quite beautiful, you are doing a splendid job."

"You're too kind, Mrs Brown," said Bert, his eyes locked on hers. She noticed then that he didn't wear a wedding ring. If there wasn't a Mr Brown she would definitely be tempted by Bert, a fine specimen of a man, and such a kind and thoughtful soul, a rare thing these days. Of course he was a few years younger, but according to the gossip she overheard in the staff room, toy boys were all the rage this season. The sound of yet another sneezing fit by Rosie interrupted their little interlude. Mrs Brown retrieved a hanky from her sleeve and handed it to the nuisance of a girl.

"Here you are, Rosie," she said.

"Thanks, Mrs Brown. Hello, Bert," she said.

Without taking his eyes off Mrs Brown, he nodded in Rosie's direction.

"Well, I best carry on," he said. "Rhododendrons need feeding and the lawn needs trimming, lovely to see you both." And with that he and his wheelbarrow were gone. The stares of both women lingered on the view of him for a little longer than was necessary as he walked away. Mrs Brown took a moment to gather her thoughts and get her breath back.

"So, Rosie, we were talking about your pay," she said as they made their way back towards the house.

"Oh, don't you worry, Mrs Brown, I shouldn't have said anything," said the girl, before handing back the used hanky. Mrs Brown stared at it for a moment, then pushed it into her pocket, making a mental note to throw it in the bin once inside.

"Not at all, I want you to feel able to talk to me whenever you have any concerns. As you know, times are tough for a lot of people at the moment, but let me see what we can do, how about that?" said Mrs Brown begrudgingly. Her words surprised herself, but then being around Bert always brought out the best in her.

"That would be lovely, thanks, Mrs Brown," said Rosie, a little more upbeat than before.

"You're welcome, and Rosie," called Mrs Brown before turning down the corridor towards the conservatory, "perhaps some anti-allergy tablets might be in order, it doesn't do to have you sneezing all over the residents during the summer months."

"Yes of course, Mrs Brown, I'll see to it and pop into the pharmacy on my way home."

THIRTEEN

Moira looked at her seventeen year old self in the mirror. It had been almost two years since she was diagnosed. A lot had changed, but she looked almost exactly the same, at least on the outside. She frowned at her reflection, a mixture of disappointment and disapproval. Her hair was longer and Mother had let her start wearing a little mascara, but otherwise she remained unchanged, unnoticed. She flushed the hospital toilet and washed her hands twice, keen to be rid of the germs and dirt of the train and the swarms of commuters that filled it. The hospital in the city seemed much the same as the local version. It was a little bigger and shinier, she supposed, as she made her way back towards the waiting room. She had waited over a year now for an appointment to see the specialist doctor for treatment. Moira wasn't entirely sure what the treatment would involve, seeing as she wasn't sick. She sat alone and afraid of what she was waiting for.

"Dr Wise will see you shortly," said the receptionist. Moira had been waiting for over an hour, but her book sat abandoned in her lap, the same corner of the same page folded down as first thing this morning. She found herself unable to do anything other than stare at the walls while she waited. She ignored the exotic looking fish in the dirty green tank, the loud TV and the six month old magazines. After months of wasted hours with Grey Shoes Man, Mother, Father and Dr Goodman had decided she should come and see a doctor in the city about not being able to have children. She had to wait until after her exams, because they were more important than everything, according to her parents. Everyone else in the waiting room must have come to see a different doctor, because they either had children already or were fat with pregnancy. Moira couldn't help but stare at the women with their enormous tummies all sitting in a row opposite her. She stared at the hugeness of them, their tummy buttons turned inside out and poking through their tops. She listened intently to their inane mutterings about morning sickness and the cost of childcare. She watched the way they held their backs when they stood and found herself staring while a woman breastfed a baby right next to her. She was surely in the wrong place, but the receptionist didn't seem to think so.

"Make your way to room four, please," prompted the impatient voice behind the desk. Moira realised that she hadn't moved since being called. She stood and gathered her things, then followed the finger of the receptionist, as it pointed down a hallway on the left. She felt alone and afraid and then angry at herself for feeling that way. For a moment she wished Mother was here. She shook her head until she didn't want anyone, until she knew she didn't need anyone and knocked on the door of room four. A voice on the other side instructed her to enter.

"Hello, Moira, I'm Doctor Wise, come in and take a seat," said the doctor. He looked kind, and a little bit wise as his name suggested. Moira did as she was told and sat in the seat he had gestured to. There was no nurse, there were no squeaky shoes, there was nothing and no one but the two of them, sitting in room four, looking at each other for the very first time. Doctor Wise took off his glasses and leaned forward in his chair. Moira sensed he was trying be friendly, but automatically leant back, sitting up straight, her face as far away from his as the chair would allow.

"Tell me what you know about your condition so far," he said, his body mimicking hers and sitting back a little to allow for some space between them.

"I know I can't have children," she said. The words were a little louder than she had intended, as though her voice had a volume control all of its own.

"Well, yes and no. You have a very rare condition known as Rokitansky Syndrome. It affects people in different ways. I'm going to do some tests over the next few days. We'll be able to find out a lot more about how you will be affected and what you can and can't do. You're going to stay at the hospital here with us for the rest of this week, if that's okay with you. I see you've brought a bag along, but if there is anything else you need, the nurses will help you."

"So I might be able to have a baby?" asked Moira, a sudden rush of hope pushing her forward to the edge of the seat.

"Maybe. Your doctor at home has referred you here to

me because the condition you have is very rare—he doesn't know how to treat it. I've met lots of girls like you from all over the world, you are not alone. The condition can be far more severe. From what I understand, your ovaries and kidneys are healthy and functioning. In many ways you are very lucky." Moira didn't feel lucky. "Let's get you settled in your room and see what's what. Do you have any more questions for now?"

Moira wondered if she did, then mocked herself for having such a ridiculous thought. Of course she had questions, so many that she didn't know how to begin to ask them and for the first time it seemed she might have met someone with some answers.

"How did I catch it?" The words formed themselves and slipped out of her mouth and into the room unknown to her. A tear escaped her right eye and slid down her cheek. It was unusual for her to cry. Mother always said it was best not to, especially not in front of strangers. She wished Mother was here. She wished someone was here. She wished she wasn't alone.

Doctor Wise took a tissue box from his desk and passed it to her. He smiled, though Moira couldn't see what there was to be happy about.

"Moira, you didn't catch this, you were born with it." Moira paused and thought about his words.

"So it was Mother's fault?" she asked. It all made sense now, that's why Mother was so upset.

"No, it was nobody's fault. When you were in your mother's womb, before you were even you, when you were just a tiny embryo, something happened to tell your womb not to grow."

"Why?"

"The truth is, we don't know. Your condition is as simple and as complicated as you choose to view it. For many girls with your condition they have far more serious complications—other parts of them didn't grow properly. With you, that's not the case, your ovaries, your fallopian tubes did exactly what they were supposed to do. But for some unknown reason, your womb just stopped growing. Let me be clear on this. Your condition isn't your Mother's fault, it certainly isn't your fault, it isn't a result of anything that anyone did. Unfortunately in life we just have to accept that sometimes these things can happen, and accept it you must. We are all born different."

Moira stared into his eyes and tried to take in everything he had said. She tried to believe the words he had shared with her. She tried to accept that this wasn't her fault, but she couldn't.

Moira's room was white and square with four beds in it. Her bed was on the right next to a window. The other beds all had pregnant women in them. They smiled at her when she came into the room. She meant to smile back, but instead she just stared. The nurse who had led her here pointed to the bed and drew a large green curtain all the way around it.

"My name is Ruth," said the nurse. She was small with dark skin and a bright white uniform. She had kind eyes with no wrinkles and Moira was completely baffled as to how old or young she might be. No nurse had ever told Moira their name before, this one was different. "I'll be looking after you while you stay with us. If there is anything you need, you just pull this cord here, you see?" she said pointing up at a red cord dangling from the ceiling near the top of the bed. Moira nodded. "We're going to start some exercises this afternoon, but it's nothing to worry about," said Ruth. Moira felt worried. She hadn't come here to attend gym class. "First things first, take off your socks, shoes, jeans and pants and pop on this stylish gown. When you're ready, hop up on the bed and put this paper sheet over you. I'll be back in a jiffy," said Ruth. She snapped back the curtain, stepped out and whipped it back behind her and was gone.

Moira did what she was told. She removed her clothes folding them neatly in a pile on a chair in her cubicle. Then she sat alone beneath a blue paper sheet on the hospital bed, surrounded and protected by the green curtain. Her bare feet were cold. She could hear the other women in her room, moving about, turning pages of magazines, but in between their noise, the silence swallowed her. After an indeterminate length of time, Ruth returned.

"Now then, have you ever had sex, Moira?" she said, as though these were normal words for a stranger to put together in a sentence. Moira was more than a little taken aback by the question.

"No," she whispered, looking at the curtain as though she could see the other women through it.

"Don't worry, nobody else can hear us," said Ruth. One of the women in another bed outside the curtain sneezed. Moira heard the sneeze loud and clear. If she could hear the other women, they could hear her. She wanted to tell

Ruth that she was born without a womb not without a brain, but she did not.

"So no sex?"

"No," whispered Moira again.

"No boyfriend?"

"No. Well yes, sort of, but we don't do that," said Moira. She was unsure if she ever wanted to do that with anyone, let alone Steve who had become more than a friend, but was still very much just a boy.

"Right, well your vagina is a little short, so I'm going to show you some exercises so that when you do have sex, it will be a bit more comfortable for you." Moira processed the words. They sounded horrific. "You're lucky, we have to operate on some girls but we can work with what you've got."

Ruth opened a box she had placed on the end of the bed. She took out two glass ornaments, they were the shape of a small, thin cucumber chopped in half. "There are six of these in different sizes. I want you to take the smallest one and pop it inside you, just see how far it will go in," said Ruth, passing her the smallest glass cucumber. Moira took it and held it and didn't move. "Whenever you're ready," said Ruth. *Ready for what?* wondered Moira.

"I'm sorry, I don't understand," said Moira.

"Just push it in and see how far it goes," said Ruth matter–of–factly.

"Push it in where?" asked Moira. Ruth blinked and looked at her as though she was dangerously stupid.

"In your vagina," she said. Moira's eyes widened. Was the woman mad? "Or I can do it for you if you like?" said

Ruth as though she was offering to pour milk over her breakfast cereal. Moira blinked and her mouth formed an involuntary O. "Why don't I show you how, back in a jiffy," said Ruth.

The nurse disappeared behind the curtain again and reappeared as if by magic moments later with a pair of gloves and what looked like a tube of toothpaste. There was a *thwak* sound as Ruth pulled on the stretchy gloves until both her hands were covered in an off-white, stretchy second skin. She then opened the tube and squirted some clear gel onto the end of the small glass ornament.

"Lie back on the bed and spread your legs for me, there's a good girl," said Ruth. Moira was still processing the words she had spoken.

"Ready?" said Ruth.

No, thought Moira. "Yes," she said quietly.

"Good, lean back, bring your knees up, then relax them to the side. Relax," repeated Ruth, one hand on Moira's knee, one hand holding the glass object between her thighs. Moira tried to relax. "Wiggle your toes, it will help to relax you, this shouldn't hurt a bit." It did. The hard glass object entered Moira down below, it pushed inside her and felt cold and strange. She wiggled her toes, it made no difference, her knees tried to close, Ruth gently held them down.

"There we go," said Ruth. "All done, that's good. You don't have too much stretching to do at all, so let's try the next one," she said. She repeated the squirting of the gel and the inserting of a larger glass object, this one hurt even more. "Right, I want you to put your hand down here and

117

hold it. Keep the pressure on, I'll be back in five minutes, okay?"

"Okay," said Moira. She tried not to cry and stared up at the discoloured ceiling. She pushed her index and her middle fingers on the end of the slippery glass, holding it in place inside her. She did her best to ignore the pain and tried to block out the sound of the women on the other side of the curtain chatting about the weather.

"You all packed?" asked Ruth, drawing back the curtain around Moira's hospital bed. She had been scanned, prodded, poked, stared at and stretched and was definitely ready to leave. The night before, Moira had lain awake listening to a woman in a bed behind the curtain in the early stages of labour. She had listened to the woman moan and cry out in pain and had eventually cried herself to sleep. She realised this was probably the only time in her life when she would spend a few days on a maternity ward. She had asked Ruth why someone who was being treated for a condition which meant she would never have children, was being treated on a ward where other women waited to give birth. Ruth had simply shrugged, she had said it was unfortunate but there was nowhere else for Moira to go. Moira had somewhere else to go now, Moira was going home.

"Yes, I'm ready," she said, sliding down off the bed and putting her trainers back on for the first time in three days.

"Good, remember what I said, keep stretching! And if you have any questions or you're worried about anything you just get in touch, we'll be here."

"Thank you," said Moira.

The automatic doors of the hospital slid open and spat her back out into the world. She walked to the tube station and started on the long journey home. She felt different somehow, changed; a new version of herself retracing her steps back to where she belonged, back to the people who knew her, or at least knew who she had been.

FOURTEEN

"Have you done it yet?" called Tori up the stairs.

"No," yelled Harry.

"Do you want me to help you?"

"No thank you," he replied, a little too quickly. Tori considered the options. They were due back at the hospital in forty minutes. It was at least a half hour drive. Harry had already been up in the bedroom for fifteen minutes trying to fill his specimen pot. It wasn't even a big pot. She paced up and down the hallway before concluding she should just leave him to it and not say anything else. Then, without meaning to, the words slipped out of her mouth and up the stairs to her husband's ears.

"Why don't you try looking at a magazine?" she called.

"What, like one of yours? Let's see, I could read all about the top ten sights not to miss when exploring South Devon? You're right, I'm rock hard!"

"Not one of my magazines fool, you know...a men's magazine?"

"Do you mean porn, darling?"

"Yes, I mean porn, okay, there, you got me to say it out loud."

"I don't have any bloody porn magazines!" he yelled.

She looked over to the dining room table where there was a copy of Woman and Home. She didn't think that would help either. They had never really discussed porn before, but she had always imagined he must have a secret stash hidden away somewhere, she thought all men did.

"How about some internet porn? I could turn on the computer and see if I can find something? I'm sure if I put the word porn into Google something will come up..."

"You're really not helping, darling," interrupted Harry.

"Sorry," she called up the stairs.

"Can you just go somewhere else? I'm finding it hard to...concentrate when I can hear you pacing backwards and forwards down there."

"Okay, okay, I was only trying to help. We need to leave in ten minutes."

"Great, thanks for that."

Tori sat herself down at the dining room table. She had drunk several glasses of water as the doctor had instructed. Her bladder was nice and full and ready for the ultrasound. The only problem now was that she was desperate to pee. She crossed her legs and started flicking through Woman and Home to try and distract herself. The double page spread about garden water features didn't help matters.

"Right!" called Harry, running down the stairs, "let's go!"

"Okay!" said Tori, grabbing her coat from the hook on the back of the door. There was an awkward moment when Harry handed her his pot. She wrinkled her nose without meaning to and regretted not wearing rubber gloves.

Once in the car, Tori placed Harry's pot between her thighs, as instructed by the doctor to keep it at the right temperature. Once in position and wearing her seatbelt, she did her very best to try and think of anything but going to the toilet, which turned out to be all she could think of. Harry drove as though their lives, not just their future, depended on arriving at the hospital on time.

After the challenge that was finding a parking space in the hospital car park, they made their way back along the warren of corridors towards the Assisted Conception Unit. The rude woman who had greeted them that morning had been replaced by a tall, unwell-looking man. He stood towering over the desk and grimaced at them as they approached.

"Can I help you?" he sneered at them.

"Yes, I have an appointment for an ultrasound with Dr Sydney," said Tori.

"And I have a...pot for her," said Harry, producing his sample.

The unwell-looking man turned his nose upwards in disgust, his huge nostrils flaring at them both as though Harry had just taken a shit on the desk. Surely this guy was used to seeing this sort of thing, thought Harry. He started to doubt whether the man actually worked here, wondering if he might just be a lost patient who had wandered in from the psychiatric ward.

"Thank you," said the man, his skin looking ever so slightly green under the fluorescent lighting. He took Harry's pot between his thumb and index finger and held it to the light before putting it in a white paper bag. "Take a seat, I'm afraid Doctor Sydney is running a little late," he said, before returning his attention to the paperback he had been reading.

"Oh...do you know roughly how long she might be?" asked Tori, looking longingly at the toilet sign just down the corridor.

"No," said the man, without looking up from his book.

Tori and Harry waited in the waiting room. It seemed like the thing to do. Then they waited some more. People came and went, time passed slowly and names were called, just not theirs. Tori's need to go to the bathroom was becoming unbearable. She tried sitting in different positions, crossing and uncrossing her legs, reading magazines and walking up and down the corridor but nothing helped. Harry, far more relaxed now that his contribution had been safely delivered, found the situation strangely amusing.

"Why don't you ask him if you can just pee a little bit? I could get you a bottle of water from the machine to top it up again after..."

"Don't say the word water!"

"Sorry. Do you want me to ask him if you can use the toilet?"

"For God's sake, don't say the word toilet either!" snapped Tori.

"Sorry," said Harry again. He tried not to laugh, he knew it would be wrong to, but his mouth had other thoughts. His lips curled up at the end and before long his silent smile gave way to a muffled chuckle.

"Are you laughing at me?" said Tori, glaring at him

now.

"No, of course not," said Harry, unable to stop himself. The unwell-looking man on reception looked over at them, adopting a look that said *be quiet*, before making an angry *shhh* sound and shaking his head as though he might be suffering from a seizure.

"Don't you think the reception guy looks like he might need a doctor?" said Harry.

"Well he's in the right place. I think he looks a bit like Spock—check out those pointy ears," whispered Tori.

"You have a point. Shall I see if I can find Doctor Spock a doctor? Or us for that matter...our appointment was meant to be over an hour ago."

"Nah, this is a hospital, you won't find a doctor round here," said Tori with a smile. "Alright, I give in, I'm going to ask Spock if I can pee, just a little, before I wet myself," said Tori before walking very carefully over to the reception desk.

"Can I help you?" the unwell-looking man sneered once again, without looking up.

"Yes, I wondered if it would be okay if I used the bathroom?" asked Tori.

"Down the hall, on the left." His eyes acknowledged her then, looking into her own as though he had never seen her before. The fact that she was still stood there caused them to narrow.

"No, I meant because of my scan. The doctor told me to drink lots of water and not go to the toilet....so that my bladder is full...for when she does the scan," babbled Tori, not sure how much detail she needed to give by way of explanation. Sick-looking Spock stared at her as though she were perilously foolish. He let out a sigh, a breathy garlic whiff reaching out across the desk to slap some sense into her stupidity.

"So the doctor told you not to go to the toilet before your scan, and you're asking me if you can go to the toilet before your scan?" he said, flaring his nostrils again. It was a good point and reasonably well made.

"Right, I'll sit back down in the waiting room then," she muttered. "I don't suppose you know how much longer we might be waiting for?"

"No," he said. And with that their interaction was over.

"What did he say?" asked Harry as she retook her seat.

"He said I can't pee."

"Oh," said Harry.

"Oh, indeed."

"Victoria?" called a nurse with a clipboard who had appeared from nowhere like a uniformed angel sent from heaven.

"Yes!" said Tori.

"Room nine when you're ready please," said the nurse before squeaking her way back wherever she had come from.

"Shit!" whispered Tori.

"What now? This is good, we're next," said Harry.

"I know, I know, it's just I was so excited when she called my name I've pissed myself a little bit."

"My wife, ladies and gentleman," said Harry, before he and Tori stood and made their way towards room nine and their future.

Tori lay on the table while Dr Sydney sat next to her and squeezed some cold gel on to her tummy. She rolled the ultrasound wand over her skin.

"I can't see anything," said Dr Sydney. She frowned intently at the small screen she was staring at, whilst moving the wand back and forth. Whatever she could or couldn't see was not making her happy. Harry sat at the far end of the room and followed the doctor's gaze to stare at the small monitor. Tori watched both their faces, hoping for a positive display on either, but they continued to frown as though the film they had paid to see would not start and things were not getting any clearer.

"I'm sorry, I'm going to need to do an internal scan, would you like to use the toilet first?" said the doctor. Tori no longer cared what the doctor did to her, as long as she could use the toilet first.

"Yes, please."

"Just down the hall on the left, come back when you're done." Tori slid down off the bed, pulled the gaping nightgown around her and shuffled out of the room. When she returned the room was quiet. Harry and Doctor Sydney had clearly been interrupted, though what they had said she did not know and would forget to ask about later.

"Bend your knees and try to relax," said Doctor Sydney. Tori tried and failed. It wasn't easy when the doctor was about to push what looked like a kitchen blender inside her.

"No, still nothing," said the doctor after a long and painful few minutes. Tori was feeling desperate now, she knew it made no sense but couldn't help wondering if something had happened to her ovaries, whether perhaps they were of no use to her now either. She turned away from the monitor and concentrated on not crying instead.

"Hold on just a minute," said Doctor Sydney, more to herself than anyone else in the room. "I've got one!" It was as though the woman was on a fishing trip and had got her first bite after a long day. "Your ovaries it would seem are a little high, but I've found the right one, and it looks good to me," she said, squinting at the small screen. Tori felt relief rush through her. She smiled at Harry who in turn relaxed a little and took from his wife's smiling face that this was good news.

"And there's the left," sighed Doctor Sydney, a sense of satisfaction in her voice. "Both very healthy looking, no cysts and a good size, they were just hiding from us. Right, all done, you can pop your clothes back on now."

Tori did as she was told. She dressed and came back to sit next to next to Harry, who squeezed her hand affectionately as though she wasn't broken. She looked at him. His eyes said, *I love you*. Her eyes said it back. She tried not to cry, again. Sometimes this was all too much. Sometimes this was just too hard.

"Right then," said Doctor Sydney, oblivious to the moment and comprehensively interrupting it without further ado. "There's good news and bad news. The good news is medically speaking everything is looking pretty good. The lab have had a look at Harry's sample, you can see here on the screen that everything is as it should be." Tori and Harry both looked at the computer screen, there was a graph and a series of words and numbers that meant absolutely nothing to them at all, but they both nodded and smiled as thought the screen had said ten out of ten and the doctor had given them a gold star. "Your ovaries are high up, Tori, but they're there, and not only are they there, but they're healthy, very healthy. According to what I saw on the screen today and the results of your blood tests here, you have the ovaries of a twenty-one year old and there is no reason why we shouldn't be able to take your eggs, Harry's sperm and make some embryos," smiled Doctor Sydney.

"What's the bad news?" interrupted Harry. Tori would have rather he hadn't asked. She didn't want to hear the bad news, whatever it was.

"The bad news is that your only option to make all of this happen is IVF with a view to surrogacy. The PCT, that's the Primary Care Trust responsible for this area does fund IVF, but not for the purpose of surrogacy. I need to double check, but after a few initial phone calls, I don't think we can treat you here."

"I don't understand, we've already been to three different hospitals," said Tori. The walls seemed to be coming in closer, the room felt smaller and she was aware that her knees were trembling.

"What it means, is that we can apply for funding for IVF, but, because it would be for the purpose of surrogacy, as in you couldn't carry the child yourself, I fear the PCT will reject the application. Even if they granted funding, which I'm sorry to say is highly unlikely, because you need treatment for both the IVF and the surrogacy, we can't do that here. I'm sorry." Harry and Tori sat in silence. Neither knew what to say.

"I really am so sorry," said the doctor again. She was.

"How much would it cost? If we paid for it ourselves?" asked Harry.

"You mean if you went private? Around nine thousand per cycle."

"Nine thousand pounds?" asked Tori, just to clarify.

"Yes around that, possibly a bit more. You would still have to join a waiting list for treatment and of course you would have the surrogate costs on top," added Dr Sydney. Harry shifted in his chair.

"We've waited quite some time already and we're aware of the surrogate costs. That would mean us spending over twenty five thousand pounds just to try for this baby. That's more than I can earn in a year. Why didn't someone tell us that before? How are we supposed to find that kind of money? I don't understand why we don't get funding?" said Harry, his anger increasing the volume of his voice. He wanted this to work because he wanted a child of their own, but above all, he wanted this to work because Tori wanted it and primarily he wanted her to be happy.

"Can't we apply for funding anyway? Just see what they say?" pleaded Tori. She was desperate now. She could sense how this was going to go, they both could. They had been told it was the end of the road before, and she just wasn't willing to hear it or accept that. She didn't think she would ever be ready to give up.

Doctor Sydney observed them quietly, looking from one to the other. She wanted to comfort them but it wasn't in her power to do so. She had become a doctor to help people, recently she found she helped people less and less. She spent her days delivering bad news instead of babies. This was not how things were supposed to be.

"Yes, we can apply anyway and see what happens," she said, and did her best to smile and look hopeful. Whatever happened with the patients sat in front of her, she didn't want to be the one to tell them that the road had come to an end.

FIFTEEN

Mrs Brown found herself staring down at her own hands. She barely recognised them. Her dead leaf-like skin endured an autumnal fragility that was both unfamiliar and unwelcome. Aged flesh wrapped in a carpet of age spots masquerading as freckles. Her fingers looked like misshapen old twigs, they were thin, so much so that her rings twisted freely around them. Above all they hurt. Her hands, like the rest of her body, were tired. She was in desperate need of a manicure and perhaps a few extra cod liver oil tablets. She stared past her hands at the pile of papers still stretched out, untouched on the bureau. They were to blame for much of her discomfort, all this letter writing was taking its toll on her body and mind. It was late. All but one of the residents had been put to bed and bed was all she herself could now think of. Her body ached with pain and her mind was weary from the day's troubles. She couldn't find a way to give Rosie a pay rise, but knew she couldn't go back on her word now. She would have to find the money from somewhere. Perhaps she could find the money tomorrow.

"Good evening, Mrs B, you're up late," said Adele, the overnight care assistant. Adele was a large woman from

Barbados. She had the face of a beauty queen and a bottom any hippo would be proud to call its own. She was large and loud and didn't suffer fools gladly, which was one of the many reasons Mrs Brown had hired her. Adele's arrival meant it was even later than she had thought.

"Hello, Adele, yes I've had a bit of a late one, lots of paperwork to get through. I'm going to stay the night rather than drive all the way home and I think I'll head off to bed very soon."

"You've been staying here a lot lately, Mrs B. Would you like a cup of cocoa? I'm making one for myself anyway?" asked Adele.

"Oh go on then, why not, might help me sleep. Would you be an angel and bring it to my room?"

"Of course I will, you look shattered. I'll be along in a few minutes."

Mrs Brown made her way down the maze of quiet corridors, past the sounds of sleep, towards her room on the ground floor. She opened the door, pleased to find the bed made but otherwise things exactly as she had left them. This was her home away from home, all that was missing was Mr Brown. She undressed, unfolding tired limbs out of her red woollen dress before hanging it carefully back in the wardrobe. She thought she had put something else on that morning, but she had clearly changed her mind. She was definitely over-tired now and in desperate need of a good night's sleep. That would sort her out, no doubt about it.

In the top drawer of her chest she found a neatly ironed and folded nightgown. With additional effort she stretched her arms high above her head and let the gown fall down around her. The cool cotton slid down her body with ease and she realised she must have lost weight. She washed her face in the small porcelain sink and dabbed it dry with a thin pink towel. She stared at herself in the mirror, barely recognising the old woman who stared back at her with equal measures of curiosity and dismay.

She surveyed her small, neat room. It wasn't much to look at, but it was after all only somewhere to sleep. She had spent too many nights here recently, putting her work and this place before herself, her family and her home. She needed to come up with a plan and see if she couldn't spend more time there and still run the place, without having to hire in any more unaffordable staff. She was getting too old for all this and she knew it. She shuffled over to the dressing table and took a closer look at the lady in the mirror. She watched as the woman applied some face cream, then slowly pulled out the pins holding up the neat grey bun on top of her head. The old woman uncoiled her long hair, unplaiting each strand with care until a mass of grey curls framed the face staring back at her, and rested gently on fragile shoulders. The woman in the mirror removed her earrings and necklace and placed them in a heart-shaped mother of pearl box. The woman's hands shook ever so slightly as she went about her business, but Mrs Brown barely noticed. She was too busy looking into the woman's pale blue eyes. Those eyes had seen a lot of things; she could tell. Those eyes spoke a thousand words between each and every weary blink. She knew this woman, knew her well, she had known her all her life.

Without warning the woman stood and turned away from the dresser, as did Mrs Brown. She hoped she hadn't offended her in some way.

It was kind of the staff to make her bed when she stayed. She gratefully made her way towards it, leaning down to peel back the patchwork floral quilt, revealing crisp white sheets. There was something sterile about the bed linen. Something about the way it smelled, which always served as a reminder that this was neither a hotel, nor a hospital. Most of all, she was reminded that this was not home and home was where right now, more than anything, she longed to be. She sat with the bedside table lamp gently lighting the gloom. She sat and stared and waited, not quite able to remember what it was she was waiting for and a touch too tired to care. There was a light knock at the door. Mrs Brown stared at the door handle and held her breath. She had forgotten to lock it, anyone could be out there and here she was sitting in bed in her nightdress. The door handle turned and a dark figure looked into the gloom.

"You still awake, Mrs B? Sorry it took me so long, Mrs Pike pulled her cord on the top floor, took me an age to get up there and check she was alright. Still, here's your cocoa now, and with a bourbon biscuit just ripe for dunking, better late than never, I always say. I'll leave it on the side there to cool down for a bit," said Adele, waddling into the room to place the drink where Mrs Brown could reach it. This was a slight invasion of personal space and crossed a boundary which Mrs Brown was not entirely at ease with. But it was late and she was too tired to make a fuss. Adele

134

meant no harm and it probably wasn't necessary to remind her that she was her boss, not a resident at Godalming Lodge.

"Is Mrs Pike okay?" asked Mrs Brown, taking the cup from the bedside table and dipping the biscuit into the hot liquid.

"Oh yes, she's fine. Think she just woke up in the night and forgot where she was the way the residents do sometimes when they first move in," replied Adele, making a beeline for the door.

"Good. Thank you for the cocoa, hope you have a quiet night."

"You too, Mrs B, sleep well now," said Adele, and with that she was gone.

Mrs Brown finished her drink and placed the empty cup back on the bedside table. She scooched down into the bed, with the sheets still firmly tucked around her. It was a mildly strange habit she had developed since first spending the night here. She felt safer this way. Without the sheets trapping her in the bed, she found she awoke from her dreams falling. She didn't want to fall. She reached out to turn the lamp off before quickly sliding her arm back down underneath the covers where it was warm and safe. Above her the house slept. Twenty-four rooms filled with twenty-four separate souls, that had come to end their lives together here under the one same roof. It was not a happy thought, but it was a true one. She hoped when her time came, there would be a more satisfactory ending. She didn't mean to think about death so often, but in her business it was hard not to. Death walked the corridors of Godalming Lodge both day and night. Every whistle of the wind or creak of a floorboard, she knew it was him sniffing about the place, for he was forever lonely and looking for a new soul to take with him for company. Death mostly made night calls. One by one the residents would go to sleep, but with alarming frequency they did not all wake in the morning. Were she not so tired, Mrs Brown would have thought about death a little longer, but her eyelids were heavy and had thoughts of their own, mainly thoughts about sleep. She allowed them to close and found herself in a dream. In the dream she was flying, soaring through the air. She held on tight and hoped she would not fall.

SIXTEEN

Moira pulled off her faded cotton night dress, folded it twice and placed it under the pillow of her neatly made bed. She dressed in what she hoped would make her look vaguely attractive and brushed her long hair until it was free of knots and tangles. She applied some moisturising cream to her face, some Vaseline on her lips and a little mascara. It was so hard trying to be someone else when she didn't know who it was she was supposed to be. She stood back to examine her work in the mirror. For the briefest of moments she felt pleased with the girl who stared approvingly back at her, but doubt was never too far away. Her reflected twin developed a worried frown and looked altogether less like whoever it was they were trying to be.

Steve was waiting for her at the station. It had only been a few days since she last saw him, but excitement bubbled up inside her. The thought of his attention and touch quickened her strides until she was almost tripping over herself to get where she was going. She was late, time had delayed her. She ran up the station steps, weaving her way through the slow walking passengers all on their way to somewhere else. Her eyes found his. He looked happy to see her. She felt a rush of something a lot like love.

"How are you?" Steve asked. He was nervous,

awkward.

"Fine, good," she said. She took the lead and kissed him on the cheek. He looked embarrassed, as though he had been kissed by his mother in public. "Where are we going?" she asked.

"You'll see," replied the boy.

"Okay," she said simply.

"I've got the tickets already, we should go before we miss another train."

"I'm so sorry I'm late." She had been stretching, but not in a way he would understand.

"Don't worry about it, I'm sure you'll be worth the wait," he said and took her hand in his. It felt clammy and unnatural. It felt like they were play acting. They made their way towards the platform in silence, as though they had both forgotten their lines.

Southend on a Saturday afternoon was a blur of flashing lights, seaside sights and smells. They walked hand in hand along the pier, excited like the children they still were and carried along by the swelling tide of people with the same idea. Everything felt better at Southend, it was impossible to feel sad or lonely. They had both been coming here since they were children and it was a place filled with the simplest of happy, innocent memories. The two of them wandered aimlessly through the spinning tea cups, candyfloss stalls and brightly coloured slot machines. They became fat with the sights and sounds and smells, greedily gulping them down, not wanting to admit they were already full, not wanting to stop. After pausing to tie his laces, Steve took Moira's hand in his again. It felt awkward, but she appreciated the sentiment and liked that he didn't mind passers-by knowing that they were together. He wasn't ashamed to be seen with her, or at least the person he thought she was. They soaked up the smell of salty sea air and let themselves be themselves. They strolled along the pier eating fish and chips with miniature plastic forks and if Moira hadn't known better, she'd say she felt happy.

"Do you want to go get a drink?" Steve asked.

"I've got one," said Moira, holding up her can of coke.

"A real drink," said the boy. The penny dropped unhurriedly with Moira.

"Sure," she said eventually, having had time to consider the suggestion. The words had meant far more than was implied, the words had consequences. Her response would preordain her destiny. These things had to be considered; all words, whether spoken or written should always be cogitated, it was a simple case of due diligence.

They made their way towards a homely old pub on the seafront. Moira wasn't quite old enough to drink yet, but the landlord either didn't notice or didn't care.

"You okay? You seem a little different?" asked Steve, putting a small white wine down on the table in front of her. Moira's cheeks flushed, her mind filled with panic. Could he somehow tell? The thought made her uncomfortable and she gulped down the wine faster than was sensible.

"I'm fine, just a bit tired is all."

"Well so long as you're not secretly seeing someone else behind my back," said Steve, a flash of something like danger in his eyes. He nervously imitated laughter before taking a sip of his beer. She was keeping secrets, but not the sort he could predict or guess. A boy about their age stumbled into their table, interrupting the moment. Steve's glass started to fall but he caught it before too much of the drink was spilled. His reactions were fast. His hand caught the glass, his legs stood, his face changed.

"What the fuck are you doing?" he said to the boy, his face full with rage. The hand that had caught the beer now clenched in a forewarning fist.

"Sorry, mate, I tripped," said the stranger. The smile he had worn also faded. "I'll get you another drink..."

"No, it's fine. Just watch where you're going," said Steve, back to being himself just as quickly as he had changed into someone different. Moira was shocked by this side of him. She had seen it before but chosen to forget, as she would again now.

The rest of the evening passed more easily. Steve and Moira talked about everything and nothing and by the time her third glass of wine was empty, she felt noticeably more relaxed and a little under the influence.

"We should head home, I told Mother I'd be back in time for dinner and it's already well late. I'll be in trouble again."

"When aren't you?" said Steve. "Come on then, before we miss the last train home," he said, downing his pint and standing to leave.

She saw it in him then for the first time, they had both changed. They had both grown up. Steve was no longer the boy who was a friend. He was something more. He was the boy who would be the first in his family to go to university the following year, he was the boy who she could almost be herself with, the boy she loved. They walked hand in hand once more, different but the same.

The train spat them out at the station and they began the winding walk home, back to where they had come from, laughing loudly at nothing at all in the cool darkness. Orange glowing street lights lit the way along quiet streets. They ran out of words around the same time as they ran out of man-made light, relying on the illuminated moon to guide them through the shadows. The light drizzle that had slowly dampened them grew up into a rain shower and then rapidly translated into a full on downpour. Moira's parents' house was only a mile or so from the station, but the rain was heavy and they were barely half way there.

"Come on, we'll take a short cut across the fields," said Steve.

"It will be muddy," said Moira protesting on behalf of her new trainers.

"It'll be fine," Steve insisted. His shirt was already soaked through. The cotton clung to his chest, which looked larger, more defined than she had imagined. Moira had seen the weights in his bedroom, but until now she hadn't noticed that he'd been using them.

"It's private property," said Moira noticing an angry looking red sign and holding back while he pulled her hand.

"Owned by a farmer who is already tucked up in bed a whole town away...I really don't think he'll mind us taking a little short cut. Come on, don't be a chicken," he laughed.

"Okay," she said and laughed too. The wine surged through her body, slowing her down. The rain was falling heavily now and slapping at her face. She could barely see where they were going, but she let him lead her. They ran and they laughed in the darkness until she fell. She fell hard and the laughter stopped. Only the rain and the sound of the wind in the corn field remained.

"Shit, are you okay?" Steve asked, a worried frown forming on his youthful face. He bent down next to her in the corn. She thought about it, then laughed some more, it seemed the thing to do. She was okay, she felt great. She kissed him then, just reached up and kissed him. The rain fell on their entwined bodies, in the middle of the field. They kissed more passionately than they had ever dared before. Two childhood sweethearts, no longer children, no longer so sweet. His hands held her face as his tongue danced inside her mouth. Moira felt dizzy, she felt warm despite the cold rain and above all she felt alive. His hands moved under her bra and he kissed her neck. His mouth moved lower and he hungrily kissed her breasts while she stared up at the stars through the rain in the night sky. Her hands found his belt buckle. They had never done anything like this before, and yet it felt natural, automatic. Moira wasn't scared, she wasn't cold, in many ways she wasn't Moira.

When he entered her it hurt. For a moment she remembered the hospital, but with every second, the hospital felt further away, a distant memory. The present felt dreamlike. Naked, in the middle of a field in the pouring rain, Moira lost her virginity. They made love for an indeterminate period of time. It hurt, but she felt wonderful and when he came inside her and collapsed on top of her, she thought this must be how it felt to be normal. They lay next to each other then, holding hands, panting. The star-filled sky looked down on what they had just done. Moira felt the hot liquid seep out of her as a trickle oozed down her thigh, mixing with the rain, washing her pain away into the dark, sodden earth.

SEVENTEEN

"What do you want to drink?" asked Coxy.

"I don't know. Anything. Wine?" replied Tori, too tired to take on the responsibly of decision making. She examined the friend sat opposite her. It was a brief inspection, but she observed the carefree way in which her perfect hair fell about her shoulders, her manicured nails, her clear skin, and her new clothes. She reflected how Tori used to look, before her life was taken over. She looked down at her own dry hands with their unpolished nails, folded together in the lap of the tatty old skirt she had thrown on that morning, without a second of consideration or care. She assessed the tranquil air her friend breathed with ease and noted how much younger she looked, dismayed by the knowledge that they were in fact the same age.

The friend returned her stare and exchanged the evaluation. The friend saw that she was tired and changed. She was a version of herself that neither of them liked, that neither of them particularly wanted to spend time with. But being a good friend, she put none of this into words. It was a silent exchange that neither would acknowledge for it was beneficial to no one.

"Wine it is, you guard the table, I'll get a bottle and bring it over," said Coxy before turning away from the truth of her friend and heading off to flirt with the handsome barman.

Tori did as she was told. She didn't have the energy to argue or to explain to Coxy for the hundredth time that she wasn't supposed to be drinking too much at the moment. The doctor had said it was best to drink no more than half a bottle a week before treatment. Without funding there would be no treatment, but she couldn't give up, not yet. She would have a glass to be polite and because she wanted one. Then she would let her friend finish the bottle. Tori had known the woman at the bar for as long as she could remember. Coxy recently joined the same company and worked on a political magazine four floors up. They were seeing a lot more of each other again, it felt like the old days when they had been students together. It felt familiar and safe, it felt good. They had grown apart but the shared memories of growing up held them securely together through brief periods of incompatibility or change. Tori could be herself with Coxy, the self she sometimes forgot ever existed.

"What's the matter with your face?" said Coxy, plonking the drinks on the table and sitting down.

"Nothing, just a bit of a bad day that's all."

"Don't give me that crap, what's happened?" said Coxy, before downing half a glass in one gulp. Tori thought about telling her friend the truth, she knew she should tell Harry first, but keeping it all in was eating away at her. Coxy knew everything that was going on anyway, she was one

145

of the few people Tori didn't have to put on an act for. She took a sip of her own wine, then reached down and took a letter out of her handbag.

"What's this?" asked Coxy, taking the letter from her hand.

"Read it," said Tori and watched her friend's facial expressions as she did just that.

"Okay, I've read it, I still don't understand, what is it?"

"It's from the PCT."

"The what?

"The Primary Care Trust." Coxy continued to stare blankly back at her. "They are the people who decide whether we get funding for IVF."

"Oh," said Coxy, looking down at the letter again.

"Yes, oh."

"Haven't you been waiting forever for these cocksuckers to get back to you?"

"Six months."

"Six months, then the fuckers go and say no? Why are they saying no? My hairdresser is having IVF and she hasn't even got a steady boyfriend, if she got bloody funding, why can't you?"

"It's complicated," said Tori.

"Bullshit, it's bollocks is what it is. Write back to them and tell them to look at it again. How else are you going to pay for all this? Sell your house? Work on street corners?" said Coxy.

"I don't know. We've talked about selling the house..."

"I was joking! You can't sell your house, that's nuts."

"Harry has started teaching full time again, so that will

146

help a bit."

"What about his writing?"

"He's doing it in the evenings. Even with the extra income we were always going to have to find another pot of money to pay for the surrogate. Not that we have one of those either yet."

"Why? How much are you going to pay her?"

"Fifteen thousand or thereabouts," said Tori, taking another sip of her wine. She'd never talked about how much all of this was going to cost before with anyone other than Harry. Coxy's mouth fell open. She was silent. It was a rare, brief moment when she had nothing to say. It didn't last.

"Fuck me! Fifteen grand! I'll carry the sodding baby if you pay me that much!" Tori couldn't help but laugh at this. Coxy was many things, but maternal was not one of them.

"You drink like a fish and smoke like a chimney," said Tori, smiling for the first time that day.

"Okay, I'll give you a discount. Ten percent off *and* I'll throw in some free babysitting when the kid is born, what do you say?" Tori laughed. Somehow Coxy and a glass of wine had cheered her up when she didn't think it was possible.

"Where have you been?" asked Harry. He stood in the doorway with anger etched on his face. He had clearly been waiting and had opened the front door just as Tori was about to slot her key in the lock.

"Just a quick drink with Coxy after work, had a bit of a rubbish day..."

"You didn't eat, did you?" asked Harry.

"No, why...?" said Tori. Still sulking just a little, he took her hand and ushered her through to the dining room. The first thing she noticed were the candles, they were everywhere on every surface. The table was set for two and she could smell something pleasant wafting in from the kitchen.

"I've made you a surprise dinner, that's why," said Harry, kissing her on the cheek and helping her out of her coat.

"Oh, you should have told me, I would have come straight home! It's not ruined, is it? What's the occasion?" she said.

"Had I told you, it wouldn't have been much of a surprise now would it? And who says there needs to be an occasion for me to cook the woman I love a meal?" asked Harry. They both smiled at this, a silent acknowledgement of his tendency to burn things rather than cook them. He pulled her into his arms and kissed her softly on the forehead.

"Okay, you got me. The occasion, my beautiful wife, is that it is two years since we got married."

"Oh my God, have I forgotten our anniversary? I can't have, it's not until the end of the month..."

"Okay, it's next week, but I wanted to celebrate a little early."

"Oh," said Tori, flooded with relief. She had forgotten many things lately, including her own name some days; there had just been a little too much going on, a little too much to deal with. The memory reminding her that she needed to tell Harry about the funding popped into her head, briefly spoiling the moment. She ignored it long enough for it to hide away at the back of her mind, almost but not quite forgotten.

"Now then, I want you to sit down and relax," said Harry, pulling out a chair. "There is a bit of a theme to tonight, but I'll let you see if you can guess what it is rather than spoil the surprise."

"I thought this was the surprise."

"Yes and no," said Harry with a smile. "A glass of Rioja?"

"Yes, why not, I only had one drink at the bar. Crikey, I feel spoilt," said Tori, as Harry poured them both some wine. "Cheers," she said, clinking her glass with his.

"Now I've made tapas, I've never made them before so bear with me," he said bringing a series of small bowls in from the kitchen. It all looked and smelt delicious.

"This looks great, you should cook new things more often," said Tori. "I think I've guessed the theme...everything is Spanish!"

"See, all those people who said you were slow, they were wrong," said Harry with a grin. He pulled an envelope out of his pocket and slid it across the table.

"What's this?" asked Tori. She had already received one unwelcome envelope that day.

"Open it and you'll see," said Harry, taking another sip

of his wine and looking very pleased with himself indeed. Tori did as she was told. Inside there were two tickets and a letter from a hotel. A Spanish hotel.

"What have you done?" asked Tori, delighted and terrified at the same time.

"I've booked us a little trip to Rioja for our wedding anniversary," said Harry, relieved that he didn't have to keep it a secret any longer. He had always struggled to keep anything from Tori. Her reaction and the expression on her face wasn't quite how he had imagined it.

"But, how? When? I mean we don't have the money. We're supposed to be saving and what about getting time off work?"

"It's all sorted. I spoke to your boss about it weeks ago. He gave me the idea actually, asking you to write about somewhere from your desk again. You wrote such a wonderful article about the place, I thought we should go and see it for ourselves." Tori didn't look nearly as happy as he had hoped. She didn't look happy at all, so he persevered. "And the money thing, don't worry about it. I know we are saving, I haven't forgotten, but I'm back full time at the school now, I got my tax refund for last year and I just wanted to spend a little bit of that on something nice for us." She started to quietly cry. As the tears slowly and silently rolled down her cheeks, a splattering of tiny raindrops started to decorate the exterior of the dining room window.

Tori stood and went to get her handbag, then pulled out an envelope of her own. Without words, she handed it to him. He frowned, almost snatched the letter from her and

150

read it. She knew instantly from the way his face changed that she shouldn't have given it to him. She had spoiled the moment forever now, but she simply couldn't carry the burden alone any longer. She sat back down at the table, full of regret, unable to look at the face of her husband, fists of dread clenched on her lap.

"I don't understand," he said. Although they both knew that he did.

"We didn't get funding," she clarified for them both.

"Why not?"

"As it says in the letter, it isn't their standard policy to fund anything associated with surrogacy." Harry put the letter that had ruined everything down and looked at the uneaten tapas getting cold on the table. He felt full of anger, but didn't want this to spoil their night; this was supposed to be a happy occasion. This was not how he had imagined things would play out. Tori was not supposed to be crying again. He took a breath and closed his eyes for a moment.

"Well, we were expecting this anyway. I know it's taken a long time to arrive, but Doctor Sydney always said it was a long shot. We'll sell the house," he said. He sincerely hoped that the words he had offered would be an end of the baby talk that evening, but realised he was optimistic to do so. The rain was falling heavier now outside.

"What? We can't sell the house, it's our home! I spoke to Doctor Sydney this afternoon, she thinks we should appeal...." As Tori spoke, something inside her husband snapped. Something that he had buried deep down within himself could no longer be contained. It wasn't his fault. It wasn't her fault. They would tell themselves later that is was just one of those things.

"Appeal? What for? So we can wait another six months for a room full of faceless bastards to tell us we can't have a baby. What do they know? They don't even know who we are! We're just case numbers on a sheet of fucking A4 to them!" Tori cried because of the letter and cried because Harry was not Harry anymore and it was all her fault. He noticed how hard Tori was crying now, he tried to calm himself down for her sake. He came round to her side of the table and crouched down next to her, passing the rain-lashed window and ignoring the howling wind outside. "Look, I thought this was going to happen, it was only a matter of time. We've saved quite a bit over the last few months, but it was never going to be enough. I don't want to wait anymore, do you? I am sick of having this hanging over us, feeling like my life is on hold. I'd like to try for this baby before we both retire. I had an estate agent round a few weeks ago, had the place valued. We've made a healthy profit. We're not rich, far from it, but we can sell this place. We'll have a bit of money to buy another house, maybe something a little bit smaller, and still have some money left over to try for the baby," he said. He had hoped it wouldn't come to this, but it had and he had made the decision for the both of them.

"I love you," said Tori.

"I love you too," said Harry. "Now eat your tapas before everything is completely cold. This was supposed to be a happy occasion! Not only do you have an amazing husband who is whisking you away for a romantic holiday to celebrate our anniversary, but we've also found a way to try for our baby. The answer was there all along," he said patting the walls. The rain stopped.

"But you love this house, it's our home," she said.

"I love you more. It's just a house, just bricks that's all. Home is wherever we say it is. Home is you and me. Everything is going to be okay," he said.

"Do you promise?"

"I promise," he said, sitting back down and taking a sip of his wine. He wondered whether that last promise would be one he would be able to keep. The storm was silenced for now.

EIGHTEEN

Mrs Brown was having a rather good day. The sun was shining and she felt happy with herself and her surroundings. She had slept well the night before, got up nice and early and had managed to get so much done already. She smiled to herself and concluded that she deserved a well-earned rest. Today was Friday after all and Fridays at Godalming Lodge were all about personal grooming performed on and by strangers. Yellow old toenails on twisted, gnarled feet were clipped and thin, colourless hair was cut into meaningless neat lines. Enormous old ears needed to be carefully cleaned of wax and some of the women, as well as the men, needed their faces shaved. The inability of the residents to do these things for themselves, did not mean that they no longer needed to be done. Mrs Brown decided to take a break from the paperwork; she would deal with it later. She heaved herself up and out of the chair, feeling a somewhat lighter and more carefree version of the woman she knew herself to be. She cancelled the plans she had made for her time that afternoon, acquitted herself from the self-imposed guilt of not working and went to investigate what the rest of the house was up to.

At the back of Godalming Lodge, on the opposite side from her little room where she stayed from time to time, was the mini salon. She had had the room converted a few years ago when they extended the utility room on the other side of the building. Describing the space as a salon, was perhaps a stretch too far for the old imagination, but it was what she liked to call the room. There were two washbasins with two seats in front of them and a couple of mirrors on the wall. Sally, the peroxide blonde visiting hairdresser, was hard at work washing May's hair. She was a busty woman in her forties with an aggressive looking bob, Sally not May, who was old as the hills but still sharp as a pin. May's eyes were closed, she looked serene and was clearly enjoying the head massage.

"Hello, Mrs Brown, how are you?" said Sally cheerfully as Mrs Brown came a little closer, to take a better look. This room made her feel proud. It was small touches like this that made Godalming Lodge so very different from the other care homes. It was the little things in life that reminded the residents that they were still alive, they were still human. Nobody should ever outgrow the little things that life just gives away.

"I'm well, very well thank you," she replied.

"Do you fancy a quick trim yourself while I'm here?" asked Sally.

"Oh dear, does it look that bad? I have been a bit preoccupied lately. I haven't had a lot of free time to deal with it...but no, I couldn't possibly," said Mrs Brown who had only ever had her hair cut at a proper salon. It wasn't that she didn't think Sally was up to the job, but this was for the residents, not the staff and that included her.

"It's no bother at all and May is my last client for the day, so it won't take long," Sally persisted. She was a kind woman.

"No, honestly, I'll pop to the hairdressers next weekend when things quieten down a bit..." Sally frowned at her then and shook her head.

"Now then, Mrs Brown, I think we both know that isn't true," she said. Mrs Brown knew she was right. It would probably be weeks before she really had time to get away from the place. She couldn't remember the last time that she actually went into town to get her hair done. May's eyes opened as did her mouth, which had been firmly closed in a peaceful smile until now.

"Oh just get your hair done, woman, and stop dithering. Why would you look a gift horse in the mouth, all those things you think need doing will still be there waiting for you later. Just learn to say yes and let people do something nice for you once in a while," she said before closing her eyes again and resting back in her chair. Mrs Brown couldn't help but laugh at the old woman. She may be getting on a bit, but she hadn't lost a single marble and always spoke her mind.

"Is that a yes then?" asked Sally with a cheeky grin.

"I think it had better be, don't you, or I'll be in trouble with May and that will never do," smiled Mrs Brown.

"That's good news, take a seat and I'll be with you soon."

Mrs Brown, for once, did as she was told and sat down in the seat next to May. She wasn't sure whether it was the right thing to do or not, but she was here now and how bad could it be? Yes Sally was here to look after the residents, but like she said herself, May was the last one for the day and if she didn't mind, then Mrs Brown shouldn't either.

"How are you, May?" she asked, and realised that she had a genuine interest in the answer.

"I'm good. My eyes are playing up a bit and I've run out of new audiobooks, but my niece promised to bring something along next time, so I can't really complain. I think compared to a lot of people here I've got it quite good. And today is a nice treat. Sally says I'll look just like Marilyn by the time she is done with me."

"Is that so?" asked Mrs Brown.

"Spitting image," said Sally with a wink.

"Are you still missing home?" Mrs Brown asked. As soon as the words left her mouth she felt a sudden stab of regret. It was probably her own thoughts of missing home that had caused the words to escape her in the first place.

"You know I didn't really want to come here," said May simply. Mrs Brown knew only too well.

"I didn't think I needed to be here, still don't," said May. "I look around me and I'm surrounded by old people; some so old they don't know who they are any more, some so senile they think they're someone else. I'm not like these people, I know I'm not. I may look like them on the outside, but on the inside I'm still me. I miss my home so very much. But I understand why I'm here. After the last fall I think I gave everyone a bit of a scare. Though I still say it was the ice under the snow, nothing else that caused me to slip; could have happened to anyone. My eyes might be going but I'm not blind yet," she added.

"It's difficult sometimes, the transition, but I promise you this is a good place to be, a safe place."

"I know, I know, you don't need to give me the hard sell. I know you love this place and I'm not saying it isn't a lovely home, it just isn't my home. Do you know what I mean?" Mrs Brown did know what she meant. She understood completely. She often felt bad for May and wondered, along with her, whether she really did belong here after all. But she was here now, and her old home was no longer her own. Mrs Brown thought better of expressing her thoughts on the matter.

"Right, let's get you washed, young lady," said Sally. Mrs Brown leaned her head back and closed her eyes. She rested her body, emptied her mind and let time move freely forward without holding herself or it back. Sally carefully unplaited her long grey curls and began to wash away her worries.

While having her hair cut, Mrs Brown almost forgot where she was. Sat next to May, chatting away with Sally, if it weren't for their three reflections in the mirror giving the game away, it could easily have been another place and time; just three women having a gossip and a catch up over the noise of an angrily hot hairdryer. Sally combed and snipped and brushed and dried Mrs Brown's hair, until she barely recognised herself. Her grey hair was long and straight and almost shiny. She looked much younger and much better than the woman who had stared back at her in the bathroom mirror that morning. May's hair was a halo of neat curls around her face. She looked happy, which was how Mrs Brown liked to see her. It was how she liked to see them all.

"How we doing in here then, ladies?" chirped Rosie, bursting into the room like a constipated duck, tits first, arse slow to follow behind. Mrs Brown was convinced she was always helping herself to the biscuits. Especially the custard creams, they always seemed to get through more packets of those than anything else and she was certain she knew why. Quite sure of it in fact.

"Oh, Mrs Brown, you've had your hair done, you look lovely," said Rosie as though she were speaking to a toddler. Mrs Brown was only too aware that she still hadn't got back to the girl about that pay rise.

"Thank you, Rosie," she said with a smile that hurt her face. She hoped she would turn on her heel, go back where she came from and stop ruining things. But she didn't.

"May, shall I take you back through to the lounge?" she asked. It was a kind question, but one Mrs Brown felt sure she knew the answer to. May didn't need help finding her way back to the lounge or anywhere else for that matter.

"Yes please, dear, that would be lovely. Good to see you Mrs Brown, glad you agreed to let your hair down and give the mane a wash," she said, standing up with ease, something Mrs Brown rarely managed herself. May read Mrs Brown's confused expression and smiled kindly.

"As I said earlier, my dear, sometimes you just have to let people do something nice for you," and with her final words of wisdom, she took a gormless Rosie by the arm and walked off down the hall, as if the pair of them were heading for the altar.

"Bye, May, see you soon," Mrs Brown called before it was too late.

"Who's May? I'm Marilyn!" she said without looking back.

NINETEEN

Moira opened her eyes and instinctively rubbed the sleep out of them with the back of her hand. She felt the grains of slumber loosen from her lashes and brushed them gently from her cheek. She was at home in her own bed, staring up at the familiar swirls and patterns on the ceiling and she could not remember ever feeling this happy. She felt herself at last, or at least a self she was happy to be. She felt fearless and all her doubts and worries were forgotten specks on the horizon, invisible to the well-rested naked eye. She sat up and effortlessly leapt out of the bed, there was no need to stretch. She almost skipped to the window to open the curtains, relishing the warmth on her skin as the sunlight streamed into the room. She caught sight of her reflection in the glass and almost liked what she saw. Today was going to be a good day. Today, Moira was eighteen years of age. She was a female adult and she felt quite undamaged, nearly complete and almost normal. Her heart was whole and strong.

"Good morning, birthday girl," said Father as she entered the kitchen.

"Happy birthday," said Mother, with watery eyes. They had been waiting for her. "I've made a cooked breakfast, thought we'd celebrate with a fry up," said Mother sliding up out of her chair and marching towards the oven with purpose. She looked pleased to have something to do. Moira noticed how they smiled at her. They looked at her differently now, as though they might be a tiny bit pleased that she was there. She sat herself down at the table and ignored all the questions her parents didn't ask.

"I know you want to see Steve, and that's fine of course, but you will be home for dinner won't you?" asked Mother.

"We've booked a table at the new Italian, wanted to take you out to celebrate your eighteenth in style and..." Father paused, looked down at the table, he looked as though he had just smelt something rather unpleasant and was trying not to vomit, "...put the past behind us," he finished, pleased with himself that he had delivered his words in the right order.

"We thought we could all make a fresh start, as a family, move on with our lives, celebrate," added Mother with uncharacteristic enthusiasm. Moira nodded her agreement, partly because she wanted to leave the house as soon as she could politely do so and partly because she hoped what Mother and Father hoped for was possible. She wished for a fresh start too. She had buried the memories of her last hospital appointment somewhere deep down inside herself, as though it had all happened to someone else, someone who looked a lot like but wasn't her. After breakfast Moira kissed Mother and Father goodbye and left the house, knowing that what she was about to do went against their wishes. She was an adult now, she had to make some decisions for herself and her mind on this matter was made up.

She spotted Steve from quite a distance. He was a tiny dot on their favourite bench by the lake in the park. It was a wintry day and the open lawns and neat rows of flowers were less inviting than normal. The lake looked murky; a sinister, bottomless, black pool of still water beneath grey clouds, hanging like dirty stage curtains over a miserable scene. The sky had darkened as though it were almost night, not the middle of the day. The wind howled and blew away Moira's confidence, a web of doubt craftily weaving itself, as the dried dead leaves danced like stringless puppets at her feet. She paused briefly and did up her jacket, her fingers struggling with the buttons and numb with cold. Nevertheless, she knew the show must go on. She sat down on the bench next to him. His eyes met hers, he smiled, held her hand and kissed her on the cheek. Doubt disappeared without warning and Moira knew she was doing the right thing.

"Happy birthday, beautiful," said Steve, tucking a stray hair behind her ear.

"Thank you," she said, feeling her cheeks blush. Nobody had ever called her beautiful before, including Steve.

"I got you a present..." he said, taking a small parcel wrapped in pink paper from the inside pocket of his jacket.

"Great, I love presents, but there's something I wanted to tell you first," said Moira.

"Is it that you love me, and I'm gorgeous and you think that I'm the best boyfriend ever?" he asked with a grin.

"No," said Moira, an awkward laugh escaping her. She was still surprised by the word boyfriend. It caught her off guard despite all the months she had had to get used to the term.

"Well in that case you better open your present because then you will want to tell me all of the above," he said holding the pretty gift out in front of her.

Moira obliged, taking the present from him and feeling the delicate tissue paper in her hands. She untied the silky bow, and unwrapped the parcel to reveal a small square box. She felt a rush of excitement and fear about what the box might contain.

"Go on, open it," urged Steve.

So she did. The box flipped open to reveal a shiny gold ring.

"Before you flip out, it isn't an engagement ring or anything. The lady in the shop called it an eternity ring. I just thought that sounded kinda cool, what with me about to go off to uni and everything. You know, like a pledge that we'll be together, forever."

Moira didn't say anything, just stared at the ring.

"Don't you like it?" asked Steve, a worried frown forming on his brow.

"I love it," said Moira, "It's beautiful. It's the best gift anyone has ever given me, it really is!" she said with tears in her eyes.

"Cool, well look, don't go all mushy on me, you look like you're going to squirt some tears, no need for that!"

"I love you," she said. And she really meant it.

"I love you too," said Steve, not able to meet her eyes when the words left his mouth. Not yet comfortable or believing of the emotions he felt for her. "Is that what you wanted to tell me? That you loved me?" he asked, his eyes smiling, his words kind, his hands warm on hers.

"No," said Moira, the smile falling from her face like a leaf from a tree. "There's something else..."

"For a minute there I thought you said someone else, that would kinda suck..." said Steve.

"I'm serious," she said, and Steve too lost his smile.

"Is something wrong?"

"Yes. Yes and no. Do you remember a couple of years ago when I was off school for a few days?"

"No."

"Yes you do. I was off school, then I came back, was lost in the woods, the police found me, I came to your house in the middle of the night..."

"Oh yes, I remember, you were weird for a few months..."

"Thanks!"

"Any time..."

"Well there was a reason I was behaving a bit strangely. Those few days I was off, I was in hospital. I'd had an operation." Steve's expression changed, his eyes narrowing as he processed her words.

"What for? Are you okay?"

"It's complicated..." Moira felt less confident now, she couldn't seem to find the right words. She had rehearsed this in her head hundreds of times, but now, in the reality of the moment, she felt as though she was falling and there was nobody there to catch her. "Before I left the hospital, the doctor told me something that really upset me. It was difficult to take in. Since then I've been to a hospital in the city to see another doctor, he was great, he explained things a lot better..."

"Do you have cancer? Are you dying?" interrupted Steve.

"No! Nothing like that," said Moira, trying to reassure him.

"Then what is it?" he asked. It was such a simple question, so without further delay Moira gave him a simple answer to match.

"I have a rare condition that means I won't ever be able to have a baby of my own." That was the first time Moira had said those words out loud. She had heard them in her head, formed them in her mind, imagined how they would sound, but had never spoken them before. Steve just stared at her, as though she hadn't said them at all.

"Did you hear me?" she asked, worried by his lack of response and the loosening of his hand's grip on hers.

"Yes, but I don't understand," he said. His hand let go of hers completely now. He wiped it on his jeans as though he were wiping any trace of her off his skin. Her hand dangled alone and awkward.

"I was born with a rare condition that means I can't carry a baby. I can't get pregnant," she said. Amazing herself with how simple the explanation sounded. How few words it took to explain something which for her had been so massively life changing.

"Why didn't you tell me?" he asked. It was a legitimate question, though it wasn't one she had expected.

"I don't know, Mother and Father thought it would be best if I didn't tell anyone."

"Why?"

"I don't know."

"Didn't you think maybe I had a right to know?" She processed his words and considered them. He was her boyfriend and that was why she wanted to tell him, that was why she was telling him now. They weren't together when she found out and they weren't married now. They were teenagers. She hadn't lied to him. Her mind was suddenly very busy. She examined the strange look on Steve's face and tried to compose a response without crying.

"I don't think you had a right to know...it was personal. But I wanted to tell you, which is why I'm telling you now," she whispered. Fear blew into the park, whispering what she already knew. This had been a mistake, she could tell from his eyes. She should never have told him. Mother and Father were right.

"You didn't think I had a right to know? I thought we had a future together. I've had sex with you!" yelled Steve, his voice filled with rage.

"So?" asked Moira, her eyes were already filling with tears despite her begging them not to do so.

"So, if you can't have children, are you even a girl? I mean, what are you?" His words sliced into her. Everything was starting to blur. She felt sick. This must be a bad dream, it had to be. She just needed to wake up.

"Of course I'm a girl, don't be so ignorant," she managed to whisper.

"Ignorant? At least I'm not a freak," he said. He stood then and looked down at her. His hands in his pockets, his

167

eyes cold and dark like the lake.

"You shouldn't have lied to me," he yelled.

"I didn't lie to you," she cried.

"Well you didn't tell me the truth either," were the last words Steve ever said to Moira. He turned and walked away from her, down the path, around the lake, out of the park and out of her life forever, taking his eternity ring with him.

A middle

TWENTY

Tori surveyed the sea of boxes that was their home. The house was sold. It had taken a few months, but the deal was finally done. She shuffled her way along narrow strips of floor to get to the front door. It no longer felt like home, just a temporary space with a strong sense of déjà vu. Every room had been filled with cardboard towers containing the hastily packed contents of their joint lives. Harry had gone to collect his father from the station. It wasn't great timing, but her father-in-law's visits were few and far between, so they hadn't had the heart to say no. She had presumed it was them at the front door, but it was just the postman who habitually delivered the morning post mid-afternoon. She thanked him for the parcel and the letters and went back inside, quickly rushing to the kitchen to check on the lunch she had been preparing. Once satisfied that nothing was burning, she returned her attention to the post. After ignoring the bill-shaped correspondence, she opened the last of the envelopes. It was from the hospital. She was in two minds as to whether to read it now or later, but her eyes moved independently along the words and made the decision for her. The letter was from Doctor Sydney. The Primary Care Trust had read her appeal letter.

Harry had said not to bother, but she had sent the letter anyway. It had only cost her time and the price of a stamp. She had cast a lonely figure sat staring at a blank word document on an elderly laptop all those months ago. The screen had blinked back at her, patiently waiting for her fingers to type some words to fill the empty space. The words which came first were both incorrect and insufficient. The delete key had been made use of. If only words that were spoken, could be so easily erased. The words that came next were the right ones. They were true. The letter had been printed and folded and put to bed inside an envelope. It had been posted and forgotten, she hadn't expected a reply. She had committed those words to paper because she needed them to know who Tori and Harry were and what their decision to not grant funding had meant to them. She wanted them to know how hard the last few years had been for them, how very badly they wanted a child of their own and what they had been and continued to go through. She wanted them to know that she was born with the condition that meant she couldn't carry a baby of her own, that she couldn't get pregnant. That it wasn't her fault that she needed their help, and that it wasn't Harry's fault for falling in love with her. Above all, she wanted them to know that they weren't just names and numbers on a piece of paper.

As she read the words of their reply, her hands began to tremble and the tears rolled freely down her cheeks, until the collar of her dress was dark with damp. Doctor Sydney had written to say that the PCT had read the letter she had sent them. They had read her words and had responded with some of their own. They had reviewed their decision and under the special circumstances, they were going to fund two rounds of IVF. Tori sat down on the kitchen stool, her legs were not able to carry her. She read the words again to make sure she had not misunderstood them. But there it really was, in black and white; they had the funding they needed. She heard a key in the lock and voices in the hall. She wiped her eyes. This was not something she wanted to share with Harry's father. This was too personal. This was about the two of them, nobody else. She slipped the envelope into a kitchen drawer and carried on as though this was just another day, even though it was far from that.

Lunch dragged on. Tori listened patiently to her father-in-law's latest news. He didn't ask about how things were going at the hospital, he never did. It wasn't that he didn't know what they were going through. Nor was it because he didn't care. He just could never find the right words, Tori and Harry both knew that. The last couple of years hadn't just been hard for them.

When their visitor had left Tori beamed from the inside out knowing it was almost time to share the news. She washed up some dishes while she waited for Harry to return from dropping his father off at the station, willing him to be back soon. When she heard the car in the driveway, she pulled off her rubber gloves and took the letter out from its hiding place. She ran to the front door and opened it before Harry had even got out of the car.

"What are you so happy about? I know the old man can

be a bore but there's no need to openly celebrate when he leaves!" he said, kissing her as he stepped into the hall. She handed him the letter. "What is it?" he asked, wary now of all and every piece of written correspondence.

"Read it and you'll see," she said, following him into the lounge, where he sat down, unfolded the piece of paper and read what was written on it. She sat down next to him, then watched and waited.

"I don't understand, how is this possible?" he said, looking up at her with wide eyes.

"I wrote to them to appeal the decision,"

"I thought we decided not to bother?"

"You decided not to bother. I thought it was worth a try."

"Well what did you say to change their minds?"

"I just told them the truth. I told them we really wanted a baby and we couldn't even try without funding. I told them we were selling our home. I told them there was nothing I wanted more, that it wasn't my fault I couldn't carry my own child. And I told them what a wonderful father you would be one day and that I didn't want you to go through life not having a child of your own because you fell in love with the wrong girl." Tori found herself crying. It happened a lot lately.

"Don't ever say that, and don't ever think it. I did not fall in love with the wrong girl, I fell in love with you. With or without children, I wouldn't want to be with anyone else, ever. Do you hear me?" he said taking her by the shoulders. He held her then. He cried some tears of his own, though he did not let her see. The house had not sold

174

for as much as they had hoped, even with funding, things were going to be very tight. He tried to protect her from the words and the worries that collided inside his head as much as he could.

"This is great news," he said when they finally came apart.

"I know, things are going to get easier," she said. The phone rang interrupting their moment.

"Leave it," said Harry.

"It's okay, I'll get it. It's probably just your father forgetting his glasses or something," said Tori. She stood and left to stop the phone from ringing and to find out who or what was causing it to do so. Harry watched her as she went, she looked happy and he wanted to hold onto the moment. The woman he had just held reminded him of someone he used to know and love. He didn't want her to leave the room. He didn't want her to leave him. He sat and stared at nothing for a moment, silently gathering his thoughts and trying to determine how he felt about them. He re-read the letter, in the same way that Tori had a few hours earlier, checking the words to make sure they were true.

When Tori came back into the room, her face was altered, changed. He couldn't read it, he couldn't read her, which was rare and it made him uncomfortable. He liked to think he knew everything about her and that he was the only one who really knew who she was.

"What is it? Who was that?" asked Harry, hoping there was no bad news to darken the rare glimmer of hope in the house.

"It was the woman from the agency," whispered Tori.

"Oh right," said Harry, wondering if the latest cheque he had sent to renew their membership had bounced.

"We've been chosen by a surrogate. Her name is Fiona. She wants to meet us this weekend."

TWENTY ONE

Mrs Brown was dreaming. She knew she was dreaming, because her hands didn't hurt and these days, that only ever happened in her dreams. It was a hot summer's day, she was walking along a river, she felt light and comfortable, she felt happy. The sky was a perfect cloudless blue, the tepid air was vanilla scented and she could hear the distant sound of children's laughter being carried downstream on a warm care free breeze. She could see a familiar blur in the shape of someone she knew a little further ahead. She couldn't quite make out who they were but she knew that she needed to reach them. She called to the shape, but it didn't stop or turn around. She hurried on to try and catch up, before it would be forever out of reach, before it would be too late. It was someone close, someone she wanted to see. The faster she walked, the further away the person ahead seemed to get. She decided to run. Now, if there was any doubt before, she knew she was dreaming. She hadn't run like this for years. The long grass tickled her bare legs and tried to hold her back and slow her down, but on she ran, faster and faster. The river and trees and blue sky were a blur all around her, as she tried to reach out to her companion. No matter how fast she ran, she couldn't quite catch up with them. Every hurried step seemed only to increase the distance between them and her. As she grew breathless and weary the blue started to rapidly darken. She ran on, despite the heavy raindrops that started to fall. The rain fell hard and fast until she could barely see the person up ahead, or the pathway beneath her feet. Mrs Brown stopped to catch her breath. She closed her eyes, only for a moment, and when she opened them, everything was black. She suddenly felt very alone and very afraid. She reached out for Mr Brown, but he was not there. She cried out for help, but if anyone heard her, they did not answer. She took a step forwards in the darkness and felt herself fall. She screamed and heard her own voice echo back at her. She reached out aimlessly with her arms, but could feel nothing. Mrs Brown kept her eyes tightly shut to the dark; if this was the end she did not want to see it coming. She could hear a siren in the distance but it was too late, she was falling.

The sound of the siren grew louder and louder. Mrs Brown opened her eyes to a tangible reality and found herself firmly in her bed at Godalming Lodge. Her surroundings made themselves known and melted back into place. Her breathing began to decelerate and she immediately felt foolish. Just as she allowed herself to relax a little and feel grateful that the dream was just that, fear began to swell within her, as she realised that the sound of the siren was still present in this dimly lit version of reality. The crunch of tyres on the gravel driveway outside penetrated her thoughts. She knew what the sound signalled. Death had either been to visit while she slept or he was lurking in the shadows. She turned on the lamp and examined the clock, holding it right up in front of her face so that her eyes could attempt to make sense of the big and little hands. It was three in the morning. That was not a good sign. She hauled herself out of the bed, straightening her limbs as fast as they would allow. With an adrenalin-fuelled effort she stood. Her tired feet found their slippers and she shuffled towards the foreseeable misfortune. She unhooked her robe from the back of the door, wrapping it tightly around her in a pitiful attempt to protect her dignity and overcome the coldness of this time and place. She took a deep breath and stepped out into the gloom to greet what she knew would transpire to be an unknown sorrow.

The first thing Mrs Brown saw when she neared the front of the house was the total eclipse of Adele's arse, waddling on ahead to open the front door. The ambulance crew came into the hallway and followed an agitated and breathless Adele up the stairs to the first floor landing. The three of them hurried past Mrs Brown as though they did not see her, as though she herself were a ghost. She pinched herself then, just to be sure she wasn't still dreaming. The pinch hurt so she felt it safe to presume she was awake and she was real. Without conscious thought she silently followed them up the winding oak staircase to the first floor, heavily relying on the solid banister to help haul her upwards. Each step required an enormous amount of effort; she did not have a good relationship with these or any other stairs. The air felt increasingly musty as she made her ascent. She tried to cover her mouth and nose with her left hand, while her right continued to grasp the

179

banister. Her white knuckles angrily penetrated her skin with the effort of each step. Death was close, she could smell him.

The house was silent now, as though nothing at all had happened. She felt like she was sleepwalking through time and space as she floated onwards and upwards, wondering if this was an out of body experience. She reached the landing and could see an open door at the end of the corridor, shedding a triangle of unnatural light onto the gloom of the hallway. The silence was louder than the sirens had been. She followed the light, becoming aware of her own breathing as she approached the open doorway. Room Five. She knew this room. She knew its occupant. Room Five belonged to May.

May endured the latter years of her life with a quiet charm that was rare. Mrs Brown had been there for May's first day at the home and remembered it well. The memories returned to her and played themselves over in her mind, slightly frayed at the edges as she crept her way closer to the door of Room Five. May's niece had been the one to sign the paperwork and deliver her here to her new life at Godalming Lodge. Before that she lived on a dwindling country estate—the home her father had passed on to her when he died. She had lived there alone for over fifty years, keeping herself to herself, no bother to anyone. But the large Victorian house had outgrown her, until it dwarfed her very existence. Her niece, Elizabeth, had come to the conclusion it was too much for her elderly aunt to manage. Conversations with the rest of the family were had. Eventually, after a bad fall and once enough time and words had followed, May was convinced, coerced and conned into giving up her home, her fortune and her independence and moved into Godalming Lodge. Mrs Brown had taken a dim view of the proceedings when they occurred but couldn't have altered things even if she had wanted to. May, like so many here, had enjoyed a fascinating and full life before old age and some slippery ice imprisoned her here. She was a celebrated and talented musician and had performed in orchestras all over the world. Her first and only husband died young, she had never wanted to remarry. She was betrothed to her work, until her eyes failed her and the arthritis in her hands prevented her from playing. Like so many of the souls that silently slept in the rooms along the creaking corridors of this tired old house, May had enjoyed a secret life, before her death sentence caged and silenced her stories forever inside these walls. Unlike the others, May was someone who was still living, not just waiting to die. She was more than just a client, over these last few busiest of months she had become the closest thing Mrs Brown had to a friend.

Mrs Brown heard her heart beat loudly inside her chest; it echoed off the peeling, papered walls. Perhaps May had just taken a tumble, that's what landed her in here in the first place. Maybe things weren't as bad as she knew they might be. As Mrs Brown grew closer to the door of Room Five, her heart continued to beat like an unsteady drum. She instinctively held her breath as she turned the corner, so quiet and small that she remained unseen, unheard and unnoticed, until Adele backed out of the room, almost walking into her.

"Oh, Mrs B, you frightened the life out of me," whispered Adele. Her choice of words was unfortunate. "What are you doing up at this time of night?" She was clearly trying not to wake the other residents with her hushed tones. How they had all seemingly slept through the siren was a miracle of sorts. Mrs Brown didn't respond to Adele. She couldn't. Her heart and mind were fixed on the scene in front of her. Through the open doorway, she could see her friend May lying dead on the floor of Room Five.

The paramedic knelt over May's body performing CPR. It was a waste of time. May was gone. Mrs Brown had seen enough dead people to know that's what she was. May's body lay on its back with one arm stretched out above her head, as though she had been reaching for something. Her faded floral nightgown drowned her tiny frame to blend in with the carpet, two childlike feet in over-washed mauve bed socks poking out from underneath. Her mouth was open as though in mid-sentence, her eyes were wide and staring at the ceiling as though it had offended her in some way just before she died. Perhaps it had, artex was far from popular nowadays.

"What happened?" asked Mrs Brown, still unable to take her eyes off May.

"Truth be told, I'm not sure," said Adele. There was a lack of emotion in her voice which perturbed Mrs Brown. She had to remind herself that Adele dealt with these situations with such regularity, that they were the normal sequence of events she had come to expect. It was all in a night's work for Adele. On the night shift, she came to know the residents less well than the other staff, her role was simply to watch over them while they slept. "She pulled the cord about an hour ago. I came running up the stairs," Mrs Brown doubted that part, "I found her like this, just lying on the floor, not moving. I couldn't find a pulse so I called an ambulance."

"You did everything you could," said Mrs Brown.

"I'm sorry," said the ambulance woman. She had stopped her half-hearted attempt to bring May back from wherever she had gone. She was addressing Adele and didn't seem to see Mrs Brown standing there at all. "Time of death, three twenty-five am," she said to her colleague, who wrote the numbers on a pad. "Have you called the next of kin?" she asked Adele.

"I'll do that," replied Mrs Brown. All three turned to look at her then.

"No need, Mrs B, I can see to that, no real point in waking them up now in the middle of the night anyway. The lady in Room Five will still be dead in the morning." Mrs Brown reluctantly agreed that the phone call to May's niece could wait until then, but she made sure Adele knew that she wanted to be the one to make it. It was only right that she should be the one to contact the family, not someone who hadn't known anything about May, not even her name.

TWENTY TWO

Moira took one final look around at the familiar surroundings that had been her room. She felt as empty and tired and pointless as the archaic furniture. Forlorn pine ghosts stared quietly back at her, dejected reminders of a shared past. The bed had been stripped bare to reveal a naked, elderly mattress. The empty wardrobe doors gaped open, displaying nothing but a few spindly wire hangers on the rail inside. The drawers in her dressing table were also barren and empty. Her books were no longer on the shelf. The contents of her room had been packed away into two old suitcases. They were already in the boot of Father's car, ready and waiting to go. The room that had been home felt more lonely and sad than ever before. Moira was glad to be leaving it.

Today was the day that Moira was leaving home, never to return. It was the day she would say goodbye to her old self and her old life and start a new one. Mother and Father were pleased she was going to university; she would be the first in the family to do so. Mother and Father were pleased she was leaving; it was something they all agreed on. Moira had a new outfit for the occasion, a brown suede mini skirt and a tight black top. She had straightened her hair and put on a little of the make-up that Mother had bought for her birthday. Her hair was shorter now, a neat shiny bob. It suited her; a polished new version of herself. Mother was delighted about the hair and make-up, less so about the short skirt.

"Have you got everything," asked Mother, coming into the room. She had caught her daughter admiring her own reflection and found the moment strange. Mother was happy to see that the room was empty. This wouldn't be Moira's room for much longer, she wondered what it would become instead, what things might replace the emptiness.

"Yes, I think so," said Moira, turning to face Mother, who looked so much sadder than was normal. Moira could tell she had been crying. She thought Mother might like it if she cried too, to show that she was sad to be leaving, but she didn't, she couldn't and she wasn't.

"Come on then, Father is waiting in the car," said Mother before disappearing back behind the door and rushing down the stairs. Moira took one final look around then followed her out.

The car journey to a new chapter was long. Mother and Father sat up front, Moira sat in the back, the three of them united in their silence. They had both wanted to come, both wanted to deliver her. Moira stared out of the window as the house she had grown up in became smaller and smaller until it was completely gone, as though it had never been there at all. She couldn't stop herself from looking up at Steve's old house as they drove past. They hadn't spoken since that day in the park, her eighteenth birthday. She had never seen him again. She wondered where he was now and then wished she didn't care. They drove past her old school, the church, the supermarket, the post office, the park. She stared at them all intensely, as though committing them to memory one last time. Once they reached the motorway she stared straight ahead, held in place by a worn seatbelt, holding a box of precious things on her lap. Mother started to say something, she offered her a sweet. Moira wasn't listening. Father started to say something too, a long list of things he wanted her to remember. Moira had forgotten his words before he had finished saying them.

The residential halls block appeared larger and more imposing than Moira had expected. The tall grey building looked unfriendly and uninviting but Moira couldn't wait to get indoors. Inside this building was where her new life would begin, she felt sure of it.

"Right then, I'll get the bags, shall I, which floor are you on?" asked Father, climbing out of the car and making a big demonstration of stretching his legs. Moira hoped nobody was watching from the windows.

"The top floor I think," said Moira, climbing out of the car with her box.

"Top floor. Great," said Father, with a hint of sarcasm which was unusual and yet suited him. "You head on up, your mother and I will be there in a moment."

"Okay, it's flat 13F," she said, not waiting for Mother to disagree. Mother was still sat in the car. Moira could see her through the window, wiping her eyes with one of the tissues that could always be found tucked up her sleeve.

186

Moira made her way up the cold, stone steps. She could hear the sounds of life behind each closed door that she passed. Music and laughter spilled into the corridor, but so far there was nobody to say hello to. When she reached the top floor she walked right to the end of the building, until she stood outside a solid looking white door. There was a silver thirteen and the letter F on the front, confirming she was in the right place. Her fingers found the key in her pocket and without further hesitation, slotted it into the keyhole. The lock turned and she pushed the door open. Immediately a face appeared behind a doorway inside the flat.

"Hello?" said the voice of the girl glaring at her. This was not the welcome she had been hoping for. Moira kicked herself for not having knocked on the door. She knew she was sharing the flat with other students, but it hadn't occurred to her that they might arrive before she did.

"Hi, I'm...I have a key, sorry I didn't knock," she stammered.

"Hello, I have a key, nice to meet you," said the girl, coming out of the doorway now, with her hand held out in front of her for Moira to shake. She had enormous curly blonde hair that seemed to have a life all of its own as it bounced along the hallway to meet her. She wore a miniskirt with black tights and trainers like Moira, as though they were both wearing an unofficial first day of university uniform. Her face was round and kind-looking. She seemed friendly, she seemed nice. Moira panicked again when she realised she couldn't shake the hand, what with all the box and key holding going on. The girl spotted the conundrum and laughed.

"Here, let me help you with that," she said, taking the box. Moira held on a fraction longer than she meant to, afraid of letting go of her things. "After all, we are going to be flatmates and one day soon I'm sure we'll be the very best of friends. I'm Sophie, what should I call you?"

"My name's Moira."

"Moira? Oh no, I don't like that at all. I had a horrid old aunt called Moira, stank of cabbage and farts the whole time, she's dead now. Moira will never do, we'll have to come up with something else."

Moira didn't know what to say, so decided to say nothing at all.

"Come on, I'll show you your room. It's the smallest one I'm afraid, what with you being the last to arrive and everything, but it's right next to the bathroom, and my room, I think that's a good thing and you've got a massive window overlooking the fields which isn't so bad, better than overlooking the car park, I suppose. Do you have any more stuff?"

"Yes, downstairs in the car," said Moira. Sophie said something in reply but she didn't hear her, she was too busy looking at her new room. Sophie was correct in her observations, the room was small, but it was perfect. There was a bed in the corner beneath a huge window with wonderful views of the countryside. At the other end there was a small desk and a wardrobe, and tucked behind the door was a little porcelain sink. The walls in the room, like the rest of the flat were all a standard issue shade of magnolia. They were covered in a galaxy of tiny Blu-tack remnants, where a previous resident had hung their posters to cheer the place up and make it their own. The curtains reminded her of the hospital. She shut the seed of that thought out of her head before it could grow, and decided she would buy new curtains as soon as possible. The carpet was a dark woven affair, it was not soft beneath her feet or at all pleasant to look at, but she didn't care. This was going to be her home for the foreseeable future, and it was perfect.

"I haven't made my mind up about the other two girls yet. They seem a bit square if you know what I mean," said Sophie. Moira didn't, but she found herself nodding anyway.

"They've gone to the library or some bollocks but they should be back soon. I've been desperate for you to arrive, I knew I'd get at least one cool flatmate," said Sophie. Moira felt ridiculously overjoyed that this stranger thought that she was cool. "What are you studying?"

"Journalism," said Moira.

"Cool, I'm doing politics, I thought about doing journalism," said Sophie.

"Well you are good at asking lots of questions," said Moira. Sophie's face fell, and for a moment Moira was petrified she had offended her in some way. Then Sophie nodded and smiled.

"Yep, good at answering them too, which is pretty much what politicians have to do, answer lots of difficult questions. Who knows, maybe I will be a political journalist one day, that would be cool, the world is my oyster!"

Moira liked the expression. She understood it to mean that a person could be anyone they wanted to be. She was going to start being the person she wanted to be from today.

"Do you smoke?" asked Sophie. Moira panicked slightly, unsure of the correct answer.

"No," she said shaking her head and wrinkling her nose without meaning to.

"I do, but I'll do it out the window so don't sweat it. Do you drink?" Moira didn't drink much, but she did drink.

"Yes," she said, confident this time that she knew the right thing to say.

"That's good news, and see there's another thing we have in common. I knew it, we are going to be the very best of friends," said Sophie giving her a big hug. Moira wasn't sure whether they would be best friends in the future or not, but she liked to think that they might. She felt a surge of happiness as this stranger, her new friend hugged her. She had arrived. She felt at home already.

TWENTY THREE

Tori sat in the front seat, she stared out of the window but did not see anything that she saw. Harry sat by her side, staring at the road ahead. It was going to be a long journey. Neither of them had slept well the night before and both were tense with nerves. Tori had barely slept at all, waking at frequent intervals from dreams about faraway places. They were on their way to meet a stranger, who they hoped might become so much more. Neither of them had any words to comfort the other, but silently they shared their hopes. The same apprehensive thoughts bounced around their two heads, heavy burdens on their still young shoulders.

Tori reached down into the handbag by her feet and took out the letter. She had read it so many times that she almost knew every sentence, word for word. For some reason unknown to anyone, including herself, she needed to read it again, one more time. It was partly revision, but she also just had to be sure that the words were real. The stranger's letter explained why she had chosen them out of all the couples who were registered with the agency. She had been sent the details of eight couples in total. The letter had reminded them that they weren't alone, they weren't the only ones going through this, even if it often felt that way. The letter from the stranger had made Tori cry. Harry had wanted to cry watching her read it. He had grown accustomed to watching his wife have her heart repeatedly broken. He felt powerless to stop it from happening again, unable to mend her. Rain started to fall, Harry flicked on the windscreen wipers to sweep away the sky's tears. There was no equivalent to stop his wife's. Transparent streaks danced on the horizon as the road ahead remained unchanged. Harry hoped the stranger might mend Tori's broken heart and return his wife to her original factory settings. He missed the woman he had married. They drove in silence for most of the journey, the fear in their hearts was so much louder than any of the songs they didn't hear on the radio that day.

Tori had taken longer getting ready today than she had for her own wedding. Trying to find the perfect outfit, desperate to be whoever the stranger might hope she would be, not wanting to disappoint her. She was terrified of saying or doing anything that might make her change her mind and decide not to help them after all. Harry had observed her routine, saddened when she applied colour to cheeks that used to glow all by themselves.

"This is all going to be okay, you know," said Harry, finding some words at last when they were half way there. He took his left hand off the steering wheel and placed it gently on her leg in a way that he hoped might reassure her. He wasn't sure how to reassure himself. His hand was soon uncomfortable, it didn't know how to behave on foreign turf and wished to retreat.

"Hope so," said Tori. She had imagined this moment for such a very long time. She had imagined the stranger too, who she would be, what she would look like, what they would say to each other when they met.

"We just have to be ourselves, that's all," said Harry. It had sounded like a good thing to say in his head. Sometimes lately he struggled to remember who being themselves meant being. There were so many different versions of them now, they were the couple at the hospital, they were the couple who pretended everything was okay to family and friends who knew better, they were the couple who were friends, but rarely lovers anymore and he was the author who had gone back to school to pay for the family they still did not have. The version of them that Harry missed the most, was the selves they had been before all of this started. When they were happy just being Tori and Harry.

"Be ourselves? Are you mad? We need the woman to like us!" said Tori. Then she laughed. It was an insignificant little giggle at first, but it grew and took her over. He took his eyes of the road ahead for just a moment to look at her, he loved it when she laughed. It was a rare phenomenon lately, a little glimpse of who she used to be and who she might be once again when all of this was over. And it would be over soon, one way or another. They both knew that.

Tori was terrified of the journey coming to the end. They had agreed if the meeting went badly, or things didn't work out with the stranger for any reason, they would take it as a sign that it just wasn't meant to be. The end of the journey could be closer than Tori could bear. Nobody could ever say that they hadn't tried. At least nobody who really knew what they had been through the last couple of years. They had both become drained of almost everything that they were.

When they were only ten miles away from the stranger, Harry pulled over to put some more petrol in the car. They didn't have quite enough fuel left to complete the journey and he needed a moment to catch his breath.

"Do you want anything to eat?" he asked before he went to pay. He already knew the answer, the words seemed a necessary politeness, a thin veil of normality.

"No thanks, not hungry," replied Tori, checking her make-up in the small mirror in the visor. Not too much, not too little. It was strange watching her construct an image of what she thought she should be. He worried about her not eating; she was rarely hungry these days. Her clothes looked too big for her and he had noticed her getting thinner.

"You should try and eat something, you haven't eaten all day," said Harry.

"I can't," said Tori, looking up at him now. She looked like she might cry, he knew better than to push her further. His strong, beautiful wife had morphed into a weeping willow. If the wind blew too strong, she might just fall down.

"Okay, but I'm hungry, I'm going to get something," he said. He didn't.

Only a handful of close friends and family knew where they were going. The rest thought they had gone away for a romantic weekend. Harry smiled at the notion of this being a romantic experience; romance was a stranger to them both in this place and time. It was Tori who insisted that nobody knew the truth. The cracks were beginning to show, though both pretended not to see.

Having imagined this day in her head so often for so very long, it was hard for Tori to accept that the events of the day were truly unfolding. She felt dreamlike, and expected to wake up at any moment. They didn't know an awful lot about the stranger they were about to meet. Tori's mind wandered, her imagination busy filling in the blanks without permission. The stranger had sent them a photo, so at least they knew what she looked like. She was pretty and had kind eyes. She was slightly older than Tori, which was the way Tori had always imagined it, as though she were an older sister, part of an anonymous extended family helping them to start their own. The stranger had a husband, three beautiful children and a dog called Oscar. Their family was complete. Tori tried to refrain from jealousy. She knew if she gave in to her cravings for it, it would only consume her. The stranger had everything she wanted. Harry's phone beeped for the second time on the journey. He glanced at it, taking his eyes off the road for just a second.

"Who is that?" asked Tori.

"No one," Harry replied, slipping the phone back into his pocket.

The stranger lived far away, in a place that they had never visited before, where the sights were fresh and new. Tori observed what a beautiful corner of the country it was while the wind in the cornfields blew them a Mexican wave of a welcome. They drove on through unfamiliar streets, a bunting of birds forming a tightrope of phone wires above them. The pavements below were scattered with people going about their business, unaware of the silent parts they were performing in what had so far been a terribly sad play.

Tori imagined the stranger taking the dog for a walk or popping to the local shops they passed with a big swollen belly, breathing the clean air and carrying their baby inside of her. She liked imagining the stranger pregnant, she liked imagining that all of this was going to work, that everything they had gone through would be worth it. She wanted to believe that everything Harry had endured because of her would be for a reason. He had tolerated test after test and produced sample after sample. She had convinced herself he was coping until she overheard him talking on the phone with a friend the week before. He spoke in hushed tones of how humiliating and awful he found each of the visits. She tried not to eavesdrop, but it was hard not to want to listen to how he really felt about it all. He said he'd had enough. That was when she had stopped listening, when she forced herself to walk away and busy herself with something else, somewhere else in the house away from him for a while. Whether he had had enough of the clinic or of her she never knew because she never asked. She needed this to work and soon. She knew he couldn't take much more, his smiles had faded, as had his love for her, or so she felt. They never talked about the things she overheard that afternoon, she couldn't bear to do so. His words that day were not meant for her ears, she shouldn't have heard them.

They pulled up outside the stranger's house. The robotic voice of the satnav confirmed that they had arrived at their destination. Tori went to check the mirror one last time. It wasn't vanity, if anything it was quite the opposite. She had never felt quite good enough, not quite up to scratch; as though her imperfections on the inside could somehow be seen on her face. Harry stopped her from pulling down the visor.

"You look beautiful, you don't need to check again, you look perfect, not that she'd care if you didn't. She's going to love you, okay, now stop worrying," he said. Sometimes Tori loved that he knew her so well. He could read her thoughts and predict her words without her ever having to speak them. Sometimes he was a little too close. Sometimes she feared he could see her too clearly and might not always like the things he saw. She tried to be the woman she thought he wanted her to be. She tried so hard to be different versions of herself for the each of the people in her life. Sometimes she couldn't remember who she was, which version she was meant to be. Sometimes the last couple of years all felt like make-believe, as though she was performing in a play where every so often, she forgot the lines. If that was the case, then this moment, them stepping out of the car and walking up to the stranger's front door was definitely the opening of the final act. One way or another, she reminded herself that though not the end, it was the beginning of whatever the end would be.

"I love you," she said, without having really meant to.

She meant the words, though she realised they didn't say them to each other as often as they once had.

"I love you too," said Harry. "Are you ready?" Given how long they had been waiting for this moment, they really should have been. But Tori didn't feel ready at all. Part of her desperately wanted to just turn around and go home and pretend none of this had ever happened.

"Yes," she said hesitantly. It was the word she knew he wanted and needed to hear.

"Good, come on then," he said getting out of the car. She resisted the urge to check the mirror one last time and stepped out of the car and into the unknown. She stood on the pavement and looked up at the house where the stranger lived. It was a good looking home, a safe place for her baby to grow until he or she was ready to be born. Harry held her hand and they walked forwards together. She hoped he would remember the script and all the things they had agreed it was best not to say. The stranger felt like their last hope, their last chance.

Tori had rehearsed this moment a million times over. She had imagined meeting the stranger long before she had met Harry. This journey was theirs, but she had started thousands of miles away, long before he joined her on the path. She would smile, remain composed, say hello in a friendly manner and perhaps shake the stranger's hand and say, "good to meet you." That was how it had been in the film of all this that played in her head sometimes, when she lost herself in a daydream imagining how all of this would be.

Before they reached the front door, it opened. The

stranger stood and smiled at them. They both recognised her instantly from the photo she had sent. Time froze while they squeezed each other's hands, their feet welded to the pavement, unable to take the last steps, too late to turn back. Time started to move forward once more, slowly and gently urging them forwards. The stranger's husband came to stand behind her in the doorway, followed by their three children, all of whom came to stand in front of their mother to get a good look at the lady she was going to help. They stared open-mouthed at the couple she was going to try and save, though she didn't know it. Oscar the dog was the last to make an appearance. He pushed through them all, took one look at Tori and came straight out to say hello. He bounded down the path, his tail wagging furiously, happily whacking both their legs. He licked Tori's hand as she reached down to stroke him.

When they finally stood in front of the surrogate the hello Tori had rehearsed was forgotten. The two women hugged and examined each other properly for the first time. They cried a union of multi-purpose tears then held each other once more. Words weren't necessary. Fiona smiled and welcomed them both inside her home. It was a better hello then Tori had imagined or rehearsed. It was a better hello than she had dared hope for.

TWENTY FOUR

Mrs Brown got out of the car and took in the scene in front of her. The church was of the traditional variety, old and grey and crumbling. It was small enough to be quaint and charming, but with a steeple tall enough to look down on all those that were gathered beneath. She remembered a time, not so long ago it seemed to her now, when all of her friends were getting married. For a few years, life was one big party. They attended wedding after wedding, a celebration of love and life, with everyone she knew looking forward to the future. How different things were now. She looked around at the fellow mourners, all respectfully dressed in black. There were no parties any more, only gatherings of grief that were a chance to reflect on a life that was over and a reminder to the living that life was indeed short. The autumnal leaves danced in the church car park. They were all either dead or dying, like so many of the attendants. Adele heaved her frame out of the car and waddled round to be by Mrs Brown's side.

"You alright, Mrs B?" asked Adele. She had been taken off the night shift to attend the funeral. One of the staff always attended the service when a resident left for good. Mrs Brown was distracted. It wasn't that she hadn't heard, it was only that she didn't know the answer. Firstly, she despised being called Mrs B and until Adele's appointment a few months ago had never suffered the indignity. Secondly, she wasn't entirely sure of the honest answer, and she liked to think of herself as always honest, especially when in such close proximity to a holy building. Mrs Brown did not feel entirely alright today and so felt it inappropriate to say that she did. She felt quite far away from alright and everything she knew and loved. She felt empty and alone and somewhat bewildered by the chain of events that had led her here, to stand on this spot, in front of this church, surrounded by and overwhelmed with grief. She felt it then, a tear that formed in her right eye, before it rolled down her pale cheek and splashed on the pavement. Adele saw it too, the tear spoke to her and answered her question on Mrs Brown's behalf.

"Come on, let's get you inside," said Adele, bustling her towards the entrance of the church. As they neared the large wooden doors, she felt herself shrink. She felt small and humble and afraid. Afraid of what lurked inside and afraid of what came next.

Inside, the church seemed much larger than it had appeared; a sort of holy Tardis. The heavy oak doors were held open by a single metal hook, hanging onto the stone walls, serious and straight with the strain of it all. Smell was the first of her senses to be infected by the place, it positively stank of age and tradition. Adele dipped her finger in the supposedly holy water and crossed herself with it. Mrs Brown ignored the performance, she had no intention of partaking in the charade she believed religion to be. The cold stone floor was hard underfoot and the rows of empty wooden pews seemed stern and uninviting. Mrs Brown instantly recognised May's niece sitting in the front row. She was accompanied by a man and a small child. May's children were noticeably absent. One now lived in Australia and the other was apparently on a skiing trip and unable to come; too busy to attend their own mother's funeral. Mrs Brown wondered why she was surprised by this, they hadn't made an effort to visit their mother while she was living, why should they bother now she was dead? Mrs Brown sat four rows from the front with Adele by her side and observed the handful of others who had come to pay their respects. She gripped the order of service in her left hand. It pained her to do so, her clawed fingers trembling determinedly with the effort.

The service was mercifully short. A spindly looking vicar reminisced about what a wonderful woman May had been, despite never having met her. Her niece read a spurious poem and talked about how much she missed her aunt, despite only coming to visit once in the last six months. When it was all over, May's coffin glided through red velvet curtains on its way to wherever via a giant incinerator. Some music began abruptly in a wretched last ditch attempt to give her a meaningful send off. "Wish me luck as you wave me goodbye," sang the voice of Vera Lynn. An elderly woman in the front row decided to sing along. What had been a miserable scene, distorted into something comically wretched and ghastly. People shifted in their seats, glancing sideways to see if their neighbours were equally uncomfortable. May had always hated Vera

Lynn. The woman in the front row soon forgot the words but clapped her hands and waved goodbye as instructed by Vera, whilst everyone else just sat and stared as the coffin, and May was swallowed up and gone forever.

There was a small gathering after the funeral at the home of May's niece. It had been May's home once, though you would not have thought so to look at it now. The old Victorian building looked just as May had described from the outside, but the interior had been transformed into a characterless modern shell of a home, without an original feature in sight. Blank, white-walled corridors led to minimalist rooms. As Mrs Brown surveyed the shiny unused kitchen, she felt as though any trace of May had been wiped from the earth long before her passing. A sea of unfamiliar faces, very few of whom had been at the church, passed in and out of the main living area, none of them saying so much as a simple hello. It was as though their young eyes could not register or acknowledge anyone over a certain age. Youth was attracted to youth. Mrs Brown couldn't help but feel that the people present were not here to mourn May. They were here to get drunk with May's niece and have a good old poke about the renovated property.

"David's grandmother is on her last legs," said a tall, red haired, beanpole of a woman. "We're pretty sure she'll leave us her old bungalow when she goes. It's a complete shit hole, but it's on a great plot of land, I reckon if we knock the place down and build a four bedroom house on it, we'll make a fortune."

"We will," confirmed the man Mrs Brown took to be

203

David.

"Awesome," said the chubby blonde they were talking to. *Awesome?* thought Mrs Brown.

"I only hope it happens soon, we want to start a family in the next couple of years and it would be great to get it all sorted before then," said the beanpole.

"I totally understand," said the chubby blonde, a small slither of a smoked salmon canapé residing on her gloss-stained lower lip. Mrs Brown didn't understand at all and found herself feeling mildly nauseous. She couldn't determine whether it was the food or the conversation making her feel sick to her stomach. Either way, she decided it was time to get out of here. She saw Adele's behind edged between two tables of food and made a beeline for it.

"Mrs Brown, there you are, do you want something to eat? There's loads here," said Adele through a mouthful of food.

"No, thank you, Adele. I think I'd like to head back. I'm not feeling so good."

"Right you are, Mrs B," said Adele, hastily wrapping some cakes inside an unfolded napkin and slipping them into her handbag.

"I'll just pay my regards to May's niece, then I'll meet you by the car," said Mrs Brown, ignoring what she had just seen and setting off to deliver the words she had come to say.

Mrs Brown found her laughing and joking with a group of men in the dining room. She stood unnoticed for too long before frustration and impatience got the better of her.

She gave a little cough, just loud enough to warrant an interruption to their joke telling.

"I'm so sorry to interrupt," she lied. "I just wanted to say goodbye and offer my sincere condolences again for your loss. Your aunt was a lady who will be sadly missed."

"Oh thank you. How kind of you to come all this way," said the niece. Her words were spoken slowly as if meant for a child or someone hard of hearing. Mrs Brown was neither. She had nothing further to say to the woman, and felt sure the woman had nothing else to say that she either wanted or needed to hear. Without further ado, Mrs Brown turned on her heel and began to make her way out of the characterless house.

"Who was that?" asked one of the men in a hushed whisper.

"Oh just a little old lady who lived at the old people's home with Aunty May. She wanted to come. Sweet really," said May's niece quietly but loud enough so that the words reached the ears of everyone close by. Mrs Brown didn't bother to correct her.

TWENTY FIVE

"Do you have something I could borrow to wear tonight?" asked Sophie. She started rummaging in Moira's wardrobe without waiting for a reply.

"Sure," said Moira. She took another breath and opened her mouth to try and express her concern about Sophie stretching her clothes. Her flatmate's chest was considerably larger than Moira's, she was considerably larger than most girls in that department. Moira couldn't think of a polite way to make the point, so discontinued her goldfish impression and returned her attention to the book she had been reading.

University had been the fresh start that Moira needed. She had found new friends, a new life and a new self. She was early for every lecture and worked hard to make a good impression. She was getting good grades and enjoyed learning new things, surrounded by new people, who only knew the version of herself she had recently become. She had a job as a barmaid at a local hotel and felt proud and comfortable with her newfound sense of independence. She was thin, noticeably so, but it was more to do with her inability to cook rather than deliberate dieting or a lack of funds. Her slender frame accentuated her fragility and the exposed high cheekbones prettified her face, attracting looks from plenty of male students and lecturers around the campus, not that she noticed. All Moira could see when she looked in the mirror was a broken disappointment, camouflaged in new clothes and pretence. Moira would rather spend her money on pretty outfits and shoes than food, and for this, among many other reasons, her flatmate Sophie adored her.

"What's in this box at the back? Have you bought new shoes and hidden them from me?" asked Sophie, on tiptoe now, trying to reach the top of the wardrobe. Moira, who had only been half listening while studying her journalism law text book, froze.

"No, they are just private things," she said, unable to hide the fear in her voice. Sophie latched on to her tone, in the annoying way she always did. Sophie had a knack of figuring out whatever Moira didn't want to talk about and insisting they do just that.

"Private things? Is it a box full of love letters from boys you went to school with?" she teased. Sophie seemed to be very much under the impression that Moira had had lots of boyfriends before coming to university. Moira had never felt the need to correct her or inform her that there had only ever been one.

"No," she said, trying her hardest to seem indifferent, although unknown to Sophie she felt physically sick. Her glass dilators from the hospital were in the box. She felt like an idiot for leaving them in the wardrobe but there wasn't anywhere else to put them. If Sophie found them, she probably wouldn't even know what they were, but Moira could do without the questions she would no doubt ask if she did. She felt sweat forming on her brow. She hadn't even used the damn things since she got here. She wasn't planning on having sex with anyone anytime soon, if ever again.

"Is it a box full of giant dildos and vibrators?" Sophie asked with a giggle. She'd been on the vodka already that day. There was rarely a moment since they'd met when Sophie hadn't been intoxicated, although to be fair, Moira was doing a pretty good job of keeping up.

"Yes, that's what they are. Why don't you wear the blue dress?"

"The new one? I can't do that, it's still got the tags on, you haven't even worn it yet." The diversion was working.

"Sure you can, I'm wearing my black dress tonight anyway. It will look good on you!" Sophie's eyes shone.

"Well if you're sure?" she asked, her fingers already stroking the soft blue fabric.

"Sure I'm sure, why don't you try it on," said Moira. Sophie began her departure on cue then paused in the doorway as though she had forgotten her lines before making an abrupt about turn. Moira was losing patience but made a determined effort to keep her cool. "Yes?" she said, prompting Sophie to speak and wishing she would hurry up out of the room and away from her and her things.

"Sorry, one last thing then I'll be out of your hair," said Sophie, for once picking up on Moira's tone. "Do you have any spare tampons? My period's come early and I'm almost out, don't want to ruin the dress..." Moira took a second to gather her thoughts, the answer was no, but she couldn't just say that. She had as much need for tampons as the boy in the room below.

"No, sorry, I erm, I've run out too," she could feel her cheeks were bright red with the lie. She felt sure that Sophie must know her secret. Moira's mind raced away from what was rational, and concluded that Sophie had asked about the tampons in order to expose and humiliate her, that deep down she sensed something wasn't right, that Moira wasn't the same as other girls. This was it, she'd have to find somewhere else to live, maybe change university, what if Sophie told everyone? Mother and Father were right, nobody must know.

"No worries," said Sophie and left the room without another word.

Moira let the breath she'd been unknowingly holding escape her body and unclenched the fists she had inadvertently made. Her parents' words echoed in her head, round and round until she was dizzy. Nobody must know, not now, not ever. She felt relieved that despite the mistake of the box in the wardrobe and the lack of tampons her secret was still safe, her new self still intact.

Later that night, one club, two bars, three glasses of wine, four vodka and cokes and several shots of green liquid later, Moira lay alone on her bed in the dark staring up at the ceiling. She felt as though the room was moving and wondered when, rather than if she would be sick. They had not left the club alone that night. Sophie had met a boy called Roy, or was it Ray, his name didn't really matter. He wasn't the first and she was quite sure he wouldn't be the last to enter their flat and her friend. Roy or Ray had sat in the middle of the back seat of the taxi home, with Sophie on one side and Moira on the other. Roy or Ray's hand had been busy under the blue dress and between Sophie's legs for the latter half of the journey, with Sophie making little gasps while it was there. The pair of them didn't seem to mind that Moira was in the car, or that she and the driver could see and hear what they were doing. She could still hear them now on the other side of the wall. It sounded like he was killing her in there, but the sound of Sophie's gullible squeaking bed, made this just like every other weekend.

Moira had more friends than ever before, but she felt desperately alone. She found it hard to sleep at night, even when the squeaking bed next door was silent and still, even when her flatmates and the rest of the students in the building slept and dreamt. She could have brought a boy home too tonight. There was a boy in the club she rather liked the look of, but what then? It would never be the same as it was with Steve, that night in the field in the rain. She couldn't see how anything would ever be that special again. And what if they somehow knew that she was...different. What if being inside her felt different to being inside someone like Sophie? What if her skinny, barren body gave her away? The club had been loud, her ears were ringing. She tried to remember whether she had

had fun or whether she had only been pretending. It was so hard to differentiate sometimes, between who she was and who she was trying to be, between how she really felt and how she thought she should feel. No, she had had fun, on reflection she was sure of it.

There was a knock at her door. She ignored it.

"Pssst, it's me, Soph, are you still awake?" Moira lazily stood up and shuffled to the door. She opened it just a crack to see a half-naked Sophie in the hallway. Moira was torn between the shock of seeing Sophie stood there like that in her underwear and the relief that she had at least removed the new blue dress she had borrowed before doing whatever it was that they were doing in there.

"I am now, what do you want?"

"Sorry, hope we're not making too much noise," she said with a drunken giggle. Her eyes were bloodshot and her lipstick was smeared all over her face. A pissed Miss Piggy sprang to mind. "Do you have any spare condoms? I've run out and he wants to do it again!"

"No, sorry," said Moira. Sophie looked devastated.

"You must have, you're the organised one!"

"Well I don't, I'm sorry," said Moira, wanting to close the door now.

"Fine, I suppose miserable old nuns don't need them, frigid cow!" said Sophie. She sulked back to her own room, slamming the door behind her. She probably wouldn't even remember this little episode tomorrow. Moira had become quite used to her friend's drunken tantrums.

Moira did not consider herself to be frigid or nun-like. She just didn't see the point in letting every boy on campus who wanted to sleep with her do so. The giggling and the grunting soon started up again on the other side of the wall. Moira hoped her friend was at least using some form of contraception, Roy or Ray looked like a dirty oik to her, who knew where he might have been or what nasty diseases he might have, it didn't bear thinking about. She made a mental note not to sit on the toilet seat again without lining it with toilet paper. Mother had always said you could catch all sorts from toilet seats, she didn't want to put Mother's theory to the test. The sounds emanating from the room next door, and the images they produced in her mind, made her feel a little ill. Along with all the alcohol, the chain reaction that resulted from the situation made her head hurt and the room spin.

Moira closed her eyes and tried to sleep but she couldn't find the off switch. If she could only learn how to stop thinking, stop worrying, stop analysing everything people said and did over and over. Long after the noises next door had stopped and silence drew over the flat like a quilted cloud, Moira still lay awake, her thoughts playing an incessant game of ping pong in her troubled mind. Later the thoughts would slow down, if not stop altogether. Later her eyelids would grow so very heavy that she could no longer stare at the ceiling even if she wanted to. Later on, she would only see black and think of almost nothing. But that was later. For now, as she lay in the dark, thinking and worrying and silently crying, she felt so very alone and hoped life wouldn't always be this lonely. Later Moira would rest and sleep and live to worry another day but for now she lay awake, holding herself in the dark, wishing the arms wrapped around her belonged to someone else, anyone else. Wishing that she was loved.

TWENTY SIX

Tori sat and stared at her laptop. She re-read the email stretched out across the screen in front of her. No matter how hard she stared at the words, they would not change. Their new home was small but perfectly formed. It wasn't quite as pretty on the outside and it was a little further away from the train station, but it was in the same town, and in the right catchment area for the best schools. This was good news for the child they hoped would one day live in this house with them and it also meant Harry could walk to work in less than ten minutes. The money they had left over after the move was squirrelled away in a savings account. It wasn't quite enough to meet all of the surrogate's expenses. They still needed to find an extra five thousand pounds, but they were much closer than ever before to having the child they longer for.

"Do you want a drink?" asked Harry, sticking his head around the study door. His words made her jump, but his presence calmed her. She turned to face her patient husband. Her head lifted but her heart sank. The indistinct emotion she first felt soon transpired to be despair, and it filled her up until it was hard to breathe. She wanted to deal with this alone, to carry the burden and protect him from the worry that consumed her and stole her sleep, but her eyes filled with the tears she had tried so desperately not to cry, and gave her away.

"What's the matter?" asked Harry, rushing to her side. She covered her face with her hands and reluctantly started to shed tears of pure desolation, her body trembling as she fought to keep the sobs inside her. Harry knelt down next to her chair and held her.

"Look at me, what's the matter?" he asked again, more gently, cupping her face in his hands. He caught her worry like a virus, it was already all over his face now too.

"The clinic wants more money..." she tried to say, through the tears.

"The clinic what?" asked Harry, his tone already toughening. There were words in this house now that could change the temperature of a room within seconds. Clinic was one of them. Money was another. Through watery eyes Tori considered her husband. How he had changed. How much this had changed him. He looked so much older than he had before, so tired of life, of what their lives had become. This was all her fault. If they had never met, he wouldn't have had to go through any of this. This was her fault. The words repeated themselves in her head, over and over, a gleeful maddening chant rising like a wave until it was impossible to ignore and until the words were spoken out loud.

"Shhhh, stop saying that," said Harry. She stopped saying it, but she still thought it.

Tori struggled to remember how they had looked before all this began. She barely recognised the man in front of her. Harry smiled far less than he used to these days. There was more grey around his temples and dark circles beneath his sad looking eyes. She rarely noticed how she looked anymore. A ghost in the mirror of someone who looked a bit like the woman she used to be, the woman trapped inside of who she now was. Sometimes she would catch a glimpse of them in happier times, a memory in a framed photo from before they were married. She missed that Tori and Harry. They were good fun. She would like to get to know them again. She would like to get in touch but as with all relationships, sometimes too much time can pass, too much of a distance can separate people who once had so much in common. They hardly ever went out now, rarely saw friends. Their friends didn't know why, invitations came less often and friends moved away. Harry was tired most of the time, like her, he couldn't remember how it felt to get a good night's sleep. When he wasn't working he was writing. Any time off they had together was spent at the clinic. She could only look on while his dreams were dying along with her own. He was still a good man but she couldn't fail to see what all of this was doing to him, what all of this was doing to them and their marriage. This was all her fault, the words repeated themselves over and over again in her head, in case she hadn't heard them all the other times. She had heard. And she believed them.

"The clinic want more money," she whispered.

"More money for what?" said Harry. His voice was

raised and charged with a mix of anger and despair.

"The woman at the clinic says the PCT funding doesn't cover the full cost of the IVF and because the IVF is for the purpose of surrogacy, we may have to pay them up to four thousand pounds more to make up the difference," said Tori.

"That isn't what she said last week..." said Harry, standing up now. The room felt colder, Tori involuntarily shivered.

"I know, that's what I said..."

"Well they can't just make this shit up as they go along. Jesus Fucking Christ, we're both working endless days as it is, we can barely make ends meet, I hardly ever see you, everything we earn goes into paying for the surrogate and all her bloody expenses, where the fuck are we going to find another four thousand pounds? I'm sick of this shit, I really am. We spent two hours at that fucking hospital again yesterday, waiting around to see a doctor who in the end wasn't even the doctor we were supposed to see, didn't know anything about us, hadn't even read our notes, didn't have a fucking clue."

"Doctor Margolis has left to join a new clinic. We will be seeing Doctor Richman from now on. They said it shouldn't change again now, it will definitely be him carrying out the treatment and performing the operation."

"I'll believe it when I see it. How many different doctors have we had to go and see now? They're all the bloody same, they don't know who we are and they don't care. All they care about is the money! And Doctor Richman didn't mention anything then about any extra charges...what's that woman's number? The one who emailed you? I'm going to call her," barked Harry. He was barely recognisable now.

"You can't call her when you're like this, we need these people to help us..."

"Fuck these people, they're not helping us, they're treating us like a couple of mugs with pound signs on our faces. This is all a big joke to them. I've had enough, this has been hanging over us for three years. It never fucking ends, I can't do this anymore, I want my life back. Look at what this is doing to you, to us!"

The house was still and silent and waiting for whatever would come next. The tears flowed freely down Tori's face. There was nothing to say, she had no words left. Harry, or at least a man who looked like him, stood and stared and shook with rage. "I'm sorry, I've had enough," he repeated, so quietly the words barely reached her ears. His eyes broke contact with hers and she sat and listened as he left the room and walked away from her. The words had been thought before, but now that they were being spoken out loud for Tori to hear, it made them far more real, far more dangerous. He wasn't just running away from the situation, he was running away from her.

A stronger version of herself picked this woman up and attempted to put her back together. She took a deep breath, smoothed her hair, wiped the tears that she was barely aware she was crying on her sleeve, and instructed one foot to walk in front of the other. She needed to help Harry, they needed to help each other. Her legs carried her along the hall and down the stairs, towards the sound of activity in the kitchen. It could have been five minutes or five hours since he left her in the little box room they called a study, she didn't know anything anymore.

She stopped in the doorway and observed her husband. He was opening and slamming drawers and barely seemed to notice she was there.

"What are you doing?" were the words her mouth ventured.

"Looking for the corkscrew," growled Harry.

"Why?" she asked. He stopped his search and returned her stare then. It was a rather daft question.

"So I can open a bottle of wine...and before you ask why, so that I can drink it. I don't care if it's the middle of the afternoon. And when the bottle is empty, I might just open another and drink that too. Both of these plans of action are however, highly dependent on my ability to find the fucking corkscrew."

"Stop swearing. You know we're not supposed to be drinking at the moment."

"Darling, I love you, I really do from the bottom of my heart but at this moment in time I can't stop swearing for which I am sorry. Life seems to be raining shit cakes on us right now and I need a fucking drink for which I will not apologise."

"But the doctor said..."

"Tori, right now, I don't give a flying fuck what the doctor did or didn't say, any of them. I'm not committing a crime, I'm not saying I want to go out and murder someone to make myself feel better, I'm saying I just want a glass of red and possibly an evening where we don't live and breathe baby shit all night long. A few hours or do you know what, just a few minutes where I don't have to think about it anymore and I can have a glass of wine in front of the fire in my own goddam home. The home I hope we can continue to live in if we can find enough money for the mortgage this month after paying all the fuckers who are bleeding us dry." He reached behind, to pick up the bottle, it fell and smashed all over the kitchen floor.

"Fuck!" yelled Harry.

Tori surveyed the mess and the broken glass everywhere. She felt her legs buckle and she sank to the floor. She drew her knees up to her chin and held her head in her hands. Tears flowed once more, the trickles soon forming into steady streams down her now thin, pale face. She closed her eyes and cried and just wished that she could make it all stop. She looked so small. So helpless.

"Arghhhh!" Harry roared. It was an animal scream, from someone who couldn't take anymore. He felt like his world was falling down around him, he hated seeing what this was doing to her but felt powerless to change things. He was broken. His own tears started to roll freely down his cheeks, his chin, his neck, dampening his collar. Time held its breath, waiting and watching to see what would happen next. Harry looked at the back door, checking for the nearest emergency exit. Then he looked down at his wife, a crumpled heap on the kitchen floor, surrounded by shards of green glass and a pool of red. Somewhere, somehow he found the strength deep inside himself to be the man she needed him to be. He stepped over the glass and bent down to be with her.

"I'm sorry. I'm so sorry," he said to her bowed head. Her crying was louder now, noisy sobs filling the kitchen. "Tori, come on, come here, look at me," she still did not respond. She too was broken now, it was his fault. She needed him to be strong and he'd let her down. He couldn't do this anymore. He needed to be stronger. Somehow. He reached down and grabbed her arms, pulling her up to him and holding her close.

"Come on. It's going to be okay. I'm sorry, everything is going to be okay," he whispered over and over, his words drowning out the carousel of words already in her head, until she could only hear Harry. Slowly her sobs started to recede. He held her tight and wouldn't let go. "Why?" was the only word in his head now. Why was this happening to them? Nobody had the answer.

"I need you," she whispered.

"I know, I'm so sorry...I just lost it."

"It's okay..." she managed to say.

"It's not okay, it won't happen again."

"It will. I can't do this on my own. I need you."

"And I'm here. One hundred per cent. We will find the extra money. We will get through this together."

"Will we?"

"Don't say that, you know we will, we just have to keep going. Sometimes it all just feels a bit overwhelmingly shit, that's all, but we'll get through it, I promise."

"Like when it's raining shit cakes?" asked Tori, and for the first time in a long time, the corners of her mouth turned upwards and she smiled. Only a small smile, as though her lips had forgotten how.

"Yes, exactly like that, all this baby stuff is sometimes like being caught out in a shit cake storm, in your underwear, with no umbrella."

"And what are shit cakes exactly?"

"Very bad things, best not to think about it really," said Harry. He released her just a little and she looked up at him.

"I can't do this on my own," she repeated. Her eyes swollen and her face a puffy pink patchwork quilt of blotches from all the crying.

"You don't have to, we'll get through this together, I'm here for you."

"I love you."

"I love you too and I always will. Now I want you to go and sit down, we're not going to think or talk about the baby for the rest of the evening. You are going to choose a takeaway and I don't want to hear about the price or how unhealthy it is. I don't care what the bloody doctor said to eat or not to eat. And just so you know, regardless of what Doctor Richman said, I am going to have a glass of bloody wine just as soon as I manage to open a bottle without smashing it all over the floor."

"Okay, I suppose one glass won't change things, he did say we could have half a bottle a week if we wanted to..."

"Exactly...there's my girl."

"One condition."

"What's that?"

"Pour me a glass too."

TWENTY SEVEN

Mrs Brown sat and stared out the window. It was a bitterly cold and thoroughly miserable day. The slate sky was dark and angry and a soundtrack of howling wind blew in time, while rain lashed indignantly against the trembling glass panes of the conservatory. She had so much to do, but felt so very tired today. A little bit down and lonely admittedly, but more than anything else, just tired. Tired of waiting to spend time with Mr Brown, tired of dealing with all of this on her own. Tired of Godalming Lodge and its staff and the paperwork and tired of the residents. She looked down into the lounge at them all sitting there and took that last one back. She couldn't be tired of them, life itself was tired of them and about to let them go. If she didn't care about them, who would?

She turned to look out of the window again. Bert was on leave and the garden was already missing him. She missed Bert too. There were no fresh flowers on her bureau today, just an empty cup of tea and the impatient pile of papers waiting for her to pay them some attention. She just needed to pull herself together and get on with it. The weather seemed to reflect her mood and only served to drag her down further into a cave of self-pity. Maybe she should go home for the afternoon. Sleep in her own bed for the night. She could take all the paperwork with her and do it there. Her heart felt slightly lighter in her chest just at the thought of it and she knew instantly that it was the right thing to do. She hadn't had a break from this place for days, no wonder she felt a bit blue, it simply wasn't healthy. With a newfound surge of enthusiasm for the day she gathered her things together and stood up.

"Hello, Mrs Brown, do you have a minute?" said the girl. Mrs Brown sat back down. It was so perfectly typical; whenever she tried to escape from the place someone, or something was always there to stop her. She recognised the girl's face. It was a pretty one. She had spoken to her before, though for the life of her she could not remember her name or what she was doing here. She must be a visitor. It was Saturday after all. She tried to hide her irritation and smiled back at her, whoever she was.

"Of course..."

"It's Emily, do you remember?" said the girl. If only they knew how many people she had to deal with on a daily basis, although the little grey cells were indeed starting to stir. Of course she remembered. Thank goodness, Mrs Brown was a terrible liar at the best of times.

"Yes of course, dear, you came to visit your grandmother," she said, failing to hide how pleased she was to be able to answer the question. Emily seemed equally delighted.

"That's right, yes," she said and sat down. Mrs Brown tried to ignore that her sitting down may lead to a lengthier interaction than was ideal or indeed necessary, but didn't want to be rude.

"And how is she, your grandmother?" she prompted.

"She's good, a bit better than before, she's remembering more and seems well."

"That's good," said Mrs Brown wondering what the girl wanted to talk about in that case. She struggled for a new line of conversation, digging deep into the depths of her memory for inspiration. The girl's ring twinkling in the light triggered something.

"And your wedding, you were planning your wedding last time we met?"

"A few months ago, yes, I'm married now, it was a lovely day."

"A few months ago? Really? My goodness, how time flies! Was your grandmother able to go?"

"Yes she did. She doesn't really remember it, but I have some photos that I brought to show her. Would you like to see? In fact first, I have some other news," said Emily. Mrs Brown looked up at the clock. She really didn't mean to, but she just couldn't help it. Lovely as this girl was, her mind was made up to go home now and enjoy a little bit of peace and quiet for what was left of the day. She tried to remember her manners and summon the patience required to stay.

"Oh really?" she followed the girl's eyes as they glanced down at her middle.

"I'm pregnant," she said and smiled happily.

Mrs Brown sat back a little in her chair away from the girl. She needed to create a distance between them, but wasn't sure why. Her mouth opened and said a word.

Congratulations. It was an automatic response. Something one said when told of another's happiness, but Mrs Brown found herself feeling suddenly emotional about it all. It was as though this sweet friendly girl had just marched up to her and slapped her hard in the face.

The girl was talking animatedly, her expressions full of happiness and hope. Mrs Brown sat and stared and listened but didn't hear the words. She was somewhere else, another place, another time. Why was this girl sitting here spilling out her life story? Why did women always do that when it came to motherhood? From the very start of the journey; endless talk about trying for a baby, endless talk about what it was like to have a baby, followed by endless talk about bringing up a baby and how hard everything was for them. That's what mothers did. They spoke at you all day long about how hard everything was. If everything was so hard then why did they do it? And why did they feel the need to spend all day telling everyone else all about it? Mrs Brown had never been like that, about anything; children, her marriage, this place. Of course she spoke to Mr Brown about things, she had always shared her innermost thoughts and feelings with him. She wasn't a completely closed book, but she had never felt the need or understood the need of others to go around talking to strangers about themselves and their children all day every day. Because that's what this girl essentially was, a stranger sitting here cradling her bump, that was now so clear to see and wittering on about her unborn child.

Mrs Brown felt pain hunching her shoulders and

closing her hands. Sorrow purred beneath her feet and leapt up on to her empty lap, outstretched and waiting to be stroked.

"Are you alright?" said the girl, interrupting her thoughts but doing nothing to remove them.

"Yes, dear, of course. That's wonderful news, I'm delighted for you," said Mrs Brown and her words were true. But the girl's happiness had stirred up a sadness that had lain quietly within her; a sadness she rarely let out, a sadness she had forgotten for just a little while it would seem. She tried to lock it back up inside, but it was out now, it was impossible. It was a gloomy day that was all, she just needed to snap out of it and get away from this place. Just for a moment it all needed to stop.

The girl seemed more familiar then. Something about her eyes, the way she spoke. Maybe that was it. Maybe the girl reminded her of someone from her past and it had triggered something. A memory she would rather not have recollected from a time she would rather she didn't recall. She needed to get away from here, she was sure of it. She needed the thoughts in her head to stop. She didn't know where they were leading and didn't want to find out.

"I'm so sorry, I didn't mean to upset you. Do you want me to call someone?" said the girl looking a little alarmed. Mrs Brown wondered who the girl could possibly call. The only person she wanted, the only person who had ever known how to put her back together again was Mr Brown. A tear ran down her cheek. She was in a house full of people but had never felt so alone.

"No I'm fine, I'm so sorry, dear. I really am delighted for

you, that's wonderful news. But I'm not feeling one hundred per cent, would you excuse me?" she said. Without waiting for a response and without looking back, Mrs Brown shakily stood and left the room.

She knew she had behaved badly but pain had consumed her and she could no longer stop herself from crying. She knew her behaviour was ridiculous, she had no reason to feel this way, not now, not any more, not at her age. Something about the girl, something about her being pregnant had triggered a broken mechanism which was best left alone. It was funny, the girl in many ways reminded her of herself. If she ever had a granddaughter, she hoped she would be like Emily. Kind and polite, happy and hopeful. Her grandmother might not have wanted to come here, but at least she had someone who loved her and someone who came to visit.

Mrs Brown went into her room. She wanted to be alone and she got her wish. She was tired, so very tired. Maybe she would stay here tonight and then go home tomorrow. It probably wasn't wise to drive in the storm especially when she was feeling this tired and upset. She sat and listened to the wind bluster and bully the tree outside into battering her window with violent branches. Time passed. She wasn't sure how much or how little. She sat and she waited as the dark clouds of the day morphed into the night sky, but nobody came to find her. Nobody had noticed her tears, so nobody would come to ask if she was alright. Nobody seemed to have even noticed that she wasn't there, where she was supposed to be. Maybe she wasn't as essential to the running of the place as she had thought. Maybe they didn't need her after all. Mrs Brown lay down on the bed. She closed her eyes to the storm outside her window and the one inside her head. She tried to silence her thoughts and compose herself. She wondered who would come to visit her if she ever lived somewhere like this. She certainly wouldn't be visited by a pretty young granddaughter. How could she? She and Mr Brown had never had a child of their own.

TWENTY EIGHT

"More shopping!" exclaimed Sophie, as Moira pushed her way through the heavy door of the flat, laden with bags. Her arms ached despite swapping the bags from right to left for the duration of the walk from the bus stop. The plastic handles had formed angry red canyons in her palms and fingers, painful lines of spending on her skin.

"Not really," Moira sighed, struggling to get her breath back after climbing the stairs with her load. "Just a few essential items, and a couple of exchanges for things I had to take back," she lied. "I'll just put these away, be out in a bit," she said, sidestepping Sophie and making her way to her bedroom, closing the door behind her. She knew it was a bit rude, but she just wanted five minutes to herself. Was it really too much to ask, to be able unpack her nice new things in peace, without Sophie asking to borrow them before she'd even had a chance to wear them herself? Moira didn't think so. Sometimes she missed the solitude of her old home.

Moira's spending habits had got a little out of control since starting university and getting a job. Now she had some money of her own to do what she wished with, shopping had become like a drug to her. When she felt low, buying a new dress or a new pair of shoes seemed to be the only thing she could do to feel better about herself. She loved the compliments she received from her friends and fellow students. Unfortunately, despite living on beans on toast and working extra shifts at the hotel, her student loan and earnings just didn't cover the amount she was spending. Whenever Sophie needed more cash she called her parents. Moira hadn't spoken to Mother for weeks, but staring at all the plastic bags on the floor of her room, she thought perhaps it was time to make that phone call.

"Where are you going now?" called Sophie from the kitchen. She had a bottle of vodka and two glasses in her hand.

"Just need to make a quick call, be back in a bit," Moira replied, dashing back out the front door, before Sophie had a chance to reply.

Moira made her way down to the basement where there was a public phone in the hall. Her footsteps echoed on the cold stone floor and the lack of natural light felt a little suffocating. There was normally a long queue for the pay phone, which was part of the reason she hadn't called home in a while, or at least that was what she told herself when guilt paid a visit. The other reason, the one she was less comfortable acknowledging, was that she just didn't want to think about home at the moment. She was happier here with her new life, her new self and was content to leave the old Moira and everything associated with her behind. For some reason, perhaps luck, or maybe just coincidence, on this occasion the phone was free for her to use. She slotted in a twenty pence coin and listened to it fall and crash into some clones of itself. She picked up the receiver and was surprised to hear a dial tone reveal that everything was in working order. She let an involuntary sigh escape her lungs and impatiently punched the small, square, metallic buttons with her index finger, listening to the familiar tune the pattern of numbers made in her ear as she dialled. The phone rang eight times before,

"Hello?" said Mother's voice on the end of the line. Moira was temporarily lost for words, she even considered hanging up, though she did not know why.

"Hello?" repeated Mother, a hint of irritation in her voice.

"Mum, hi, it's Moira." They were simple words that should not have caused her such difficulty.

"Are you okay?" asked Mother after a brief pause. Her voice had softened. Moira was aware that Mother had wanted to say something else, perhaps a comment about the length of time it had been since they last spoke, but she was pleased with the words she had heard instead.

"I'm good. I've been a bit busy. We've started learning about law in journalism, it's quite hard, but it's interesting and I'm doing well I think..."

"Are you eating?" asked Mother.

"Yes."

"What have you been eating?"

"Food," snapped Moira and regretted it instantly. Mother was not fond of snappy talk or sarcasm. There was a sharp intake of breath and Moira expected to be told off, but was pleasantly surprised with,

"Did you get that cookery book I sent you?" asked

232

Mother.

"Yes, thank you," she forced herself to say. She knew the act was Mother's way of showing that she cared and she tried to appreciate it. Some unforgotten memories made feeling grateful sometimes a bit more difficult than it should be.

"I hope you're not just eating toast all the time, Moira, you'll get sick, and if you get sick you'll get behind on your studies..."

"Please don't worry, Mum, I'm fine, honestly..."

"Promise you'll tell me if you're not?" said Mother. Moira paused, she knew this was her opportunity, but the words wouldn't come. "Moira?"

"I'm here, sorry, it's a bit of a bad line," she lied, then closed her eyes and took a deep breath. "Everything is fine, I promise. The only tiny issue is that I'm a bit short of money. I'm trying to make my student loan stretch as far as it can and the money from working at the hotel on Saturdays helps a little...but I'm still a bit short." She was out of words then. All she could do was wait to hear the words that would form Mother's reply.

"I see," said Mother. That was it. Moira waited for more, but there was only silence. The guilt she felt shoved her hard, she swallowed it down until it sat uncomfortably in her empty belly. She knew things were tight at home. How could she ask them to give her more? They had already given her everything they could. She was a bad daughter, a bad person, she hated herself for making this call. She wished with all her being that she hadn't. Whether Mother wouldn't or couldn't she wasn't entirely sure, but the possibility of it being the latter killed her. She tried to rescue the situation, tried to find the words that would mean she didn't just call Mother to ask her for something she couldn't give. Her actions had made them both feel bad, for which she was horribly sorry and would be for days.

"So, I had an idea," said Moira, the words stumbling out of her mouth, unsure of themselves as she spat them out. "I saw an advert on a noticeboard in the student union, for part time work, that I think might fit in around my studies, and I wondered what you might think," Moira thought she had done well. Her words were not lies either, she had spotted an advert and she had been toying with the idea of doing something about it. The ear-splitting silence on the other end of the phone caused Moira to check she hadn't run out of credit. She hastily pushed another twenty pence into the slot.

"What kind of work is it?" asked Mother. Moira could hear the fear following her hesitation.

"It's a job as a care assistant in an old people's home," said Moira. There was silence again on the other end of the line. Then a strange sound, something she hadn't heard for so long it took her a few seconds to realise what it was. Mother was laughing. Moira didn't know what to say.

"I'm sorry," said Mother, the words struggling to break through her laughter. "Look, don't take this the wrong way, I don't think working in a care home is really you. It's very hard work and quite demanding and it takes a certain kind of person to do it." Moira felt an indignant anger bubble up inside her. She could work in a care home if she wanted to.

She held the receiver to her ear like a loaded gun and sat waiting on the bottom step of the stairs in the hallway of the basement like a smoking volcano. She had no words left for Mother now, the only words in her head would have gotten her into trouble and weren't worth the energy it would have taken to say them.

"Why don't you see if you can increase your hours at the hotel? You'll probably earn just as much an hour there and it will be...easier work," Mother said, adding another little chuckle. Moira still didn't speak. She could work in a care home, she knew it wouldn't be easy, but she could do it.

"And in the meantime, I'll have a chat with Father when he gets home from work tonight and see if there is anything else we can do to help." The guilt from before came back up into Moira's throat, the taste of it in her mouth.

"Ok, thank you," said Moira. She unconsciously stood up from the step, she wanted to leave.

"That's okay. You take care now, make sure you eat. Moira, are you still there?" asked Mother.

"Yes."

"We love you," said Mother. They were words Moira hadn't heard for a while. Tears formed in her eyes. One tear grew too heavy and spilled down her cheek. She wiped it away angrily, she didn't want Mother to be able to make her cry anymore.

"You too," she said, trying to keep her voice level. She hung up before either one of them could say anything else. She stood motionless for a moment and took a few deep breaths, then marched up the stairs back to the flat. Once inside, she headed straight for her bedroom. She ignored the unpacked shopping bags on the floor, this was after all their fault. She grabbed her handbag from the bed, turned about heel and marched back into the hallway and towards the front door.

"Hey, where are you going now?" called Sophie, leaning out of the kitchen, swinging on the two back legs of an Ikea chair.

"Out," said Moira. And with that she was gone.

TWENTY NINE

The normally redundant table was set for two. The four wooden legs wobbled and creaked with the effort of it all, dressed up in an old white tablecloth. One leg was propped up with a couple of old beermats to steady itself and a border of unlit candles separated two of everything that was required. The dinner was almost ready and so was Tori. She checked her reflection in the dining room mirror. Her nose wrinkled in disgust and a frown folded its way down her brow in dismay. She had tied her hair back to hide the split ends and put on some make up, but no amount of concealer could hide the dark circles beneath her eyes. She looked tired and trodden on.

She turned her back on the sad-looking woman and started rummaging around in drawers, searching for a box of matches. She was determined to construct the perfect setting, in order for them to share a nice evening together. They might not be able to afford a night out at a fancy restaurant, but there was nothing stopping them from making more of an effort with each other at home. Romance did not come with a price tag. Her phone vibrated on the dining room table, interrupting the search and making her jump. She checked it eagerly, thinking it was probably Harry saying that he was on his way home from work. It was Harry, but he was not on his way. He was stuck at the school working late to mark a pile of essays rather than bring them home, again. This was the third night in a row. Tori read the message three times, unable to process the meaning of the words or produce a response. She slammed the phone down on the table and stomped to the kitchen to turn off the oven. She opened the fridge door to take out a bottle of wine, then remembered that she shouldn't have any and slammed it shut. Before she had time to cry, a seed of an idea started to grow and blossom into a plan that might just be a good one. She smiled to herself and practically skipped to the larder to rescue the old picnic basket from its hiding place on the top shelf. She filled her lungs and blew away the felt of dust that had made its home on the woven wicker lid, then opened it up to find everything on the inside as good as new. She spooned the meal she had prepared into sturdy plastic boxes and placed them inside the basket, along with some breadsticks, napkins, a supermarket cheesecake and a chilled bottle of cava from the fridge. Then, without even checking her reflection or turning off the lights, she grabbed the car keys and left the house, before the voices in her head had a chance to talk any sense into her.

The school was a maze of corridors and sign posts, much like the many hospitals she had visited, but more colourful and with a more pleasing odour. She had only been to Harry's new classroom once before, but felt sure she could retrace her footsteps from that visit and find her way back to him. Her heels echoed as she marched past empty classrooms, a patchwork of children's paintings plastered the walls and the place felt slightly eerie without the sound of chatter and laughter. The basket was heavy, the weight of it hurting her right hand, but still she smiled like a child, excited to surprise the person she loved the most. As she rounded the final corner to what she hoped was Harry's classroom, she stopped in her tracks at the sound of a woman's laughter. Perhaps she had taken a wrong turn. She felt her cheeks blush at the thought of getting caught on school premises by a teacher and then thought how silly she was being; scared of getting told off by one of her husband's colleagues. Just as she had decided to carry on, she heard his voice and froze. She couldn't make out the words, but she knew they were his. She crept on tiptoe towards the closed door of the classroom and peered through the glass window, unaware that she was holding her breath. She saw him then, sat at his desk, his loosened tie around his neck, leaning back with his hands behind his head, looking happier than she had seen him for a long time. He wasn't alone, a woman in a red dress was sitting on his desk and it didn't look like he was marking much homework.

Harry didn't see Tori at the door, he was staring up Katie, one of the new teaching assistants. He had teased her all day about the blind date she was going on. Now that she had been stood up, he felt like an arse. She looked so pretty in her new red dress, just sat there on the edge of his desk. She had cried like a child when she burst through the door of his classroom ten minutes earlier, though there was nothing childlike about her or her figure. He felt bad about

239

teasing her earlier and had tried to cheer her up. The way she laughed at his jokes reminded him so much of Tori when they had first met, Tori before the IVF. Just as his mind was lost in thoughts of his wife, the girl leant forward, her pert, young, breasts level with his face, until her mouth was only millimetres from his. She looked so good, this would be so easy but all he could think about was Tori. Just then there was a sound at the door. They both turned to stare at it, but there was nobody there and no face at the glass window. Harry came to his senses and politely explained to the girl that he was a happily married man. She looked embarrassed and stood up abruptly, apologising and crying once again.

Tori didn't see the girl leave the room. She was already back in the car and on her way home, struggling to see the road clearly through the tears that were streaming down her face. A car pulled out in front of her and she slammed on the breaks. She hadn't been looking and she very nearly crashed into a tree as the driver of the other car repeatedly honked his horn in anger and fear. Tori pulled over to the side of the road and switched off the engine. She sat alone in the cold car, crying in the dark. There was only one person she wanted to call, and she couldn't call him, Harry and her mind were both working overtime.

THIRTY

Mrs Brown laughed like a girl as they sped along the winding Cotswold country lanes. The roof of the open top car was firmly down, the sun felt delightfully warm on her skin and she greedily gulped down the air that filled her mouth as they accelerated along. She felt like she was on a ride at Disneyland, the rush of wind compelling her hair to dance behind her head like an elaborate tail.

"Where are we going?" she asked.

"You'll see," replied Mr Brown with a mischievous smile from the driver's seat. It was so wonderful to be together again. Mrs Brown felt like her younger self once more, free, alive and in love. They had decided to get away from it all and drive to the country to spend the weekend together and make up for lost time. It had been Mr Brown's idea and a very good one given how long they had spent apart recently. She couldn't be happier to see him and he looked at her just the way he had when they first met. The wind continued to blow her hair into a wild mess, but she didn't care, they were together again and that was really all that had ever mattered.

"I think we're nearly there," said Mr Brown.

"Where?" she said, it all looked the same to her,

beautiful, but the same.

"Here," he replied with an amused grin on his face. He looked so happy and handsome and still so young. For a moment she felt sad, wondering why they had spent so much time apart. It had been her fault and she had paid for it dearly, she still loved him so very much. She reached over to hold his hand. He squeezed hers back. "No wonder you don't know where we are, you've never been any good at paying attention to the road ahead, there are signs everywhere if you only opened your eyes and saw what was right in front of you!" he teased. She saw a sign then, just briefly as they whizzed past another tidy hedgerow bordering a sea of lush green fields.

"Slad?" she said.

"I beg your pardon?"

"Slad. That's what the sign said, is that where we're going?"

"There's really no need to be rude. I whisk you away for a romantic minibreak and in return you just call me rude names. Well, that's gratitude for you," he said without smiling.

"Oh, do shut up," she said laughing, "dirty evil old Slad!"

"You are a dirty evil old Slad, but I still love you," he said pulling over to the side of the road as they reached the hustle and bustle of the small town. "Pit stop, back in just a jiffy," he announced before jumping up out of the car. He disappeared as though he had never been there in the first place and she was being driven around by a ghost.

Mrs Brown sat in the car and observed all the people

going about their business on the sunny spring day; parents with their children, friends, husbands with their wives, lovers hand in hand. So many people, so many pockets of life all over the place just getting on with things; so many hopes and dreams and thoughts and prayers and plans being made and broken every minute of every hour of every day. She felt so small then and silly, and so very insignificant. She had built up their own worries and problems into a giant impossible jigsaw puzzle with too many broken and missing pieces. She felt foolish for focusing too long on all the things she didn't have rather than the things she did. The car door opened and Mr Brown put a large brown paper bag behind his seat before climbing in.

"Is that fish and chips I can smell?" she asked.

"It might be. I thought we'd have a picnic," he said turning the engine back on and pulling out onto the road.

"A picnic of fish and chips?" she asked.

"Yes. Why not?"

Sat on an old rug, beneath the shade of a lonely tree, they sat together and admired the beautiful countryside. Patchwork fields stretched out beneath them, sewn together with hedges and trees, covered in polka dot sheep forming a bleating blur on the horizon. Mr Brown opened up the old wicker picnic basket. There was champagne and strawberries to accompany their takeaway fish and chips. It was a perfect picnic. Once they had finished eating, she lay her head on his lap and he held her in his arms. Her head was a little dizzy with the champagne, she felt so very tired and yet so determined not to close her eyes, not wanting to miss one second of this perfect day. She looked up at him then and reached her right hand up to touch his face, he looked almost exactly the same as when they had first met, when he was little more than a boy. How she loved the man the boy had become. She looked up at the sky, shielding her eyes from the bright sunshine that warmed her skin. The sky was an unreal shade of blue, as though they were on the film set of a Hollywood movie, as though this place wasn't real and they were merely acting like a husband and wife in love. Her eyelids were heavy, she tried to keep them open but she was too relaxed and felt too safe to fight off the sleep that would come. She was so happy that they were together again. He loved her, she didn't even need him to say it, she could tell just from the way he looked at her, it was the way he used to. She realized she had got her priorities so very wrong. She would never leave his side again was what she decided as she fell asleep in his arms.

When she awoke, it was cold and dark. She couldn't see where she was but she felt alone. She called out his name, but he did not answer. The pain in her hands was the first clue that something was not quite right. She had felt pain-free and young again in the field. She knew the truth before the lamp she hesitantly switched on revealed it. She was alone, in bed at Godalming Lodge. It had all felt so real to her, but it was only a dream of a memory, or perhaps a memory of a dream. She closed her eyes and desperately tried to get back to that place, a place where she and Mr Brown had been happy. Whether it had been real or not, almost seemed irrelevant now. It was where she wanted to be.

THIRTY ONE

Moira sat on the train staring out of the window. Exactly a week earlier, two letters had arrived in the post for her. She rarely got mail, so was admittedly curious when Sophie put them on the table that morning. She had been staring out of the rain-lashed window and eating a slightly burnt slice of toast, which she put down before rubbing her butter-stained fingers on a sheet of kitchen towel. The first letter was from the care home, thanking her for her interest but saying she did not have the necessary experience for the role. It felt like a punch in the stomach. The second letter was from the hospital. Just seeing the name of it at the top of the typed page had felt like another hard punch, a reminder of things she would rather but would never forget. The letter was an invitation to attend a support group with other girls and women with her condition. She had folded it back up quickly and slid it back inside the envelope before Sophie could see, then had taken it back out later that afternoon, when she was alone in her room with just herself and her thoughts. Now, on the train to the city, speeding through towns and villages, she was on a collision course with not just the hospital, but with her past. Moira wouldn't be Moira if she didn't wonder and worry whether this had been a good idea.

At the hospital she followed the instructions in the letter to a modest, rectangular, bright room. Sun shone through the open windows and tiny dust particles danced in the rays of light. Orderly rows of plastic and metal chairs filled the empty, cold space. She was clearly the first to arrive. Perhaps nobody else would come. Perhaps she really was alone and the only girl to have this silly condition. She sat at the back in the corner, as far away from all the empty chairs as she could. She sat and wondered who else might arrive and what they might look like. Would they look like her? Would she recognize herself in them? Would they be normal or was the afternoon going to become some sort of freak show in which she had no desire to participate.

"Hello," said a voice from the doorway. Moira looked up at the pretty young blonde woman smiling at her. "I'm Lucy, are you here for the support group?" Moira couldn't believe it. The young woman was beautiful, she couldn't possibly have anything wrong with her. She nodded, slightly lost for words and sure there must be some mistake or confusion about the nature of the meeting and who it was for. "I'm so sorry, we had to move to a bigger room. I told the girls on reception to tell people as they arrived but I may as well have been talking to a brick wall. I organized the support group..."

"You have Rokitansky syndrome?" interrupted Moira.

"No, I'm a psychologist here at the hospital. Is this your first meeting?" Moira nodded. She couldn't help but feel disappointed that Lucy was not like her. "Well if you follow me down the hall I can introduce you to everyone. It's just this way," she said. Moira stood obediently and followed the beautiful, normal woman out of the room and down the corridor. She could hear lots of voices, chatter and laughter and as she entered the room she had to stop and steady herself. There were at least fifty woman, all different ages, shapes, sizes and colours. The room was twice as large as the last and packed full of people. There were older women, some were at least Mother's age, young women in their thirties and some girls who looked even younger than her. They all looked different from each other but above all, they all looked normal; just regular, healthy looking women who you might pass in the street without having any clue that there was anything wrong with them at all.

Moira found a seat near the back between two other girls who looked about her age. She put her bag under her chair but kept her coat on, as though she might need to leave in a hurry at any moment. She sat quietly and listened as Lucy stood at the front of the room and thanked them all for coming. Lucy talked a little bit about the condition and how it could vary in different people, so that not everybody's symptoms were exactly the same. She talked about the latest research and how many girls were thought to have Rokitansky Syndrome. She said it could be as many as one in every five thousand women, but that it was impossible to get an accurate figure because so many women went undiagnosed. The numbers whirled around Moira's head and while Lucy talked about how rare it was, all Moira could think about was how many women there were out there who were just like her; she wasn't alone. A really lovely couple came to the front of the room to talk about the adoption process and how happy they were to have adopted a little boy and girl. Moira stared at them and the photos of their family that they passed around the group, they looked happy and for the first time she realised that just because she couldn't get pregnant, it didn't mean that she couldn't have a family of her own too one day.

Just when Moira thought the meeting was over, Lucy asked them all to get into groups of six and talk about their condition and their feelings with other members of the group. Moira froze in her seat, she didn't know what to say and even if she did, she wasn't sure that she felt comfortable enough with these strangers to say it. The other women didn't seem to notice her apprehension and formed a small circle with their chairs around her, while she sat still and afraid. Without waiting to be asked, the girl to her right began to speak as though delivering a speech she had rehearsed many times. The others sat and smiled and listened, so Moira did the same.

"My name is Georgia, I'm nineteen and I'm in my second year at uni. I'm studying English Literature, but I don't want to be a writer or a poet or anything like that, I want to be an actress. My periods didn't start when all my friends' did. They all kept asking me why not and eventually my mum took me to see the GP. The GP said it was nothing to worry about but referred me to see a gynaecologist at the local hospital. On the way to the hospital I wasn't really worried at all, my gran had said that she was a late starter, so I thought I was probably just the same. They did an ultrasound and said things didn't look quite right so that was when it dawned on me that something might actually be wrong. Then they did a laparoscopy and afterwards told me that I didn't have a uterus or a vagina and that I only had one kidney. I remember the doctor telling me that he had never seen anything like it and didn't even know what my condition was called! That was weird, I just thought if the doctor didn't really know anything about it, then who did? Then I got referred here and they explained things so much better. They told me my condition was called Rokitansky Syndrome of MRKH, which I find a little bit easier to say and spell! My friends and family have been brilliant and so supportive, but I wanted to come along today to meet other people like me, if that makes sense."

"You told your friends?" asked an incredulous voice. Moira's cheeks flushed red as she realised it was her own. Georgia looked at her, shrugged her shoulders and smiled.

"Yes of course! They were all really worried about me going into hospital so of course I told them what was wrong, even if I didn't understand it at the time. I think everyone was relieved it wasn't anything serious. They've all been brilliant, my best friend even offered to be my surrogate one day if I want to have children. My ovaries are there and working so it's nice to know that might be an option one day and my boyfriend is cool with it too."

"You told your boyfriend?" asked Moira, she couldn't help it now. This girl seemed to have had a completely different outlook and experience from her own.

"Yes, he came to the hospital with me and my mum.

After dilator treatment our sex life is much better than before and I even enjoy it now, whereas it used to just hurt, if I'm honest. It isn't as though there is anything to be ashamed of; I was born with this condition like all of you, I didn't catch it. And so what if I don't have a womb and I've only got one kidney? I'm healthy and I'm happy and I'm grateful for all the things I do have, there are so many worse things that can happen, don't you think?" Moira felt foolish and wished she hadn't asked those questions out loud, it was clear that Georgia had no room for them or any other negative thoughts and Moira felt in awe of her and her honesty. She didn't think she had ever met someone so brave.

"My husband left me when he found out we couldn't have children," said the woman opposite Moira. She was older, maybe late forties and looked dowdy and trodden on. The mood of the group changed and darkened. "I never told him that I had Rokitansky, I was scared he wouldn't love me if he knew. I had dilator treatment a few years before we met, so we had a normal, healthy sex life and everything was wonderful for the first couple of years of our marriage. But then, after a while, all our friends started getting pregnant. It didn't seem to be a problem at first but then as the months went on, it was. He bought me a pregnancy test on the way home from work one night and put it on the dining room table after dinner, like he had bought me a box of chocolates or something. When I asked what it was for, he explained that he thought I looked like I had put on weight and he was sure I was pregnant. I cried. Then I got angry and then I told him the truth, all of it. He

251

was furious and said I had misled him and if he had known he would never have married me. He moved out a couple of weeks ago and says he wants a divorce." Moira really wanted to say something but the words were too shy to come out. This woman's husband sounded so much like Steve and hearing another woman's story, hearing the hurt in her voice, seeing the pain in her eyes made her feel differently; it made her feel angry, but above all strong. The group sat frozen in a fearful, still quiet, until Georgia shattered the silence.

"Well then, he's an idiot and you deserve to be with someone so much better. I say good riddance to him. If someone loves you then none of this should matter. It doesn't change who we are as people. If I found out that my boyfriend only had one lung, or that his liver was missing it wouldn't change the fact that I love him! They're just body parts, that's all, they don't make us who we are and luckily we don't need them. You might not have a uterus but at least you've got a heart. Either your husband will realise he's been a fool or you'll meet someone so much better who will love you for who you are."

On her way back to the train station Moira's head was full of the voices of the women she had met and spoken to that day. She weaved her way through the oncoming traffic of commuters dressed in various shades of grey. They all looked the same, going about their business, an army of suited zombies. She felt quite determined in that moment never to become like them and for the first time in her life, she felt proud to be different, she no longer wanted to be like everybody else. Moira wasn't going to give up on life so easily anymore, she was going to do and be whatever she wanted, as soon as she figured out what that was. For now, she was going to call the care home first thing in the morning and she was going to get that job. She might not be able to have a baby but she was determined to find a way to have everything else that she wanted in life and she wouldn't stop until she achieved her goals, no matter how large or how small they might be.

THIRTY TWO

"Remind me why we have to do this again?" said Harry. He was breathless. He'd put on a little weight over the last few months, almost as much as Tori had lost. It wasn't deliberate in either case; he ate more to cheer himself up, she felt too sad to eat. They had different coping mechanisms, that was all. If this, what they were doing, was in fact coping. They moved quickly, weaving their way through the slow walking London tourists and the hurried grey blur of commuters. The sun shone lazily, when not hiding behind thick white clouds or tall buildings. It created a chorus line of dancing grey shadows on the pavement which vanished almost as soon as they appeared. One by one they became extinct when Tori walked over them, as though she had rubbed them out with her hurried footsteps.

They couldn't be late today, too much depended on it. They would be judged as they had been countless other times before, but today it was even more important to be the people they needed to be, whoever those people were. For Tori, she knew as little about the woman she thought they wanted her to be as she did about herself. She could barely remember who she really was or who they used to be anymore. The surrogacy and the IVF were all-encompassing and had swallowed her whole. All she knew with any sense of clarity now was that they really needed not to be late.

"Please hurry up. They won't let us collect the rest of the drugs if we miss our appointment. We have to start the injections today, the timing is crucial," she said without looking at Harry. They had never spoken about the night at the school. Harry never knew what Tori had thought she had seen, and Tori didn't want to think about it, or entertain the possibility that things had been how they very much looked. If they were over, then so was her chance to have a child. Harry hadn't been late home since, so perhaps whatever it was or wasn't had passed. Either way, she didn't have the mental energy to deal with anything more than what she already had on her plate right now. She knew that he loved her. Perhaps not as much as he used to, but they were okay, or at least she hoped that they would be.

"I have not forgotten what we are doing today, darling, I don't think I possibly could; seeing as it's all you talk about day and night. What I don't understand is why we need another appointment with Mr Harding?"

"Doctor Harding..."

"Mr Harding, he is not a doctor, in fact the man is nothing more than a jumped up pain in the arse."

"Fine, whatever! We need to see Harding one last time because he has final approval, he has to sign off to say that we can start the injections. You know all this, or at least you should, it's just one more meeting."

"One more interview, you mean, so that he can ask a few more intrusive, personal questions and scribble nonsense on his stupid notepad. One final humiliating chat, so that this ridiculous stranger can decide whether we are fit to be parents? I am so sick of this shit."

"I don't need this right now, Harry, I really don't. They have to assess that I, that we are mentally ready, that we can cope with what we're about to go through. Checks and balances, remember? That's what he said last time."

"Cheques and bullshit more like," said Harry, miming signing a cheque. "It's nothing but an arse-covering exercise. It's about making yet more money out of us, that's all. These people don't care. I've already sat there and answered all his stupid analytical questions once. All these people asking me personal questions, month after month, year after year. They make everything so much worse than it has to be and it's bad enough already." Tori stopped in her tracks and turned to stare at him.

"Please don't be like this, not today," she said. He stopped and stared back at her face, frozen in anguish and time, while the rest of the world hurried by. "I'm so tired, Harry." That was all she could say at first. Not that he needed to be told. He could see how tired she was, everybody could. On the rare occasions now when they did see friends, some had started asking him if she was ill. He didn't know what to say anymore. Tired of pretending to everyone that they were okay when they were anything but.

"I'm the one who has been taking drugs for weeks. I'm the one in physical pain, I feel sick and I have to have yet another internal scan today. I need you to try and be supportive..." her voice started to tremble. He couldn't bear to see her like this anymore. He wanted the old Tori back so very badly.

"I know, I'm sorry. I'm just so..."

"I know. So am I, but we're so close now. We're nearly there. Two weeks of injections to go and that's it, we'll be trying for our baby."

"I know. I just...hate them. I hate the way they treat us. All the hoops we have to jump through."

"I know, but we need them, so just remember to be polite at all times, no matter how rude or crap they are. It's not long to go now. It's nearly all over then we never have to come back to this place ever again, I promise."

"Okay, I'm sorry. Let's go do this dance one last time."

They weren't late, but Mr Harding was. So they sat and waited for over an hour in the aptly named waiting room. Every chair in the room of the clinic in the city had become familiar to them over the last twelve months. It was the only clinic that could help them, the only clinic that would. They had met Doctor Richman here for the first time over a year ago, when the first doctor they had been referred to left to start his own fertility clinic. Making babies was becoming a big business, as more and more couples seemed to need help to have a family. Tori and Harry didn't like Doctor Richman very much, but they had no say in where they would be treated or who they saw and were just grateful for the funding which made all of this possible. At their appointments with him, the doctor spoke a lot about his travels, his gun dogs and his love of fine wine and a little about their treatment. He seemed like a selfish sort of person, but at least he didn't pretend to care.

The receptionists at the clinic were always too busy gossiping to ever notice Tori and Harry or how long they spent waiting week after week. The nurses were a mix of friendly, kind, rude and thoughtless. When their names were called from a clipboard it was always fifty/fifty whether the eyes that would meet theirs would be caring or cruel. Harry had never felt so vulnerable. Tori had forgotten how to feel anything else. Mr Harding, the clinic shrink, appeared in the doorway. They followed him to their future alone together.

"Good to see you both, please take a seat," said Harding when they reached his office. There were four seats to choose from, Harry wondered which one was the correct one to take. "Let's talk about why you want to have a baby together," he began. They answered his questions methodically, they were well rehearsed at this now. Tori determined not to cry, Harry determined not to say the wrong words, not to say something that he shouldn't.

"Good to see you both," said Harding once again to signal that his gentle interrogation was over, they had come full circle and were allowed to leave his room. They were authorised to exit while he spoke to the rest of the 'panel' as he put it, permitted to wait outside for their judgment.

The nurse scanning Tori that day was a new face, as they often were. She was unsmiling and unkind. Tori lay on the table, exposed and vulnerable and realised that the experience was going to be emotionally as well as physically painful before it began. This was not the first time she had been through this, but she hoped it might be the last.

"No, I can't see anything," the nurse complained at the screen whilst shoving her faulty magic wand further inside Tori. It was humiliating and beyond uncomfortable. Tori squeezed Harry's hand and he held on to hers. "How long have you been sniffing?" the nurse asked without looking up.

"Two weeks," Tori replied.

"You haven't forgotten to sniff your drugs?"

"No," replied Tori. The thought of her forgetting any of this at any time seemed ludicrous.

"Well I should be able to see follicles and I can't," said the nurse matter-of-factly. Tori started to cry. The nurse could see the tears rolling down Tori's cheeks but chose to ignore them, chose not to be kind, chose to make things worse than they already were. She pushed the wand further inside and Tori cried out.

"Can't you see that you're hurting her?" said Harry.

"It's a little uncomfortable, but it doesn't hurt really," snapped the nurse.

"It does hurt," said Tori through her tears. "If you read the notes you'll see I have a rare condition which means my vagina isn't as long as most other women. And so you shoving that thing up me does hurt, quite a lot actually, but I don't mind if it means you can see what you need to see."

"Not my job to read notes. What's it called, what you've

259

got?" asked the nurse, temporarily distracted from the screen she had been glaring at.

"Rokitansky Syndrome," said Tori quietly.

"Never heard of it," said the nurse and went back to what she was doing.

"Can we see Doctor Richman please?" asked Harry politely.

"All the doctors are very busy, but I'll ask," said the nurse and left the room.

The door opened ten minutes later and a different nurse came into the room and took a blood sample, "Just to check what's going on," she said.

"Can we see the doctor?" Harry asked her.

"I'm afraid he's busy at the moment," came the reply.

Twenty minutes later, just as Harry was preparing to venture out into the corridor to see what was going on, a third nurse appeared. "I'm going to give you the kit for your injections but you'll have to wait for us to call you later. It seems your body might not have responded to the drugs so far, so we might need to start everything again."

"But we have a surrogate, will she need to start all over again with her drugs too?" asked Tori.

"I'm not sure," said nurse number three.

"This is pretty important to us. Is there someone else we can speak to who can answer our questions? Can we see Doctor Richman?" said Harry, trying desperately hard to keep his cool.

"I'm afraid not. Everyone is busy," said the nurse and exited stage left. Fear entered stage right and asked them how they felt now that the journey may have come to a premature end. They could not remember their lines. This was a scene they had not rehearsed.

"Does it hurt?" asked Harry later that night. They had spent the afternoon in separate rooms. Closed away from each other, closed away from themselves, alone with their fears and thoughts. Tori, who had thought that everything was lost, that everything was over, had spent hours crying. Harry had thought about trying to write. He hadn't written a word of fiction in over a year now, couldn't remember how. He stared at the blank computer screen until his eyes hurt and took a break to stare at the blank wall. He called the clinic, an hourly cycle of being endlessly on hold only to leave a message for doctors who were too busy to talk to him, too busy to give him the answers that might put his wife back together again. This had been a day off work for them both, another day of annual leave spent at the clinic. It was the only day that week that they had to spend some time together. Some day off. Harry looked forward to going to work in the morning.

They hadn't spoken much over dinner. They hadn't eaten much during the silence. They used to always have so much to say to each other. He was desperate for a glass of wine, but she couldn't, so he didn't. She was sat right next to him. He could have held her hand if he had wanted to. He didn't. She wished that he had. He was right there by her side and she missed him so very much.

"It hurts a little, but I'm okay. I'm glad you were in there with me," she whispered.

"We should complain," said Harry.

"To who? They are all as bad as each other," replied Tori.

"I'll try them again," he said, standing to leave the table and clear the untouched plates of food. As if on cue the phone finally rang. They glanced at each other, a silent exchange. Harry answered the phone, frowning in concentration as he listened to the voice on the line. She could read from his facial expression that the news was good. Everything was not lost, Tori's body was doing what it should after all. The journey was not over, not yet. Neither of them seemed sure how to react, how to feel.

"The blood tests were good. We've been approved," he said, tasting the strangeness of the words on his tongue. He had to remind himself that this was good news and couldn't help wondering whether the lack of relief he felt was because it had not really been the news he had wanted to hear.

"Shall we get it out of the way then?" asked Tori. She tried to sound positive, as much for herself as for him. She looked so small, so broken.

"I'm ready if you are," he said. He wasn't ready. He just wanted this to stop. It was killing her. But not trying would have resulted in the same conclusion. He knew that much. He had always known that, but now he just wanted it to be over. One way or the other, he just needed all this to end.

"I'll call Fiona," she said, "tell her we are starting the injections." He nodded. It had become the norm for Tori to

262

inform the stranger of everything they were doing. Two women, preparing their bodies in unison to create his child. One of them the love of his life, the other a stranger who had invaded their lives by invitation.

Together, they carefully unpacked the box the clinic had given them, spreading its contents over the large wooden coffee table. There were different coloured needles, liquids, powders, syringes and vials. Things were more complicated than either of them imagined. With trembling hands Tori took the syringe out of its plastic covering. Harry snapped a glass container like the nurse had shown them. He broke two before getting it right, tiny shards of broken glass decorated the table; it was harder than it looked. Tori got rid of the air in the syringe and sucked out the liquid from small glass container, before mixing it with the vial of powder. They repeated this four times until they had the right consistency, careful not to lose a drop. Tori changed the needle on the syringe. It was slightly smaller, a little less terrifying. But she was still scared. They both were.

"How do you want to do this?" asked Harry.

"I don't know...standing? What do you think?"

"It's up to you."

"I think standing."

"Okay."

She handed him the syringe and stood up to pull down her trousers. She rolled up her top a little to expose her tummy, then pinched a bit of skin to the left of her belly button just like she had been shown at the clinic.

"Here. Do you think?" she asked. Her voice high, like a

child, her eyes red from the latest day of crying, her brow in a tight, worried frown.

"I guess," he said, handing her the syringe and wanting so badly for this to be finished.

Tori held the pinched skin in her left hand, the syringe in her right. She knew the anticipation of the pain would be worse than the reality, but sticking a needle into herself just didn't seem logical.

"I can't do it, can you do it?" she pleaded with him, trousers around her ankles, wearing Little Miss pants, more childlike and vulnerable than he had ever seen her.

"I can't," he said, taking a step away from her without even meaning to.

"Yes you can, the nurse said you could do it if I couldn't. Lots of husbands do it."

"Well I can't," said Harry, firmer this time. He had watched them prod and poke and hurt her too many times, he didn't want to be a part of this, he didn't want to cause her any more pain.

"Please, Harry, just do it. I know we share many of the same qualities and look a lot alike, but I am not actually Wonder Woman and I can't do this on my own," said Tori. He smiled at her then.

"You can," he said. He tried to push his own fear away and banish hers from the room as he took her hand in his. "I'm right here, you can do this, I know you can."

She started to cry again then, just briefly, then she took a deep breath and it was as though she just decided to stop. Her hand was shaking so much more than before, but for a brief moment she felt strong. It was all she needed. She plunged the needle into the pinched skin and let out a tiny scream.

"Shit, what happened?" asked Harry, stepping back.

"It hurts!"

"You didn't do it at an angle, they said to do it at an angle!"

"Fuck, it hurts," she said and pulled the needle out. A small trickle of bright red blood ran down her tummy.

"Look, let's just calm down and take our time," said Harry reaching for a tissue.

A determined "No," was all she said, before plunging the needle back into herself.

"Okay," said Harry, not knowing what to do now and wishing he'd paid more attention at the clinic. "You're in, just take it easy. Are you okay?"

"No I'm not fucking okay, the curtains are bloody open, I'm standing in my knickers in full view of the neighbours with a needle in my stomach. I've had what looked like a kitchen blender shoved up my bloody fanny all afternoon and everything fucking hurts!" said Tori, through her tears.

"Shit," said Harry, jumping up to pull the curtains. He turned to her then. She did look slightly mad. He had an urge to laugh at her but resisted. "Okay, just slowly push in the plunger until its empty."

"I can't." she sobbed.

"Yes you can," he said, coming to her side once more.

"No I can't, I don't have enough hands left," she said. He looked down to see her predicament. Her left hand squeezed the flesh on her tummy. Her shiny wedding ring now loose on her finger. Her right hand held the syringe, but not in a way where she could push the plunger. "I didn't think it through, I just wanted to get the needle in."

"I can see you've never injected yourself with drugs before, you're obviously a complete novice with syringes, that is not how you hold them," he said.

"No, I gathered that," she said. "Can you push it? Please?" Harry really didn't want to, but he knew that he had to. And so he did. Slowly he pushed the plunger down. His eyes moving from the syringe to his wife's face and back. She was still so beautiful.

"All done," he said. "How did that feel?"

"Strange," was all she said before pulling out the needle. There was a little more blood, but just a spot this time. He held the tissue on her tummy as she disposed of the syringe in the yellow plastic bucket they had been given. Then he held her in his arms. They stood like that for what felt like a long time. The first injection was done. Two more weeks of injections and scans and pain and tears and one way or another, this journey would be over.

An end

THIRTY THREE

Mrs Brown found herself staring at her hands in her lap. She was transfixed by the thin, pale paper-like skin stretched over her aching bones. She had been trying to write a letter when the pain in her right hand had become unbearable. She didn't mind getting older, it was just all the aches and pains that age brought to the party that she would rather live without. She was tired, really tired. She expelled all the air from her lungs with an exhausted sigh and looked up to survey the scene around her. From her seat in the conservatory, she could see some of the residents asleep in their chairs in the lounge. Sleeping off Glenda the cook's offering of Chicken Kiev at lunchtime. At least that's what the menu had said. Even Mrs Brown couldn't bring herself to eat the meal, just pushed it around her plate for a while before telling Glenda exactly what she thought of her cooking. She had been hoping to get rid of the woman for weeks now but nobody had replied to the advertisement she had placed in the local newspaper.

The light blocked her eyes when she looked up. She squinted them and ducked her head a little to be out of the hindering path of bright rays. She could see that outside it was a pleasant day and the sun lifted her spirits. Maybe some fresh air would do her good. Anyone would start to feel a little out of sorts cooped up in here all day with endless paperwork to deal with and surrounded by an army of old souls just waiting to breathe their last breath before bidding this world goodbye. That was it, her mind was made up. She put the blasted paperwork to one side, the same piece of paper resting on top of the pile as yesterday. She just couldn't deal with it right now, it had waited this long, it could wait a few more hours. With considerable effort she heaved herself up from her chair and made her way out to the garden.

The lack of lunch took its toll on her weary body and she felt a little dizzy and lightheaded when she first stood. She was determined to get outside and enjoy the sunshine while it lasted, so she bullied one foot in front of the other, opened the door, stepped into the outside, and left Godalming Lodge, its residents and her troubles behind her, even if it was only for an hour or two.

Once outside she breathed in deeply, taking greedy gulps of the cool fresh air. She felt better already. She made her way to her favourite spot, feeling warmed and then positively boiling in the bright sunshine. The wind had robbed the white rose bushes of their petals, a mess of tiny pale footprints all over the neat green lawn. Everything else was well tended. It was a struggle to find anything to do, but even with her poor eyesight she could spot the odd dastardly weed here and there. They could normally be found hiding between the colourful rhododendrons. She smelt a bloom and felt her heart lift with the strong scent. Goodness knows how her garden looked at home. She hadn't had the time to look after it for a while now, and knew only too well that nobody else would. Mr Brown had never been one for gardening. He always said she was the one with green fingers and left her to it. He would mow the lawn though, that was a man's job. A bumble bee hovered noisily near her then buzzed off, choosing to mind its own business and get on its way. For the briefest of moments as Mrs Brown watched it fly away she forgot all her worries and felt alive. She felt free and wished she could follow it up and over the fence. She gently persuaded her body to crouch down. Her knees groaned unhappily at the concept of kneeling, but allowed her to do so all the same.

"Hello, Mrs Brown, what are you doing down there? You'll have me out of a job!" said a male voice. Mrs Brown felt startled when she spotted the owner's shadow looming over her, despite the temporary shield from the hot sun it provided. But she softened as she recognised the voice.

"Oh, Bert, it's you, how lovely to see you. You'll never be out of a job, at least not while I'm here, you're the best gardener we've ever had. I was just doing a spot of weeding," she said blinking up at him, her cheeks flushing just a little.

"I didn't know I'd missed any!" chuckled Bert. "You really should leave that to me, Mrs Brown. It's my job and well....you'll get your nice clothes all dirty if you carry on with what you're doing," he pleaded, kneeling down on the neat grass lawn beside her.

"Oh poppycock," she replied, "A little weeding never hurt anyone."

"Very well, let me help you at least," said Bert, knowing

271

he was fighting a losing battle. The two of them sat like that, gently tugging out some troublesome weeds around the base of the rose bushes, for a good while, enjoying the warm sun, fresh air, and feel of the dirt between their fingertips. The garden was a serene haven of calm, for a while at least.

"Mrs Brown! Is that you down there? What are you doing?" hollered Rosie. She came panting over the lawn towards them, her cheeks living up to her name.

"What's the matter, Rosie?" asked Mrs Brown in alarm.

"Nothing, it's just, we didn't know where you'd gone, and we've all just been running around the house, turning the place upside down trying to find you is all," said the girl, her words tumbling out of her mouth as she tried to catch her breath between speaking them. Rosie bent over then, her podgy palms swinging down to rest on her squatting legs. Like a plump little monkey. She took some deep breaths and her face gradually turned from harsh beetroot to a softer pink hue. Mrs Brown looked on in alarm, still none the wiser as to what all the fuss was about.

"Well you've found me now, what's the matter, girl?" she asked. She couldn't help but feel irritated that her few moments of peace with Bert in the garden had been shattered by Rosie's squawking, huffing and puffing.

"Nothing, Mrs Brown, everything is fine. Would you like to come back in the house with me? It is starting to get chilly out here," said Rosie, standing up straight again, her hands now resting on her hips.

"Not particularly, no," said Mrs Brown. She no longer felt able to hide her annoyance and turned back to the flower beds, wondering to herself whether it was time she weeded out a few of the staff as well as the broomstick of a cook from Godalming Lodge.

"Well, you don't want to get mud on your dress, now do you? Are you sure you wouldn't rather come in with me?" Rosie whined.

"Why is everyone suddenly so very concerned with the state of my clothes? I am perfectly capable of deciding what I will and won't do and when I will do it, thank you very much. Now unless there is some genuine emergency, which I am so far guessing there is not, I would appreciate you all just getting on with your jobs and giving me five minutes peace and quiet for a change, if it isn't too much to ask!" said Mrs Brown, glaring at the girl and feeling quite exhausted with it all.

"Well if you're sure you'll be alright," said Rosie, looking from Mrs Brown to Bert and back again.

"We'll be fine, don't you worry," said Bert to Rosie. Mrs Brown felt sure he could see just as plainly as she could, that the girl was nothing but a nuisance and clearly missing a few marbles.

"Very well then," said Rosie and stomped back towards the house.

After watching Rosie go, Mrs Brown turned her attention back to the dirt while Bert sat quietly beside her. They sat in silence like that for a while. The perfect blue sky had clouded over a little. Finding herself in an unwelcome shadow for longer than she deemed necessary, Mrs Brown's exasperation got the better of her.

"I do sometimes wonder who she thinks she's talking

to," said Mrs Brown, returning her attention to the weeds.

"I know, Mrs Brown, I know," said Bert, bending down to help her.

THIRTY FOUR

Moira smoothed down her uniform and knocked on the office door.

"Come in," said Sue breezily. After a deep breath and a squeeze of her right fist to crush any nerves, Moira stepped inside, closing the door quietly behind her. "Moira, hello, take a seat. How did you get on?" Moira had reapplied for the job as a care assistant at Godalming Lodge. She wanted to prove Mother wrong, but above all she had wanted to prove to herself that she could do it. She thought carefully about what to say as she sat down, quickly revising the words she had rehearsed in her head. Sue's office was at the back of the building. It was small but the high ceiling made it seem less so. Overstuffed bookshelves lined the walls and a small but tidy desk over looked the immaculate gardens. The scent of Sue's perfume diluted the smell of the place, but the stench of decay still filled Moira's nostrils and lingered in her hair.

"It was hard work," said Moira after ample consideration. She paused for the duration necessary to form what she hoped would be the right words. "But I enjoyed it and I think I would like to work here...if you'll let me." She had been quite determined since she called a second time about the position at the residential care home. Sue had been reluctant to hire a student with no previous experience, but Moira had been persistent and so they had reached an agreement. If Moira would work unpaid for one weekend to learn the ropes and prove she could do the job, Sue would consider employing her. It seemed fair. There were no promises and no guarantees, but Moira felt it was worth a shot. On her first day she had felt like walking out almost as soon as she had arrived. But Mother, and Sophie for that matter, had both been so very sure she couldn't do the job that she felt compelled to prove them wrong.

"By all accounts you have done a great job over the last couple of days. You were punctual, you worked hard and the rest of the team seem to like you. As for the residents, I hear Henry proposed when you helped him into bed last night and Mrs Dennis thinks you're an angel, literally, she says you have invisible wings. You seem to have made quite an impression on them all," said Sue.

"So can I have the job?" asked Moira. She hadn't meant to sound so impatient, but she was exhausted now and just wanted to know one way or the other. It wasn't even about the money or proving a point anymore. She felt like she had achieved something over the last couple of days. She had helped people. She had done something she was proud of and above all she felt like she finally had a purpose.

"I'll happily give you the job on one condition," said Sue, looking far more serious than Moira had seen her before. "I want you to promise me that if it ever gets too much or you fall behind in your studies you will tell me straight away." She reminded her of Mother when she spoke. An unfamiliar affection stroked Moira's arm and rested on her tired shoulders. She wasn't sure what to make of the sensation so shrugged it off.

"I promise," said Moira, exceedingly happy that Sue had said the words she wanted to hear.

"And, I want you to take this," said Sue, reaching down to the bottom drawer of her desk and taking out a small brown envelope. "This is your pay for the last two days. I know the deal we agreed was that you were going to work for free, but you've earned it and you are now officially a member of the team here at Godalming Lodge."

"Thank you," said Moira and she really meant it.

On the way home, walking on tired feet, Moira managed to walk past all of her favourite clothes shops without even a moment of window shopping. She didn't want any new shoes or dresses, she no longer needed them. She had found something better to make her feel good about herself and in the most unlikely of places. She turned the corner of her road, climbed the stairs to the flat and turned the key in the lock. She was looking forward to a long hot bath and an early night. She knew Sophie would want to go out drinking and would be disappointed, but all Moira wanted to do was go to bed.

As she closed the door behind her and kicked off her shoes, she noticed a quiet sobbing sound. As she got closer to the kitchen she could see that the sobbing was coming from Sophie. She had never seen Sophie portray anything other than happiness personified. She had certainly never seen or heard her cry.

"What's happened?" she asked, rushing to her side. Sophie didn't respond. She was sat all alone bent over the kitchen table, her head resting on folded arms, jerking unhappily with each escaped sob.

"Hey, what's happened, what's the matter?" repeated Moira. She was worried now, something was very wrong.

"That's the matter," said Sophie pointing at the bin in the corner of the room without looking up.

Moira walked over to the bin and stepped on the pedal. The lid obediently flew up to reveal the contents inside. There was a banana skin, an empty can of tuna, a tea bag and a pen-shaped white plastic object that Moira didn't recognise.

"What is it?" she asked, reaching down inside the bin.

"It's a pregnancy test," said Sophie looking up. The words found their way to Moira's ears and then the kitchen filled with a disciplined silence while she tried to process them. She retracted her arm mechanically then tilted the heel of her foot. The mouth of the bin slammed shut. The secret it had revealed was back in the darkness, hidden from the rest of the world.

"You took a pregnancy test?" she said, without meaning to say the words out loud.

"Yes," Sophie said, her eyes locked firmly on the bin as though its contents might jump out and bite her.

"What did it say?" asked Moira, fearing she already knew the answer.

Sophie held her head in hands and began to sob again. Moira didn't need to hear the words.

"How? I thought you were careful?" Moira knew her

choice of words was not helpful, but that didn't prevent her from saying them. Sophie looked up angrily then.

"I am always careful, but there was that one night a few weeks ago, don't you remember? That guy from the club, I'd run out of condoms, he didn't have any, I asked you if I could borrow one..."

"I hope you're not trying to somehow blame me for this!" said Moira, feeling angry herself now. She was already exhausted from working at the care home all day, she didn't need this right now. She didn't need this ever.

"I'm not blaming you, I just can't believe this is happening to me, I don't know what to do," said Sophie, with a fragility in her voice that Moira had never heard before.

There were lots of things Moira wanted to say. The anger she suddenly felt urged her on, but she thought better of saying the things she was thinking. She had thought for weeks that something like this might happen. She had lost count of the boys Sophie had brought back to this flat. The number of nights she had been forced to listen to noises on the other side of the wall.

"It will be okay," Moira said at last, not knowing how it could be. She pushed the curls away from Sophie's wet face and gave her a tissue from her satchel which she was still wearing over her uniform.

"Have you told the father?" she asked.

"Jesus, don't say that! I don't even know whether I'm having it yet. But no I haven't told him, I don't have his number, he had mine but he never called me and to be honest I can't even remember his name." She started to cry again. Moira wanted to hug her friend but the resentment she felt stood between them and got in the way.

"It will be okay," said Moira again. They felt like the right words to say.

Later that night, Moira went to check on her friend. She knocked gently on Sophie's bedroom door and let herself in without waiting for a response that she knew would never come. Sophie was in bed facing the wall so that all Moira could see was a mass of tight blonde curls on the pillow.

"You okay?" she whispered from the doorway, unsure how far she should go, how close she could get. There were words she didn't want to hear. Words she didn't know how she would react to. Sophie, completely unaware of this, spoke them anyway.

"I think I'm going to have an abortion," she said, still facing the wall. For a long time both of them were silent and for the duration of that time, each one tried to translate what that silence meant for them, for their friendship and for their future.

"I think that's something you need to think about," said Moira quietly at last. The room fell still, like the air was gone out of it.

"I have thought about it," said Sophie, too quickly. The silence returned and stayed a little longer. "Will you come with me?" were the words that Sophie said next. When those words reached Moira's ears, everything stopped. Sophie turned to stare at her, wide eyed and expectant, waiting for her answer. Moira had imagined what it would be like the first time one of her friends was pregnant. She had never imagined it would be like this. Sophie was pregnant. It was something that Moira could never do. Sophie wanted to get rid of the baby, pretend it had never happened. It was something that Moira would never have done. She tried not to judge her friend. She tried to think of a way to not let this come between them. Time wouldn't wait, it sped ahead while Sophie looked up at her, waiting for an answer that Moira didn't know. Then, meeting her friend's eyes, the answer came for both of them.

"Yes, of course," she said, after less time and thought than she anticipated she would need. "Is there anything I can get you?" she said.

"No," whispered Sophie. "Will you turn out my light please?"

"Yes."

"Moira?"

"Yes?"

"Thank you."

THIRTY FIVE

"How you feeling?" asked Harry.

"Okay," said Tori quietly. "Are we alright for time?"

"We're fine. We won't be late. Just try and relax," he said. They were driving to the clinic today rather than travelling by train and tube. Doctor Richman had said that Tori wouldn't be well enough to take public transport after the operation to harvest her eggs. There were fifteen follicles on her ovaries now. Apparently this was a good thing. Her tummy was covered in green, blue and yellow bruises from the nightly injections. There were dark circles beneath her eyes, she wore no make-up and there were strands of grey brushed in with her dark ponytail. Doctor Richman had told her not to dye her hair during treatment. Tori did everything Dr Richman told her to do.

Harry felt sick about the thought of her going under anaesthetic today. He tried not to contemplate the thought of her never waking up. She wanted all this, not him, not really, not anymore. He just wanted her back. He wanted things back the way they used to be. They were both afraid now at all times, afraid this wouldn't work, afraid that it might. Their fear had become an unwelcome lodger who paid no rent and made constant demands of them both.

Harry reached over to take Tori's hand but then thought better of the idea. He couldn't stop himself from thinking that she probably didn't want to hold his hand, that she didn't want him at all anymore, only the baby. After a moment's indecision, he awkwardly placed his hand that had been hovering above hers back on the steering wheel. She noticed this and thought about putting her hand on his leg. She tried to think of some simple way to show him how much she loved him, but wasn't sure how, or whether he wanted her to touch him right now. They had forgotten how to be with each other. They had forgotten why they were. Sometimes it really felt as though he didn't love her anymore, that he hated her for dragging them through this. The baby they didn't have had taken over their lives. It was all she thought about, there was no room for Harry, or how he felt. And he felt lonely. Terribly lonely and terribly afraid of the operation and of what was to come. Neither of them reached out to the other. Both regretted not doing so and wished the other had.

"I'm frightened," Tori whispered some time later. She said it so quietly that it was almost inaudible, but Harry heard her, reached over without hesitation this time and squeezed her hand tight. He took his eyes off the road, just for a moment, to look at her.

"Me too. But it's going to be fine. We'll be okay." She meant she was frightened of the operation. He knew what she had meant but had fears of his own.

They arrived early at the clinic. They parked and went inside, hand in hand, wondering when they would leave and how they would feel when they did. Tori changed into a gown and they sat together waiting in silence, behind a curtain, in a cubicle. When Doctor Richman arrived, he smiled uncomfortably at them, like a schoolboy arriving at an exam he forgot to revise for. His follicly challenged tanned head and his intermittent teeth were a familiar if not thoroughly welcome sight. He checked the paperwork before saying their names. They had all met countless times but he still didn't recognise them. He didn't remember their names and had never known their story. He was too busy writing his own. He knew that they knew this, but it didn't matter. He would still be paid at the end of the month.

They waited in silence for them to take Tori away. Harry wasn't allowed into the operating room, he would have to wait alone once she was gone.

"If anything happens..." she started to say when Doctor Richman returned to collect her.

"It won't, don't say that, don't even think it," said Harry.

"I know, but just in case..." she said, tears starting to roll down her cheeks.

"Everything will be fine, I'll see you soon, they do this every day it is just routine..."

"Well it's not routine in your wife's case, it's actually quite complicated," interrupted Dr Richman. "You did sign the consent forms and waivers in case of organ damage didn't you?" he added without the hint of a smile. Tori and Harry both stared at him. It would have been funny had he been joking, but unfortunately humour was not a quality he was known for.

"Yes we've signed everything," said Tori motioning to the thick stack of paperwork on the table next to them. His behaviour had made her angry and her anger made her strong. She turned to Harry once more. "You're right, I'll be fine and I'll see you very soon. I love you," she said, quite simply. It was Harry who had tears in his eyes now. He did his very best to blink them away. "I love you more," he said and kissed her forehead before watching them lead her away from him. Tori had written him a letter and left it on the bed at home. A letter for if something went wrong, saying all the things she wouldn't be able to say but that Harry would need to hear. She hoped to destroy it later, she hoped it was a letter he would never have to read. She went through some doors and he couldn't see her any more. He sat alone in a cubicle and waited for someone to return his wife.

Tori refused to take off her wedding ring, so a cranky nurse covered it with tape. She felt by wearing it that Harry was somehow with her, not stuck on the wrong side of the swinging doors down the corridor. She climbed up onto the operating table and lay down, observing all the masked faces around her. They spoke about her as though she was not there and very soon she wasn't. As the anaesthetic flowed, Tori's eyes grew heavy. She started to dream. Harry started to pray to a god he didn't believe in. He would have prayed to anyone that would return his wife to him. The wife he married.

When Tori woke up she knew instantly where she was. Harry's face was next to hers, full of fear and drained of colour until she fully opened her eyes.

"How many?" she said.

"Oh thank God! How are you?"

"Fine, how many?"

"Don't know yet, how do you feel? Are you okay? Are you in pain?"

"I'm fine. Why don't we know yet? Did they not get any?" The curtain screeched open and Doctor Richman stuck his head into their cubicle, invading their space.

"How are we?" he said.

"Fine. Thank you," said Tori, forcing herself to be polite.

"Well the operation was a success. You've done very well. Perhaps a little too well!"

"What does that mean?" asked Harry.

"Well we've managed to get twenty eggs, which is a great harvest!" Tori felt elated.

"Thank you so much!" she beamed at the doctor in a way that made Harry feel nauseous.

"Why would that be too well? Is that too many?" he asked the doctor.

"It's possible we may have over done things a little with Tori. I was unavailable to do the operation two days ago, we were in the south of France, I'm sure you understand. Ideally we should have operated then and the delay has meant a little hyper-stimulation of the ovaries, but it should be fine. As a precaution I'll get her to sniff the drugs a little longer, calm everything back down. You're free to leave after an hour or so when you're ready. You'll need to take the painkillers for a while. Bed rest for the next forty-eight hours. You're going to be in a bit of pain when you stand up I expect, I'm afraid I accidently went through your bladder trying to get to your ovaries to get the buggers out. Really don't do *anything* for the next couple of days, you'll only make things worse if you do. We'll give you a ring later, let you know how many embryos we get." With that, the curtain was drawn, the first act was over and Doctor Richman left the building.

They waited and then waited some more. People came and went but nobody would say the words that they wanted to hear. The last nurse to pop her head around the curtain and take Tori's blood pressure had said she would come back and let them know when they could leave.

"I just want to go home, please can you help me?" said Tori looking up at Harry from her bed in the cubicle.

"I know you do, but maybe we should just get the doctor to check you one more time before we go anywhere, just to make sure everything is okay..."

"We've been waiting around for hours, I feel like crap, I'd just rather be at home in my own bed, that's all, can you help me get my knickers on?"

"Okay," he said defeated. When they first met Harry had spent a great deal of time trying to get Tori's knickers off. He couldn't help lamenting over how much their lives had changed. He helped her sit up. The pain had become steadily worse during the last hour, but there were too many drugs in her system to give Tori any more painkillers just yet, according to the last nurse. The curtain swished open and another new face of another nurse they had never laid eyes on before appeared beside the bed.

"How are you doing?" said the round faced petite lady. She seemed nice enough.

"I'm feeling better, I'd like to go home if I can," said Tori.

"Well I think we'll just get the doctor to sign off on that

before you go anywhere." Harry clenched his fists but tried to sound calm.

"With respect, the last nurse said that over an hour ago and we've just been sat here waiting ever since. We've been here for hours now and we were originally told we could go at lunchtime, do you know where the doctor is or how much longer he will be?"

"And do you know how many embryos we have, they said we would know by now, but we haven't heard anything..."

"Oh that's strange," said the nurse, "I think Doctor Richman had a lunch meeting at another clinic, so he might not be back for a while. Let me call the embryologists and see how they are getting on. I'll be back soon," she said and was gone. Curtain and case closed.

"Please can we go?" asked Tori.

"Yes, okay," said Harry, feeling defeated and wanting to get out of there himself. He helped her to dress then he helped her to stand and held her arm tightly as she took her first steps.

"Are you okay?"

"Yes, I'm fine, I promise," said Tori. She slowly shuffled her feet in front of each other one at a time and tried to ignore the pain she was obviously feeling.

The nurse appeared at the end of the corridor and marched up to them with her big smile and clipboard.

"I see you're off then," she beamed as though they had just won the lottery. "Doctor says that's fine, by the way. He's been held up at a luncheon with colleagues so won't be back until much later so no point you hanging around if you're feeling up to leaving." Tori had carried on shuffling towards the exit, desperate to leave throughout the conversation. "Would you mind just signing the release form to say that you felt well enough to go and didn't want to wait for the doctor to check you over?" she said thrusting out the clipboard and a pen.

"It would have been nice if a doctor, any doctor had checked her over, but seeing as we've been waiting for that to happen for five hours now while Dr Richman has been indisposed..." His anger egged him on and Harry had plenty more he wanted to say to the nurse, to all of them in fact, but he felt something change and his fear slapped him hard and silenced him. Tori's grip on his arm had loosened and she suddenly felt heavy where he had been supporting her.

"Tori?" he said "Are you okay?" She looked at him then, a deep frown on her perfect face. Then she looked down. He followed her gaze to her bare legs. Everything looked fine and he didn't understand what she was doing but knew something was wrong.

"Are you okay?" he said again. His voice was slightly louder this time, his words were spoken to be heard but she still didn't appear to hear him, she just stared downwards. He looked again just in time to see a small trickle of blood. He watched it silently make its way from out beneath her dress, down the inside of her right leg, all the way to her right foot. She was wearing cream coloured ballet pumps which was where the line of red stopped. A new red line drew itself down the inside of her left leg and stained the left shoe. Within seconds there were many lines and then there was only red. Red on Tori's legs, red on the cream shoes, red on the floor. Everything happened very quickly.

"It hurts," said Tori before her eyes closed and she collapsed in Harry's arms. Harry shouted for help. He didn't know what he was saying, the only word that he remembered was the word help, which he said over and over again while trying to hold her up. He wished she would just open her eyes and tried not to look at all of the red that surrounded them. The nurse had been quick to react. The clipboard and pen had dropped to the floor, she ran to the desk and pushed an unseen button. A light that Harry had never noticed before, despite their numerous visits to this place, began to flash. There was a noise of a bell and the double doors at the end of the corridor swung open. Within seconds there were multiple doctors rushing towards them, doctors they had been begging to see were suddenly running to help. They pulled Tori from Harry's arms and she was on the floor. Someone pulled him back. All he could do was stand and stare at her lifeless body.

Her eyes were closed, her skin so pale against the red-soaked summer dress she was wearing. The nurses were pushing and shouting and trying to move him away but he wouldn't listen to them, he couldn't hear them anymore. The clinic was the loudest it had ever been but Harry couldn't hear anything. Time froze and all Harry could do was stand and stare.

THIRTY SIX

Mrs Brown made her way inside, sneaking in through the conservatory doors and hoping to get to her room unnoticed and undisturbed. It was three in the afternoon. It was tea time. She became aware of this because seemingly all of the residents and all of the staff were in the lounge and they were all staring at her. She glanced at the clock which confirmed the time, as did the trolley of tea and biscuits in the middle of the room. Shortbread, she noticed, must be Friday. She was pleased it was Friday as she was going home for the weekend. This place could run itself for two days she was sure, and if not, she was only a phone call away.

Adele waddled towards her, her black skin in strong contrast to the rest of the room.

"Mrs Brown, you are covered in mud, are you okay?"

"Yes of course I'm okay. A little mud never hurt anybody and I am hardly covered Adele, you really must learn not to exaggerate," said Mrs Brown. "And why are you here? Not that I'm not delighted to see you given I've had to put up with Rosie all day, but it's only three o'clock, the night shift doesn't start for another five hours. That's incredibly early, even for you."

"I swapped shifts, Mrs B, I'm doing the day shift today so I can go to my son's concert tonight at the school. I've been here all day."

"Well, I haven't seen you until now, and if you're going to swap shifts amongst yourselves you really do need to tell me, it's not good enough and you of all people ought to know better."

"Yes, Mrs Brown," said Adele.

"I'm going to get cleaned up."

"Okay, let me know if you need anything."

Mrs Brown made her way past the residents, ignoring their curious stares. She took a route via the tea trolley, taking a biscuit on the way to her room. She changed out of her dirty clothes and washed the mud off her hands, watching the clean white porcelain turn a grubby brown, the pressure of the water not quite strong enough to pretend it had never been. She realised that every time she had tried to leave this place lately, something had happened to stop her. Something or someone had held her back. She was determined that would not be the case today. She sat and thought about it all for longer than she had intended, until there was a knock on the door.

"Come in," said Mrs Brown reluctantly. The door opened and Adele's face appeared around the corner.

"Just wanted to check you were okay," she said gently. "You seem out of sorts."

"I'm fine. I just needed a moment to myself was all."

"We all know you're missing Mr Brown," said Adele. She meant it kindly but the words translated into something quite different on their journey to Mrs Brown's ears.

"I can cope perfectly fine without him," she replied and on seeing Adele's expression, she softened. "But yes, I do miss him when he isn't around."

"Dinner is ready if you want some," added Adele.

"No, I'm fine thank you, Adele. I daren't risk another plateful of food poisoning this evening. I'll have something a little later, when Glenda has gone."

"Okay, if there is anything I can do, just let me know," said Adele and closed the door. What could Adele possibly do to make things better?

Alone again. Mrs Brown's mind had made itself up. She would leave now for the weekend and call them later to let them know. If she went out there now, they would all start talking at her with their endless questions and unsolvable problems and she would never escape. Regardless of whatever was going on at Godalming Lodge tonight, she was going home and straight away, before anyone or anything could change her mind. If she went to the car park they would see and delay her, so she decided to leave by the back door and walk home, she could never find the car keys when she needed them in a hurry anyway. It was a beautiful evening and still light outside. She knew the way and resolved that the walk would do her good. She picked up her bag and she left. As she walked down the garden path, out of the gate, and on to the public footpath behind the house she felt many things, but above all else, she felt free.

She walked lightly, taking greedy gulps of the fresh air and enjoying the sights and sounds around her. The trees surrendered their branches to the wind which was too strong for some of the browning leaves, so they parachuted down to join their brothers in the dirt. The sound of the wind in the trees quietly shushed the traffic in the distance, as though she were somewhere else, a less suburban place, trekking alone a rural desert. It was colder than she had anticipated, she should have really brought a jacket. So long as she kept walking she would surely stay warm enough and home wasn't too far away, just over the hill.

For a brief moment she felt lost. She stood still, unsure of how long or how far she had walked, taking in her surroundings, getting her bearings. The weather shared her momentary confusion, tiny droplets of rain starting to fall despite the sunshine. She followed the lane down to the road and turned left until everything looked the same as she had remembered. She thought back over her life and wondered whether there was anything she should or could have done differently. She didn't really believe in having regrets, what was the point? She couldn't do anything now to change the decisions or paths she had chosen to take when she was younger. There were episodes in her life that had made her incredibly sad, but she had got through them. She and Mr Brown had got through them together.

She used to be scared of the dark, but with age she had realised that it wasn't the dark she was afraid of, but the unknown. It was perfectly natural, she thought, to be afraid of what might be lurking around the corner, nobody ever really knew what life had in store for them. She had never really been one for religion. She respected other people's beliefs but she was unable to share them. As far as she was concerned when you were gone, you were gone, which was why she believed it was so very important to make the most of each and every day. It was why it was so important that she get away from Godalming Lodge, just for a while, just to live a little again without the constant stress and worry of it all.

The last of the light was slowly being pulled down around the horizon and she could see the moon up above. If she squinted, she could just make out a faint sprinkling of stars winking down on her. It was getting properly dark now, dark and still. The street lights came on to light her way and she knew she did not have too much further to go. The road beneath her feet softened and the way ahead became quite muddy. A Mexican wave danced across a field of long grass, mocking her, urging her to turn back.

"Watch where you're going," she heard Mr Brown say. She froze. It was as if he had been right there behind her. She turned but there was nobody, just an empty road. The wind rustled the leaves in the trees above her and blew the fallen leaves at her feet into a badly choreographed dance. An owl hooted in the distance and Mrs Brown reluctantly gave in to the fear that had been building with every step she had taken since she left Godalming Lodge.

She started to walk again, a little more quickly now, she slipped, only just recovering her balance in time to prevent a fall. She squinted to try and see where she was walking on the muddy road. It was then that she noticed the beautiful fur lined slippers on her feet, covered in mud and completely ruined. In her hurry to leave Godalming Lodge she had forgotten to put her shoes on. She couldn't understand how she had walked all this way without noticing before now. If anyone were to see her, they would think she was a mad old lady. She briefly wondered whether perhaps she was. It seemed like a good idea to push those thoughts to the back of her mind, so she did, and instead she hurried on towards home and Mr Brown, only now starting to doubt whether this had been a good idea.

A large building full of flats stood where home should have been. In the darkness and her confusion she had obviously taken a wrong turn and so began to retrace her steps. Larger spots of rain started to fall and she began to feel like the foolish old woman she resembled. In the distance she saw a set of headlights turn the corner and drive towards her. They grew larger as did the car they belonged to, growing too bright and blinding her vision. Just ahead of her the car came to a sudden stop. Her heart began to beat hard in her chest and fear swelled up inside her making it hard to breathe. This had been a bad idea. She should have driven. She was miles from anywhere and nobody would hear her scream even if she could. The car's headlights dimmed, a door swung open and the shape of a man climbed out. When her eyes adjusted to the dark once more she could see it was a police car and he was a policeman or at least a man wearing a police uniform. He took what she thought might be a gun, but transpired to be a torch from the glove compartment and shone it in her direction.

"Mrs Brown?" he called. Now this was very strange. She didn't know any policemen, nor did her husband, and unless she had been committing crimes in her sleep she could think of no reason how or why this man should know her name. Something was wrong, something was very wrong.

"Yes?" she said. There was little else she could say.

"I've been looking for you," he said with a smile. He seemed a friendly chap, but his words failed to put her at ease.

"Is my husband alright?" she asked. It was all she could think of.

"As far as I know he's fine, it's you I've been looking for. Got a call from Godalming Lodge and have been looking for you ever since," he said. Of course, it was something to do with the Lodge, when wasn't it? So this weekend was destined to be ruined too.

"I see," she said.

"Can I give you a lift back there?" said the policeman kindly.

"Yes of course, thank you. And you can fill me in on whatever has happened on the way," she said and reluctantly climbed inside the car.

THIRTY SEVEN

Moira had left Sophie at the clinic. She had sat and waited with her in reception and would collect her later. When Moira had seen her this morning she was pregnant with a nameless boy's baby. When she next saw her, she would no longer be pregnant, she would just be Sophie again. The same, but different.

Moira thought about Sophie all day long while she worked at the care home. She thought about Sophie in the morning, when she helped Mrs Gibson have a bath. Mrs Gibson had travelled the world when she was young and spoke about a different country every time they met, most of which Moira had never heard of but would very much like to visit one day. Moira thought about Sophie at lunchtime when she helped Mr Dawson cut up his sausages and fed them to him with some mash and gravy. Mr Dawson had a stroke a month ago. He couldn't move his right arm very well anymore. He needed help with almost everything and wasn't very happy about it. Moira thought about Sophie in the afternoon when she helped Mrs Clein into bed and hand-washed her stockings for her in the sink. Mrs Clein liked to sing. She sang all the time, except at night when you tucked her into bed and turned out the light, then she cried.

As Moira walked up the hill towards the clinic in the rain she didn't think about Sophie at all. Although she was on the way to see her friend, she could only think about herself. Who she was and who she wasn't. She couldn't decide whether she liked herself or not. She had changed in many ways over the last few months, she knew that, but sometimes, crazy as it seemed, she felt as though she didn't know Moira Sweeney. Not only did she feel like she didn't really know herself, but what she did know, she didn't really like. She had changed her hair, her clothes, her friends and her home. But the one thing she really wanted to change she could do nothing about. Some days she didn't care about not being able to have a baby. Some days she convinced herself that it didn't matter, that she didn't want one anyway. Other days she was not so easily fooled by her own thoughts. Other days she thought of little else. Not that there was anyone she particularly wanted to have a baby with, not right now anyway. But what if one day there was somebody? What if one day she wanted to have a baby with somebody and she couldn't. What then?

At the top of the hill she hit rock bottom. Tears ran down her cheeks and she felt a familiar emptiness in her tummy. She involuntarily put her hand to her stomach then, as though feeling for a kick from a child that would never be. The door of the clinic swung open and she quickly wiped her face with her sleeve. The man who came out barely noticed her and walked past without a word, back down the hill she had just climbed. She could do the same, just turn around and walk away. Turn her back on her friend and leave this place. Someone watching might have thought she could do that but she knew that she couldn't. She pushed the door open and stepped inside.

"Thanks for coming to get me," said Sophie in the taxi on their way back to the flat.

"That's okay," said Moira. She knew that Sophie wanted more than that from her, but she just didn't have the words.

"You haven't asked about it..."

"Asked about what?" said Moira, feeling a tiny hint of anger bubble up inside her.

"About what happened," said Sophie. A little angry herself now, and needing more than her friend could give.

"No, but I have asked how you are, I went with you this morning and I've come to pick you up this afternoon. I haven't asked about what happened because I don't want to know. And perhaps it's best I make myself clear now, I don't ever want to talk about this. I'm here for you because you're my friend, that's it. That doesn't mean I am okay with any of this. What happened in there was your decision and your business. If you want to talk about it, then talk about it with someone else. If you ever find yourself in this situation again, don't ask me to help you, in fact don't even tell me about it. I'm your friend Sophie and I want to carry on being your friend, so just don't tell me, okay?" The words stopped. The car was silent. The taxi driver stared at the road ahead and pretended not to have heard. Moira didn't pretend not to have heard the words but was baffled as to where they had come from. The voice had sounded so much like hers and yet so unlike her own.

"Okay," said Sophie. She was quiet and childlike.

As the car pulled up outside the flat, Moira reached for her purse to pay the fare. She felt like the grown up, it felt strange but not altogether bad. She paid, climbed out of the cab and carried Sophie's bag up the stairs for her.

"Do you want a drink?" asked Moira once they were inside.

"Yes please, coffee if there is any," said Sophie. Moira put the kettle on for Sophie and poured herself a glass of orange juice. She kicked off her shoes. Her feet ached and she was tired.

"How come you don't drink coffee again?" asked Sophie.

"I don't like it, tastes of socks and smells revolting," said Moira. She took off her coat, letting it rest on the back of the kitchen chair. Then made Sophie's drink with an upturned nose and put it on the table in front of her before finally sitting down.

"It's weird," said Sophie.

"What's weird?" asked Moira.

"Not drinking coffee is weird."

"You're weird," she said back, then smiled. Sophie smiled too. They smiled at each other. They were okay. Sophie knew never to talk about this again and Moira knew she wouldn't have to hear about it, they could both just move on with their lives and each other. The day had

301

pulled them apart but the words had pushed them back together. Without any more words, the girls sat quietly, wondering the same thing. They thought about whether their futures were entwined or whether the paths they were on would lead them to totally separate lives.

"How was work?" asked Sophie. It was unlike her to ask about Moira's work.

"It was okay," said Moira. Not wishing to go into too much detail, fearing Sophie was merely being polite.

"Yeah? What did you do?" continued Sophie. Moira sighed, thinking to herself that there wasn't much she hadn't done today. But if Sophie really wanted to know she would tell her.

"The usual, really. I got four of the residents up and washed and dressed. I helped with lunch. I gave Mrs Clein a bath..."

"Was she naked?" interrupted Sophie.

"No, she was fully clothed. Of course she was naked, stupid." Sophie wrinkled her nose. "You'll be old one day too, Sophie Cox."

"No I won't, I'm going to die young, all the coolest people do. And I don't want to be called Sophie anymore," she said.

"What?"

"All the cool people die young..."

"No the other bit, about being called Sophie."

"Yeah, I just think it's a bit boring, a bit common you know?"

"No."

"Yeah, you do. There were three people called Sophie at

302

a lecture last week, three! That's ridiculous. And there was another girl called Sophie at the clinic this morning," she stopped herself short, aware that she had strayed into unwelcome territory. Moira didn't look up.

"So what do you want to be called instead? I can think of a few names," smiled Moira.

"I'm sure you can, but I'm thinking maybe just my surname. That's kinda cool. Just Cox."

"Sounds like cocks. Or Cox, like the apple?"

"Oh no, I hate apples. How about Coxy, that would be cool, rhymes with foxy! Yes I like that!"

"Okay then, whatever you say," said Moira.

"Whatever you say, Coxy!" said Sophie. "Sorry, you didn't finish telling me about work, are there any fit, young male care assistants at the home?" Moira smiled, a little alarmed, but more relieved to hear her friend sounding like herself again.

"No, afraid not. It was just like every other day," said Moira, then after some thought, "although Mrs Clein..."

"The naked one in the bath..."

"Yes, that one..."

"See, I do listen," said Sophie. Moira gave her a look, "Sorry, all ears," she said.

"Well it was nothing really, it was just that she was telling me about her family tree and it was really interesting. She had traced her ancestors all the way back to her great, great grandfather. It just made me realise how little I know about my own family, thought I might do some research myself," said Moira excitedly. She looked at her friend for a response but didn't get one. Sophie looked as tired as Moira felt. "Do you want to go to bed?"

"What? Sorry, I was away with the fairies there for a moment," said Sophie.

"That's okay, you've had a long day," said Moira, taking the glass and the mug from the table and placing them in the sink.

"Do you think we'll be friends forever?" asked Sophie. Her words betrayed a hidden childlike innocence. She was quite unlike her normal self. A wall had come down today and it would take some effort to rebuild it.

"Yes," said Moira. It was an easy answer, having thought about the question so recently herself.

"Good, I'd like that," said Sophie.

"I'd like that too, Sophie."

"Coxy," Sophie corrected.

"Whatever."

THIRTY EIGHT

Tori opened her eyes. Pain took hold of her violently and for a moment she wasn't sure where or who she was. The repetitive pattern on the curtain looked familiar but this wasn't home, this place smelt foreign and sterile.

"Tori?" Harry's voice brought her to her senses. His eyes were red. His face was pale. She was still at the clinic.

"Oh thank God," said Harry. "Hang on, let me get someone..."

"No, please don't," she said. Her voice was audible though weak, but he was gone and didn't listen. Not this time. He returned a moment later and kissed her forehead. He took her hand in his. Some colour had returned to his cheeks.

"You gave me quite a scare there. The doctor is on his way," he said. His hand tightened around hers as though he was scared to let go.

"What happened, I don't really remember," she said. She tried to sit up but the pain in her abdomen convinced her otherwise and she lay still where she was.

"I don't really know, you were fine, we were leaving...then there was blood, lots of blood. You passed out, they lifted you up on to a trolley, your eyes were closed, they said you barely had a pulse, for a moment I thought you...They said that you'd lost too much blood, they put a mask on you, hooked you up to the monitor, gave you pain medication, stopped the bleeding. You've been sleeping ever since, you wouldn't wake up," he said. As he spoke it felt like a bad dream. All Tori could remember was the blood trickling down her legs and the stains on her shoes. She could see them next to the chair in the corner of the cubicle, still stained red.

"I'm so sorry," were the only words she could think of to say. They seemed to be the only words appropriate.

"Don't say that. I'm just glad you're okay," he said, still not letting go.

"Was there any other news while I've been sleeping?"

"The country is going back into recession," Harry joked. She didn't smile.

"You know what I mean."

"Yes, darling, we've got ten," he said and kissed her again.

"Ten?" she said. She didn't know how to react to this news, wasn't sure whether she should be happy or sad. "There were twenty eggs? Why are there only ten embryos? What happened to the rest?"

"Darling we've got ten. What are you talking about? Sometimes this doesn't work at all for people, but we've been lucky enough to get ten embryos. That's ten chances for us to have this baby. They don't know why the others didn't work, but I can't help thinking we should just be really pleased with what we've got. Personally, I'm just happy that you're okay. I was really scared."

306

She let his words float around her head for a brief moment, allowing herself time to carefully consider each one of them. She knew he was right. She knew she should be happy. But she also knew that ten embryos guaranteed nothing. What she thought she knew, and what she hadn't yet told Harry, was that she didn't think she could go through all of this again. So now, her part in all this was done. They had ten chances left and then the journey really would be over.

A day later and Tori was still in bed, but thankful that at least it was her own. She had been given a strict prescription for bed rest and no worrying, neither of which were a realistic request or proposition. She called for Harry and heard him run up the stairs, scared to leave her side, scared to leave her alone in case she disappeared.

"What's the matter?" he said, coming to the bedside.

"I need the bathroom again," she said.

"Okay, well it might not be as bad this time," he said and leant down towards her. She cautiously sat up, but the pain wasted no time and stabbed her in the stomach, tearing through her body. She cried out and wrapped her arms around Harry's neck. "It will be okay, hold on," he whispered and lifted her up and out of the bed. She screamed in agony as he carried her to the bathroom, carefully lowering her down onto the toilet seat.

"This is so undignified," she said.

"I don't care about that, you just need to get better," he replied and waited by the door. He looked away while she cried a stream of tears and pissed a river of blood into the toilet bowl.

Mid-afternoon, just as she was drifting off to sleep, the phone rang. She sat up a bit too quickly, the drugs helped her to stand and steadied her careful steps to the other side of the room. She picked up the phone and listened to the words being said on the other end of the line. She didn't say very much back, but managed to acknowledge that she understood. The words tasted unpleasant on her tongue, but she swallowed them down and digested them. She made her way back to the bed and slowly sat down, her body throbbing with the effort of it all. She put the phone on the bedside table and noticed Harry standing quietly in the doorway. Not quite able to enter the room. Afraid of being where Tori was, of knowing what she knew.

"Who was it?" he asked.

"The clinic," she said, her eyes not wanting to meet his.

"And?"

"Four of the embryos didn't make it overnight. We're down to six," she said, without emotion.

"Did they say why?"

"No, but they said the others were doing okay. They said it was time to call Fiona and arrange her travel."

"Okay, and when do they think for the..."

"She said the transfer was booked in for Monday morning and if Fiona was happy to agree to it, we should probably try with two."

"If we have any left by then," said Harry. As soon as

308

he'd spoken, he wished he could take the words back. Tori's eyes filled immediately and seconds later she was sobbing hysterically. He held her. Not knowing what to do or what to say.

Monday took its time to come and when it finally did, Tori and Harry were exhausted. Tori was still in a lot of pain and hadn't slept properly since the operation. The journey to the clinic was long. The time spent in the waiting room, longer still. There were only two embryos left now. The others had failed to divide the correct number of times. They might have started with ten, but now they only had two chances left. When the time came, when their names were called, Tori, Harry and Fiona stood and went to Room Three together.

"Now then, how are we all, little more crowded than usual," said Doctor Richman as they entered the room. "Fiona, if we could have you up here on the bed and Mr and Mrs..." he paused to check the folder on the desk.

"It's Mr and Mrs Brown," said Harry. Tori shot him a look.

"The file has another name," said Doctor Richman.

"My passport was still in my maiden name when we started coming here, so I think some parts of the file are out of date, that's all," said Tori.

"I see. Well if I could just see your identification please, passports would be perfect, you too, Fiona, and we'll just triple check that we've got the right sperm and eggs making the right embryos to go into the right surrogate. Don't want any nasty mix ups now, do we?" he said with a chuckle, "Always a bit of a nightmare when that happens!" Tori glanced at Harry. They didn't need words anymore. They both knew what they thought of this man, but if today worked, none of that mattered.

"Well the dates of birth all match so I think we're all set to go. Talk amongst yourselves, people, I'll just pop to the lab and collect the goods, be back soon."

Fiona lay on the table and smiled at them nervously. She wanted this to work for them almost as much as she needed the money if it did. She had grown to care about them a lot and more than anything she was so glad she chose them. Out of all the couples asking for help, she knew that Tori and Harry would make truly wonderful parents. She knew this had put a strain on things, but if they loved the child as much as she knew they loved each other, they were destined to be a very happy family.

A nurse entered the room, making everyone jump and stealing them away from the individual thoughts that had silenced all three. A paper sheet covered Fiona from the waist down. She lay on her back on the table, with her legs in metal stirrups. Harry and Tori stood at the head of the bed and looked at the screen on the right.

"These are your embryos," said Dr Richman, coming back into the room, with a syringe like instrument. He sat between Fiona's legs. "Now if you all watch the screen, you'll be able to see me popping them in," he said. Fiona held Tori's left hand and Harry held the other. Fiona flinched a little as they watched the tube containing their two last chances move across the screen.

"That's it, all done. They're in!" said the doctor seconds later. "In fact I can see them, just there," he said pointing to two tiny white specks on the screen. "Do you want a photo?" he asked.

Harry and Tori looked at each other. It seemed like a bizarre question and one they hadn't expected, but there was only one answer.

"Yes, please," whispered Tori. "Can we have one for us and one for Fiona too?"

"Of course," said the doctor and he pressed the button on the printer.

"What happens now?" asked Harry.

"Now all you can do is wait. It may seem like the hard part is over, but most people tell me it's the waiting that is the worst. It might feel like the longest two weeks of your life, but it is only two weeks. Then Fiona will have to come in for a pregnancy test and with any luck, we'll have some good news," he said, and smiled at them warmly. "I suggest you go home and have a drink now that you can. You two, not you," he said pointing at Fiona with a grin.

Doctor Richman was wrong about many things but he wasn't wrong about the agony of the wait. The next two weeks dragged on miserably. Harry found it difficult to sleep and Tori barely ate anything at all. She was still in pain but went back to work almost straight away, as she had used all her leave trying for the baby. They kept themselves busy but the days took their time to roll into each other. Fiona kept in touch and tried to reassure them, but at times the wait felt unbearable and they just wanted to know, they needed to know, one way or the other. Life carried on all around them and they tried to participate in it, willing to do almost anything that might distract them from the phone call that would come.

THIRTY NINE

Mrs Brown sat in her chair at the far end of the conservatory. She sat and she stared and she waited. She tried to remember what it was she was waiting for and waited for her memory to find her. She looked down at her clawed hands. The pain had become as natural to her as their twisted form in her lap. She felt sad, though she did not know why. She knew exactly where she was but found herself feeling inexplicably lost and a more than a little afraid. Something wasn't right. She heaved herself up out of the chair and made her way towards the hall.

The worn, rose-coloured carpet cushioned her shuffled steps, one at a time. She needed to be alone, and hurried as best she could to her room. Once inside she closed the door firmly behind her and sat on the bed. A small herd of cushions and pillows cradled her while she sat and surveyed her surroundings. She didn't feel any better, even here, alone, her own private fortress, protected on all sides by four solid brick walls. She felt as though she was trapped in a floral prison, though she had committed no crime. Even in here, away from the sounds, and smells of the communal lounge for the residents, she couldn't get away from the fact that this was a residential home for the elderly, a glorified waiting room for the frail, infirm, unloved, unwanted and soon to be dead. She felt sick. Perhaps she was ill. She looked around at the few personal belongings she had dotted about the place to try and cheer the room up and make it feel a tiny bit more like home. Then her gaze fell upon the photo of her husband, so real it was as though he were here in the room. She knew what he would say, she was so certain she knew that she could almost hear his voice repeating the same words over and over, it was time to go home. And she wanted to, so very much. The business had taken everything from her, her life, her love. She agreed with her husband, it was time to go home. She would deal with things from there from now on. Some things were just too important. She realised just how late it was and that she hadn't eaten all day, she had had too much to do again. She decided she had better have some lunch, she would start putting a plan in place tomorrow, to run this place from home and get a little of her life back.

Mrs Brown eased her tired body down into her chair at the table at the far end of the dining room. She was tired, almost too tired to eat, but thought she had better make the effort. Even she couldn't pretend not to notice how loose her clothes were at her waist, a consequence of Glenda's lack of culinary skills and the stress of running the place had taken a toll on her appetite. She heaved an involuntary sigh as Glenda marched through the swing doors from the kitchen, stomping purposefully in her direction. She still hadn't managed to find a replacement. She had placed another advertisement in the local newspaper, but clearly people didn't want to have to work for a living nowadays.

"You're late again, Mrs Brown," snarled Glenda. Mrs Brown guessed she had seen the advert and knew she wouldn't be here much longer.

"I beg your pardon?" asked Mrs Brown.

"I said you're late again. It makes my life so much harder when you refuse to eat with everyone else, I'll never understand why you can't just eat at the same blinking time as the others. Just as well I have some food left over, isn't it!" said Glenda, before marching back towards the kitchen, her twig-like arms swinging angrily by her side like determined frail pendulums.

Mrs Brown was lost for words. She couldn't comprehend how a member of staff dared speak to her this way. Before she had a chance to decide how to react, the swing doors burst open again and Glenda clomped towards her with a steaming tray of lunch.

"There you go, fish cakes and salad, enjoy," she muttered before turning on her heel.

"Fish cakes?" whispered Mrs Brown.

"Yes, fish cakes," snapped Glenda, turning back to glare down at her.

"But it's Sunday. Shouldn't we be having a roast? This really isn't good enough!" said Mrs Brown, finding her authority and entwining it with her outraged words as they tumbled out of her mouth.

"Firstly, it isn't Sunday. If it were, I'd be at home with my feet up watching TV, not here cooking for you. Secondly, I'm afraid the only options on the menu this afternoon are fish cakes or fish cakes. I suggest you take up

315

any complaints you may have with management."

"I don't know who you think you're talking to..." Mrs Brown started to say. But her words were only ever going to be heard by her own ears. Glenda was back in the kitchen, and the swing doors swung angrily in her wake.

Mrs Brown stared down at her unappetising plate. It was Sunday, she was absolutely sure of it. Glenda was obviously having some kind of breakdown, but she struggled to feel any sympathy for the woman. She had crossed a line today and would need to be asked to leave as soon as a replacement could be found. In fact maybe sooner. Mrs Brown would rather cook the food herself she thought, but she was too tired to sack Glenda today. What she needed was some rest, a moment's peace away from it all, away from here. What she needed, she realised with unfailing certainty was to go home and not tomorrow, right now.

Mrs Brown pushed the untouched food away from her and then held on to the side of the dining room table to heave herself up. She felt dizzy, but quite determined to stick to her decision now that it was made. She felt ill, and more than a little out of sorts, most likely from the lack of food and sleep and the stress of it all the last few weeks. She made her way to the bedroom and closed the door firmly behind her. She walked over to the window, it was a glorious afternoon out there, the sun was shining down on Bert's garden. She wondered what state her own garden must be in now at home, and thought perhaps he might be able to pop by and give it a tidy for her. She had let this place and its inhabitants consume her. First thing

316

tomorrow she would fire Glenda and hire somebody who could take on some of the responsibilities of running the place, she had done her best but it really was time to go.

She felt her heart lift a little, she should have done this years ago, still better late than never. She bent down with some difficulty and slid her old suitcase out from under the bed. She didn't have too many belongings to pack, just the paperwork, her photos and a few toiletries. The rest could wait, she would come back to collect the rest of her things next week when she was feeling up to it.

She scanned the room. It looked bare, as though she had never been here, as though she was a ghost. She felt tired from the effort of it all and could barely keep her eyes open. It wouldn't be responsible or safe to drive home and she liked to be both, so she pulled the cord in her room, deciding it would be best to just get one of the girls to book her a taxi. Moments later there was a knock at the door and the face of Adele appeared around it. It must have been later than Mrs Brown thought if Adele was already here to start her nightshift.

"Adele dear, would you be so kind as to book me a taxi?" Mrs Brown asked, before double checking the dresser drawers to be sure she hadn't left anything she may need behind.

"A taxi?" asked Adele, waddling into the room and staring at the suitcase on the bed. Tiny beads of sweat had formed on her deep furrowed brow. "Lordy, you had me worried, Mrs B, pulling the cord like that, I thought something was wrong, thought there was some kind of emergency," she said, puffing and shaking her head.

"Sorry to worry you, Adele, no, there's no emergency. I'm just ever so tired and I want to go home for a while, recharge my batteries, that's all. Could you book me a taxi for fifteen minutes' time? Thank you ever so much."

"No, Mrs B, I can't do that, you can't go home..." said Adele. Mrs Brown examined her face. She understood that they needed her, but the time had come to put herself first for a little while.

"Now, Adele, you needn't worry about Godalming Lodge...or your position here for that matter. I will continue to run the place, money is tight but we are doing just fine. I just need to spend some time at home, with my family, I miss them...and I'm tired, Adele. I'm ever so tired."

"Maybe you should just get some rest if you're tired, Mrs B. Things might seem different in the morning. Maybe just sleep on it..."

"No, I'm sorry, I'm going home and I'm going home tonight," said Mrs Brown. The two women stared at each other for a while then. Their words met in the middle of the room and were introduced to each other but did not get along.

"Okay then," sighed Adele and she turned to leave the room.

Mrs Brown sat on her bed and waited. The shadows looked down on her from all four walls, still like statues, holding their breath for the next scene. The room seemed to shrink and darken. She waited for what felt like an incredibly long time, her suitcase by her side like a loyal pet. Just as her patience expired and she was about to pull the emergency cord in her room a second time, there was a knock at the door.

"Hello," said a pretty young thing, entering her bedroom. "Do you remember me?" Mrs Brown was in no mood for visitors. She remembered the girl, though what she was doing here at this time of night and in her bedroom was completely alien to her.

"Yes, I do remember you, your grandmother is a resident here at Godalming Lodge. I'm afraid you'll have to excuse me but now is not a good time. I can get one of the care assistants to talk with you now and perhaps make an appointment to talk with me at a later date..."

"That's right, I'm Emily," said the girl, cutting her off mid-sentence.

"Yes, Emily, as I said, now is not a good time."

"I wonder could we maybe have a little chat?" asked Emily. Mrs Brown found herself wondering whether the girl was deaf, stupid, crazy or all three. Not in the mood for tolerance or patient enough to find out, she hastily reached over and yanked the emergency cord for the second time that evening. Adele appeared behind the girl in the doorway with alarming speed, almost as though she had been stood there the whole time.

"Adele, would you mind taking Miss...?"

"Harvey-Brown," interjected the girl. The word halted proceedings, but reason suggested it was a common enough name.

"Miss Harvey-Brown back to the lounge and perhaps talk about any urgent concerns she may have regarding her grandmother's care. And can you chase up the taxi company, I've been waiting an awfully long time..."

"No, Mrs B, I'm real sorry, I can't do that," said Adele.

"I beg your pardon?" said Mrs Brown, wondering whether she was dreaming or whether a second member of her staff was being rude to her face in the space of a few hours.

"I think you should listen to what Emily has to say." Emily came to sit on the bed next to Mrs Brown and Adele closed the door.

"I'm sorry, but you can't go home," said the girl, taking Mrs Brown's hand, who violently shook it away.

"Young lady, I can do whatever I want. I'm sorry if you are upset, but I really don't have the time..."

"You do have the time, and you need to listen to me."

"I don't have the time, I have a residential home to run. I'm incredibly busy and..."

"You don't run a residential care home, Grandmother. This is where you live," said the girl calmly.

Mrs Brown stared at the girl. Confusion and fear came out from under the bed. Mrs Brown replayed the lies the girl had spoken and knew them to be true. She felt dizzy. She felt sick. Then everything turned to black.

FORTY

"Where have you been? We're going to be late!" hollered Coxy from her bedroom.

"Sorry, I lost track of time at the library researching my family tree, it's amazing what you can find out. I found out I'm not really me," said Moira, taking off her hat and scarf. Rain was falling hard outside and she was soaked to the skin. She began to peel off her clothes in the hallway.

"What's that?" Coxy said, padding out of her bedroom in her dressing gown, her curls wrapped up in a towel on top of her head.

"The library? It's a large building on campus full of books that you can read, you should check it out some time, perhaps before you graduate," said Moira.

"You're funny, did I ever tell you that? I meant what are you talking about, not being you? And can I borrow your hairdryer? Jesus, you've lost weight," said Coxy, taking in Moira's frame as she stood in her underwear in the hall, a pile of wet clothes at her feet.

"Yes, it's in the top drawer. Have I got time for a quick shower?"

"No, but you better have one anyway if you don't want to see in the New Year looking and smelling like a drowned rat," said Coxy. She followed Moira into the bathroom and picked up her toothbrush. Moira turned on the shower and waited patiently for the water to heat up. She stood relaxed and at ease despite wearing almost nothing, finally comfortable in her own skin.

"So I found out my name isn't really Moira..." she said, stepping into the shower. The water was still icy, but she didn't have time to wait.

"Is your real name Harold?" laughed Coxy, spitting out her toothpaste and wiping her mouth on the hand towel.

"No, Moira is my middle name," she said, squeezing her eyes shut to prevent the shampoo from stinging.

"Okay, seriously, have you been drinking or something? What are you on about?"

"I also found out that my great grandfather was a baker..."

"Fascinating stuff...but hurry up or we'll miss happy hour altogether!"

"And I found a copy of my birth certificate," said Moira.

"At the library? I don't get it."

"No, the librarian is into ancestry too. She helped me research my family tree with records from the census and ordered a copy of my birth certificate. It arrived today."

"I still don't get it," said Coxy.

"That's because you are a simpleton, my friend. My original birth certificate says that my name is Victoria Moira Sweeney."

"Bit of a mouthful. So why have you been using your middle name all this time? I prefer Victoria, makes you sound like less of a loser," laughed Coxy. "It must be a mistake, why would your parents name you one thing and then call you another?"

"That's what I thought, so I called them," said Moira, stepping out of the shower and drying herself with the towel.

"And?"

"And it's true. Took a while for me to get Mother to talk about it, she denied all knowledge at first. But then she explained, quite matter-of-factly, that they named me Victoria on the birth certificate to keep my grandmother happy, but that she had always preferred Moira, so that's what they called me."

"Mystery solved, thank goodness! Can you get dressed now so we can get to the New Year's Eve party before the New Year?"

"Don't you think it's really amazing?"

"What?"

"All these things I'm finding out."

"Not really no. What do I call you now? Moira or Queen Victoria?"

"I don't know. Victoria sounds so formal, it's not really me."

"Well when you figure it out, do let me know."

"Yes, Coxy, will do."

The club was packed. They forced their way through the army of bodies swaying to the music to get some drinks. The floor was sticky and there were broken plastic glasses beneath their feat. Moira felt a tad too formal in her little black dress, but everything else she owned had looked ridiculously baggy on her diminutive frame. Coxy had helped put her hair up so she would look like Audrey Hepburn. It hadn't really worked. She didn't look like Audrey, but neither did she look anything like her old self. The new Moira was all but complete in her self-regeneration. She was more confident, she had given herself permission to be different and she was fairly sure she felt happy, or something close enough. Something was still missing, but she hoped she would find it one day and if she didn't, she told herself, she would be fine on her own.

Tonight she wasn't on her own, she was with Coxy and she was about to start a new year as a new woman. Somewhere inside, the girl she had been lived on, but to anyone who had known her before, she was barely recognisable, inside or out.

"What do you want?" yelled Coxy above the din as they finally reached the bar.

"Glass of rioja, please," said Moira.

"Glass of rioja, please?" Coxy repeated. "Who are you and what have you done with my friend?" laughed Coxy, before resting her breasts on the bar and catching the barman's attention.

"Two shots of vodka, a pint of cider and a glass of rioja please," she said into his ear. He smiled at her cleavage and went to get the drinks.

"So, I reckon tonight's the night. It must be your turn to pull some guy and bring him back to the flat," said Coxy with a grin. Moira rolled her eyes, she had heard this speech before. "Seriously I'm starting to think you might be gay, which is fine if you are, just don't try and take advantage of me when I'm drunk," she said, then passed Moira a shot. "Down in one, cheers!"

The night felt long. Moira was tired, but she was happy to be out. She certainly didn't want to be home alone in the flat watching Jools Holland. They danced, they drank and as the crowd counted down the last few moments of the old year, the night reached its inevitable conclusion. Cries of, "Happy New Year," left the lips of strangers and filled the room, the words tripping over themselves in a drunken melody. Coxy was in the arms of a man she had met an hour earlier, his mouth on hers. Everybody seemed to be holding onto someone else, happy smiles and words trading between them. Moira was surrounded by people but still alone. She made her way to the bar to get herself another drink. She wasn't feeling sorry for herself, but she didn't feel the need to stand and stare at them all. It was a loud but lonely start to the New Year.

She waited at the bar to order one last drink to drown the sorrows that she pretended not to be feeling. She was aware of somebody coming to stand beside her, but did not look up. One more drink and she'd make her way home, with or without Coxy.

"Happy New Year," said a voice belonging to the stranger at her side. Moira stared at the bar, unsure whether she had the energy or will to respond. She didn't feel like making small talk and was too tired to be polite. She looked to her left and was met with the face of a man she had seen before. She had noticed him around campus, they shared some of the same lectures. He was tall, but not too tall, with messy dark hair. His dark brown eyes stared down at her from behind thick framed glasses that made him look more intelligent than he was. She noticed his arms looked strong. She had an urge to touch them, but resisted, blaming the urge on the wine or the vodka or both. She stared at the stranger for a little while, with her mouth slightly open, not knowing quite what to say.

"Hello," was the word she settled on. It came out a little more frosty than she had intended.

"Can I get you a drink?" said the beautiful stranger. Moira considered the merits of the proposal. She was thirsty and short of money. It seemed like a good offer.

"You may," she said, still speaking in a voice that sounded very unlike her own but at least the words had warmed themselves up a little.

Moira sat and talked with the stranger for a while. Something a lot like love sat with them, pushing them closer together, though neither of them noticed. Talking to the stranger was easy, listening to him talk was even better. They shared a bottle of red wine and spoke about everything, it was as though they were frozen still in time while the party danced on around them. They seemed to have lots in common. They both wanted to write. They both wanted to travel. As they leant in close, to hear each other over the loud music, they seemed to fit together. Moira felt as though she might have found something she hadn't realised she was looking for.

When the lights came on and the music stopped they

were still talking. The crowds started to disperse but a lot like love stayed, pasting them together like glue. They were both content to be attached to the other, had it not been for Coxy, they would not have been interrupted.

"Jesus! I've been looking for you everywhere, I thought you'd been kidnapped...and I can see now that you were," she said, smiling at the stranger.

Moira felt as embarrassed as she would have if Mother had just marched into the club to speak to her.

"Hello, I'm Coxy," she said with a broad smile.

"Good to meet you," said the stranger with a polite but restrained expression on his face. "I better let you get back to your friend and find my own, he'll be wondering where I got to." He got up to leave and Moira felt her heart sink, she wished they could have talked longer. Suddenly she didn't feel tired at all. He turned back to her then.

"Could I get your number, maybe give you a call some time?" he said. He seemed nervous, though still to this day Moira could never understand why.

"Yes," she said, wishing Coxy would vanish.

"Great. I never even got your name," laughed the stranger. "I'm Harry, good to meet you."

"She's Victoria, and she'd very pleased to have met you too, we both are," said Coxy. Moira shot her a look as she finished scribbling her number on the back of a beer mat.

"Victoria?"

"It's Tori. My friends call me Tori, it's short for Victoria," she stammered.

"That's good to know," said Harry. He smiled and took the number. "I'll call you," he said, then turned and walked away. Tori spent the rest of the night lying awake, wondering if he would.

FORTY ONE

"I know you said it was best to keep busy, but do we really have to paint the spare room?" moaned Harry.

"Yes we do. The paint has been sitting there for the last couple of months, no more excuses, it needs doing and we're going to do it today," said Tori.

"Fine," said Harry surrendering his way out to the garden shed to get the ladder.

Tori got dressed and went to brush her teeth. She examined the woman staring back at her in the mirror. The last few days had taken their toll. She'd kept herself busy at work and at home. Today was exactly two weeks since the transfer and the day they kept free so that they would be alone. They wanted to be together when Fiona called with the result of the pregnancy test. Tori bent down to spit out the toothpaste and flinched involuntarily. The pain had been with her at all times since the operation and fear was never far away. She saw it in the eyes that stared back at her in the mirror. What she feared most was Harry's reaction. He had always said it didn't matter if they couldn't, if they didn't. But she had never been sure if that was really true or something he said to make her feel better. She tried to put the thought out of her head.

Day turned to night. The painting was finally finished and they paused briefly to examine their work.

"This will now make a perfect nursery," said Harry, pulling Tori towards him.

"Or a study," she found herself saying out loud, "I want you to start writing again." He took her by the shoulders and stared hard at her.

"We need to stay positive darling. Just a little bit longer. What time did Fiona say she was going to call?"

"Seven. When she's home from work."

"Well then, we only have an hour to wait. After three years I think we can try and keep positive for one more hour, don't you? In fact I'm going to pop that bottle of champagne in the fridge..."

"Don't," interrupted Tori.

"Why?"

"What if..?"

"Positive, remember?" he said more firmly this time and then examined his wife's expression. She looked so tired, so pale, she barely resembled his Tori, but he knew she was still inside there somewhere. They needed this to be good news. Fiona had to be pregnant. He knew the phone call would be the thing to destroy what was left of his wife if she wasn't. "Do you know you've got paint in your hair? And on your nose?" he asked, smiling down at her.

"Yes," she said and tried to smile back. "I think I'll have a shower," she added and withdrew herself from his arms and his love. She went to the bathroom to lock him out of the world she had created for herself. Steam filled the room and the sound of the shower drowned out her crying. In just under an hour he might not love her anymore.

An hour later, time had caught up with them and the moment of truth made everything still and silent. Harry had optimistically put a bottle of champagne and two glasses on the coffee table next to Tori's phone, as though positive thinking could create a positive result. She felt a little sick when she saw them but sat down next to him quietly. He held her hand. There were only a few minutes left and then their world would change forever.

"Just remember that I love you," said Harry. Tori's eyes filled with tears.

"The phone isn't going to ring," she said, avoiding Harry's eyes. They were both silent as he tried to process the words she had spoken and make sense of them.

"Why not?" he asked. Silence took hold of them and made everything so very still. She couldn't look at him. She couldn't speak. She felt paralyzed with fear, she was powerless and broken. Her tears flowed freely. "Why not?" Harry repeated. A little louder this time, his words insistent on an answer.

"Because Fiona called me two days ago. She had her period. She isn't pregnant. I'm sorry," she said with a trembling quiet voice.

"I don't understand. Why didn't you tell me?" said Harry, anger pulsing through him.

"You were at work...I didn't know how. I thought it would be better to wait until we were together."

"We've been together all day. You made me paint a nursery you knew we didn't even need? You've just been carrying on as normal when the whole time you knew?

You let me think there was still a chance when you knew that it was over?" he said, and let go of his wife's hand. What she had feared the most was beginning, he was letting her go and it would only be a matter of time before he walked away. He stood and she knew he would leave her, she had always known.

"No, I just wanted it to be the right time." She stood and followed him out of the room, her legs trembling and almost giving way beneath her.

"You've basically been lying to me for the last few days. It's sick, is what it is. It wasn't your secret to keep, it affects me just as much as you. What else have you lied to me about?" Harry said turning to face her, rage in his eyes.

"Nothing, I..."

"I thought we were doing this together?"

"We are. We were, I just..." she had no more words, only tears. She folded and began to sob as though someone had died. Perhaps because something had. Harry watched her, this broken tired woman. She was destroyed and he had no idea how he would ever put her back together again or if he even could.

"I'm sorry..." she managed in between sobs. "I'm...I was just so scared to tell you it was over. I was scared in case you wouldn't love me anymore." He softened then and shook the anger away. He started to understand what this was about. No matter how hard this was for him, how hard these last few years had been, this was about Tori. She had fought for this, she had given everything and she had lost. She would still never be a mother. She would never hold her own child. She sank down to the floor, a broken mess, her head in her hands as she cried. The sound of her crying like this was enough to make Harry shed some tears of his own. He crouched down beside her and held her tight.

"It's okay. Everything will be okay," he said, whilst at the same time wondering if anything would ever be okay again. "I love you, so very much and we are going to get through this," he tried.

She cried for the longest time and he let her and held her until it was over.

"If you want to leave me, I'll understand," she said.

"Don't ever speak like that. I love you for being you. We tried and it didn't work. It obviously just isn't supposed to be. If you want to try again we could save up and..."

"I don't want to try again," she said. He nodded slowly, taking in her words and knowing they were true.

"I don't want to try again either but I don't think we should rush to make any decisions right now. Come on, come with me, Mrs Brown," he said and pulled her up from the floor. He led her by the hand and she followed him like a child, her cheeks puffy and reddened from crying. Harry reached for the champagne and lifted it out of the ice bucket, letting it drip a little on to the table.

"Now then, this isn't quite as cold as I might like but we're going to open it anyway," he said and popped the cork before there was any time for her to argue.

"I'm not sure this is something to celebrate," she managed to say in protest before Harry handed her a glass.

"I think we've got plenty to celebrate," he said taking his glass. "The last few years have been a living nightmare, and I for one am glad that it's over. No more visits to the clinic, no more giving all our money to doctors or surrogates. No more seeing you in pain. There was a moment when I really thought I had lost you after the operation. I know we don't talk about what happened that day, but I never, ever want to feel like that again. At least not until we're in our nineties, when we'll be living in a home and I'll have forgotten my own name. I love you. I think you've forgotten quite how much and maybe that's my fault for not showing you recently. I want to spend the rest of my life with you. Being with you makes me happy and it has torn me apart to see you so sad for so long. I know you wanted a family and I know that you would have been a wonderful mother, but for whatever reason it just isn't meant to be. But this isn't the end. We still have each other and we've got a lot more going for us than most couples I know. I cannot imagine a world without you in it and I wouldn't want to. We will get through this. I know you might not believe me right now, but I promise you that we will. I love you and nothing will ever change that." He stopped because he hoped he had said enough to convince her that this wasn't the end. He stopped because she had started to cry again and because he could feel tears of his own filling his eyes. She looked so fragile, so broken and all he wanted was to fix her. He was going to put her back together, or at least he was going to try. He raised his glass.

"This is to us, to our future together. May it be long and happy and healthy from this day onwards. And no regrets. We were dreaming the right dreams at the wrong time, was all," he said and clinked her glass with his own. They both took a sip. It tasted surprisingly good.

Tori's fear shrugged its shoulders and stood to leave. Love rushed down the chimney and filled the room.

"I love you," were the only words that Tori managed to say. They were the only words that Harry wanted to hear.

FORTY TWO

Mrs Brown woke up in her bed, her eyes immediately offended by the bright light flooding into the room. She closed them and willed them to stay tightly shut. Her head was throbbing and she didn't feel at all well. She felt sick and confused. Her mind had wandered through its own back streets of memories, past tear-filled streams and towers of doubt made from bricks of worry. She reached out for her husband, hoping he hadn't already left for work, she needed him. "Harry?" she called. His name darting out of her mouth and bouncing around the room like an overexcited pet trying to locate its owner. Her claw-like fingers felt the smoothed down white sheets next to her and the truth surrendered. Mr Brown was not here, she was alone. Mr Brown had not slept beside her, he had not been here for quite some time now. The heavy, suffocating childlessness weighed down on her until she couldn't breathe. "Harry," she called again, though she knew it was in vain and knew that there would be no answer. She began to gently cry to herself, keeping her eyes firmly closed, shut to the world and everyone in it. She didn't want to see the empty side of the bed, she didn't want to see or breathe reality, she knew she couldn't bear it.

Adele came to her side, and stroked Mrs Brown's furrowed brow.

"There now, Mrs B, don't you cry. Everything is going to be okay, you hear me?" She turned then and addressed someone else in the room. Mrs Brown reluctantly opened her eyes and was alarmed to see that although her husband was not there, she was far from alone. There seemed to be several people in her bedroom, all staring at her.

"Who's Harry?" said a voice in the room full of strangers.

"Harry was her husband's name," said a young woman sitting on a chair in the corner. For the briefest of moments Mrs Brown thought she recognised her, but the moment passed and confusion and fear took hold.

"Who are you, what do you want? What are you doing in my room? Adele? Who are these people?" cried Mrs Brown, sitting up in the bed and pulling the sheets around her.

"It's Emily, Grandmother, do you remember?" said the girl, rising up from the chair in the corner like a slender ghost. Mrs Brown stared at the girl. She was surely dreaming. She was fairly sure she would remember if she had a granddaughter, she wasn't even old enough.

"I don't know what kind of trickery this is, but I won't stand for it. Adele, call the police."

"I can't do that, Mrs B," whispered Adele, tears in her eyes.

"Why not, are you in on it too? Harry, where are you?" screamed Mrs Brown.

"Please try and stay calm, I just want you to listen to

what Emily has to say," soothed Adele.

"Who is she, and who is that man?" she shrieked, glaring at the young suited man cowering in the corner.

"That's just the doctor, Mrs B. You had a bit of a funny turn last night, passed out on us. We just wanted him nearby in case you weren't well like last time."

"Last time?" said Mrs Brown.

"Last time we had this conversation," said Emily gently, cautiously perching on the end of the bed.

"Young lady, I suggest you stop deluding yourself, I don't have any children, let alone a granddaughter...Adele, call the police. Where is my husband?"

"Your daughter, my mother, is on her way, she got on the first flight this morning."

"Well now I know you're lying, we couldn't have any children. We tried, it didn't work. Adele please do something."

"She's telling the truth, Mrs B. I don't like seeing you upset, but she's telling you the truth," said Adele. Time stopped then. Mrs Brown trusted the words that had been spoken and knew them to be true. Her breathing calmed, her words untangled themselves and came out in the right order.

"Then how old am I?"

"Ninety-one in October," said Emily. Adele nodded and the young doctor remained in the corner staring at his feet. A pause settled itself between them.

"Then tell me this, how could a ninety year old run this place?" Mrs Brown demanded to know. Nobody needed to answer. Silence swallowed the room. Unspoken words floated between the cast, waiting until everyone was ready for the final act.

"I live here, don't I? I'm just like them?" said Mrs Brown, nodding at the walls that hid the other residents and the truth. Adele nodded.

"Where's Harry?" she asked, looking up at Adele and reaching out for her hand.

"I'm so sorry, Mrs B," said Adele, she hated this part the most. She had been the one to tell Mrs Brown that her husband had died the first time. It was like watching her heart break all over again every time since. Tears started to stream down Mrs Brown's deeply lined face. She closed her eyes and started to tremble.

"How long has he been gone?"

"Six years now, I'm so sorry..."

"He was here with me?"

"In this room with you, yes. You lived here together before he passed away."

Mrs Brown looked over to Harry's side of the bed. With effort she lifted her hand out from under the sheet and lay it where he should have been.

"Mrs Brown, do you remember now?" asked Adele, but Mrs Brown couldn't hear her, she was somewhere else now, somewhere far, far away. Moira stared up at the ceiling wondering where the time had gone. Tori took a deep breath, unsure why they were all staring at her. Mrs Brown closed her eyes. She started to hum softly, the tune sounded familiar to Emily, though she did not know why. "We were alone and I was singing a song for you," whispered Mrs Victoria Brown. She kept her eyes tightly closed from the reality she had tried so hard not to see. She would not open them again.

"What did she say?" asked Emily.

"I don't know, think we've lost her again. Why did she think she couldn't have children?" said Adele.

"My mother was adopted. Is there anything you can do, Doctor?" said Emily to the young man in the corner. He was looking out of the window and looked thoroughly bored with the scene before him.

"No, I'm afraid not. Mrs Brown is ninety-one, given her age, she is in pretty good health—you're obviously doing a great job looking after her here despite the advanced Alzheimer's. All we can do is wait, I'm afraid," he said. The sky outside darkened. It would not be long.

"It's not all crazy talk you know, she used to work here when she was younger, when she was a student," said Emily.

"I never knew that," said Adele.

"Mum thought she was just getting more forgetful as she got older but then the police found her sitting in a field in her nightdress in the middle of the night. That's when they came here. Granddad was in good health but he wouldn't be without her, so they moved in here together. She always loved this place and having worked here once, albeit a long time ago, it was familiar to her, a home away from home of sorts," said Emily.

"Most things that Alzheimer's sufferers say is linked to some memory, a hazy reality of something from their past. You're doing the right thing, bringing her back to the real world from time to time," said the doctor.

"I had to, she was about to break the door down trying to leave," interrupted Adele. "She went downhill fast after your grandfather died. Like she just couldn't see the point in carrying on without him. We found them wrapped in each other's arms, same way they always were every morning in this very bed. I think she knew he was dead, but she just couldn't let go," said Adele.

"But lately it's not just forgetting things and people...she thinks she runs the place," said Emily.

"In her own way, she does," said Adele. She picked up the pile of papers that Mrs Brown insisted on carrying round with her at all times. There were letters from Emily, old photos, cards and Mr Brown's death certificate. She would never believe the words printed on it, no matter how many times she read them. Adele leant down and stroked Mrs Brown's long white hair.

Mrs Brown didn't feel Adele's fond touch and couldn't answer their questions. She was getting further away with each and every moment on a journey to a place where there's no space or time. There was a knock on the door that everybody noticed but nobody heard. He let himself in, stood at the end of the bed and smiled at her. She smiled back.

"What are you doing here? Where have you been?" asked Moira.

"I've been waiting for you," he said, "Are you ready now?"

"Yes. Yes I am," said Tori. She climbed out of the bed with ease.

"Good, I've missed you," said Harry.

"I've missed you too. Let's go home," said Mrs Brown. She took his hand and followed him out of the room and out of Godalming Lodge for the last time.

The End

I feel so lost without you, though you were never here.

The future seems too lonely. The end I fear is near.

My heart was broken long ago, the chance to mend it never came.

The me I dreamed of for so long. The child I'll never name.

The disappointment in myself was never more than now.

I wish that I were stronger. I try, but don't know how.

The woman in the mirror, an ugly shadow of the girl I knew.

I don't know who to be now. I can't remember what is true.

The days turn into weeks, turn into months, turn into lies.

The waking nights that haunt me. The sadness in his eyes.

Consumed by guilt and hurt and blame. Wondering why and who.

I don't know where to run to now. I don't know what to do.

Acknowledgements

There are a number of people who have been a part of this journey. I would like to thank my family and friends, with special thanks to Charlotte Essex, Brian Grant, Alex Vanotti, Jen (Jack) Winbolt, Anna MacDonald, Jane Garvey and Julia Gibbs. I would like to thank those who helped with the research over the years for their patience and honesty and John Chandler for the front cover I had imagined for so long.

Lastly, mostly, Daniel Grant. For all the endless reasons, this novel is dedicated to you.

What inspired you to write Rokitansky?

Rokitanky, also known as MRKH, is described as a rare condition. According to the latest figures, 1 in every 4500 women are living with it all over the world. That doesn't sound terribly rare to me and yet nobody knows the cause and there is no cure. It can be heart breaking and life changing, depending on the individual and how they come to terms with the condition and yet so many people, so many doctors in fact, have never heard of it. I wanted to raise awareness of the condition and hopefully stamp out some of the ignorance about it. I know that many women feel incredibly alone when they are diagnosed with Rokitansky Syndrome, and I very much wanted, in some small way, to change that. They are not alone and I felt very passionately that there was a story to be told.

What are the central themes of the book?

The overriding central theme of the book is childlessness. The need and desire to reproduce, to be remembered when we are gone. There are four other major reoccurring themes; love, pain, fear and hope. It sounds a little melodramatic perhaps, but I almost treated the last four themes as characters in their own right. Childlessness isn't always about infertility, there is a difference and I wanted to explore that a little. As the story unfolds we are with Moira in her hospital room when she is told she will never be able to have a baby. We watch her come to terms with her condition and deal with the implications and consequences in her own way. Next, we join Tori and Harry on their journey through IVF and surrogacy. They are willing to sacrifice almost anything and everything for the child they long for, a child who hasn't been born and doesn't exist. And then we meet Mrs Brown who cares so much about the residents in the care home she runs that they are almost like her children, her family in a way. All three of the characters experience moments of love, pain, fear and hope, as we all do in life. I like to think if you have love, you can get over whatever has caused you emotional and sometimes physical pain. And sufficient hope, will always extinguish fear.

Why did you choose to tell the story with three female characters?

I studied a poem at school called 'I and Wolverine' by Jeni Couzyn. I can't pretend to remember the poem, it was a long time ago now, but I do remember how it made me feel and that was a starting point of sorts. I'm very aware that I become a different person depending on who I am with. I seem to have conjured up different versions of myself to try and be whoever it is that the different people in my life want/need me to be. I don't think that means I have a multi personality disorder, at least I hope not! I think feeling and behaving that way is actually quite common, but often people don't even realise they are doing it. Are you the same version of yourself with your mother in law and best friend for example. I think each of us as individuals can be many different things to many different people and the best way I could come up with to explore and demonstrate that notion was to tell the story with three characters instead of one.

Did you know the ending when you started writing Rokitansky?

No, I genuinely didn't know the ending when I first started writing the novel. I felt a little bit like Moira in the first chapter, "She had known deep down for as long as she could remember that something was wrong. What she didn't know was what happened next." I knew for years that I was going to write this novel one day. When I started, the ending really could have gone either way. In the end, having spent so long getting to know the characters, it became a bit of a no brainer. I don't want to give away the ending for those who don't know yet, but there was a particular message I suppose that I wanted to convey and the only way to do that was have things turn out the way they did. I still cry when I read it, which is ridiculous given I wrote it and I've read it so many times during the editing process.

Is it a happy ending in your opinion?

Yes it is, although I know that not everybody agrees with me! Sometimes we can spend our lives wishing for something that we don't have and completely taking everything else for granted. It's not wrong to want a baby. It's not wrong to have a baby! But it isn't and shouldn't be everything. I like happy endings, I get cranky when I am denied one at the end of a a book or film, but my idea of a happy ending may not be the same as yours. I am a firm believer that everything really does happen for a reason, even the bad stuff, or what seems to be bad stuff at the time.

Did you enjoy writing it?

Yes and no. That's a strangely difficult question to answer. There were parts I found incredibly difficult to write, which would haunt me for days afterwards. This is a novel, it is fiction, but there are many, many Moiras, Toris and Mrs Browns out there, having the same experiences and living with similar emotions. I experienced the same highs and lows as all writers I suppose, the joy of getting through a difficult chapter, or when the story seems to write itself and your fingers magically type it out on the laptop. The lows of almost living through the sadness of some situations as they unfolded on the page were quite intense sometimes. And then there is the sorrow of saying goodbye to characters who you have spent more time with than your friends while writing the novel!

What are you working on now?

I'm a new author which is mildly terrifying. There are lots of things that need to be done that have very little to do with the writing. I have come to realise that finishing the novel was just the beginning. There are all sorts of things, like cover design, websites and twitter that I know little or nothing about, but I'm learning. I have started on my next novel. I was lucky enough to meet and interview PD James once and she said she never, ever talks about a novel until it is finished. I think she is a woman who knows what she is talking about, so I'm going to take that advice. I'm in that really exciting stage of having lots of ideas in the middle of the night and turning on the bedside table lamp to scribble them down in a notepad I keep by the bed. It's exciting for me, but probably quite irritating for my husband.

What would you like the reader to take away from this novel?

A desire to share it so that Rokitansky Syndrome becomes more widely known about and understood. I hope that readers find the something special in the novel that I hoped they would. I've dedicated this book to my husband Daniel because quite honestly I don't think I would be here without him. But this book is also for every little girl who ever dreamed of being a mother, this book is for you.

Thank you so much for reading Rokitansky, I hope with all my heart that you have enjoyed my story. As a new author, if you would like to leave a review on Amazon, I'd be very grateful.

You can find out more about Alice and get in touch with her via her website or on Twitter. She would love to hear from you!

www.alicedarwin.com

@alicewriterland

9292817R00211

Printed in Great Britain
by Amazon.co.uk, Ltd.,
Marston Gate.